HERS TO CAPTIVATE

-VERDANTIA SERIES BOOK FIVE-

PATRICIA A. KNIGHT

ISBN 978-1-950661-11-4

ALL RIGHTS RESERVED

Hers To Captivate Copyright © 2015 Patricia A. Knight

Edited by Josephine Henke

Cover design, digital and paperback formatting by LJ Stock

Electronic book publication November 14, 2015

DEAR READER,

Thank you all for your fascination with my world of Verdantia. It warms my heart to know there are others for whom the Second Tetriarch, et al, are living, breathing characters.

I have heard your desire to know how to pronounce characters' names, terminology, and places as the author would like them pronounced, and to that end, I have included a Glossary Of Terms in the back of this book. Yeah!

If there is a term or name that I have left out that you wish to have defined simply drop me an email at:

patriciaknight190@gmail.com

Warm regards,

Patricia

Dedication

To my wonderful readers.
I'm sorry I don't write faster.

ACKNOWLEDGEMENTS:

Thanks to my usual cast of suspects! My wonderful critique group (in no particular order): Sweet M, Elizabeth, Brenda, Rachel, Stephanie and Travis. My dedicated editor Josephine Henke. And finally, my publisher, Troll River Publications, for allowing me the freedom to create this manuscript in the first place, publishing it, and then gracefully returning this title to me when our contract expired.

PROLOGUE

The planet, Verdantia—spaceport city of Arkodaenia

Tristan DeHelios slouched against a tower of packing crates that vibrated from the ever-present rumble of arriving and departing starships and gazed at a cluster of dockworkers busily unloading freight. In spite of his bored appearance, Tris listened carefully to the words of Lord Ramsey DeKieran, the gods-be-damned nanny inflicted upon him by his brother, Hel. Ramsey denied the accusation, but Tris knew better. Ramsey DeKieran was there to ensure he didn't screw up. Well … fuck Hel, and fuck the horse he rode in on. Bitter frustration seethed inside Tris. At thirty-two, he'd long outgrown the need for supervision, but Hel insisted on casting him as his heedless, immature, baby brother. Tris snorted and tuned back in to DeKieran's instructions.

"…and provide Dr. Giverny and our returning noblewomen with every possible protection and assistance." Tristan's former commanding officer and ostensible nanny stared at Tris with his eerie, indigo-ringed gray eyes. "Did you hear anything I said?"

Tris brought his hand to his forehead in a mock salute. "Yes, sir. Every possible protection and assistance, sir."

Ram straightened and uncrossed his arms with a sound of disgust. "Stick it up your ass, Tristan. I'm no longer your superior officer. For the last time, I'm in Arkodaenia because Steffania is here with her Blue Daggers, and where my wife goes, I go."

Tris arched an eyebrow. "You refused Gu-r-r-r-ley? I'm surprised he let you live." He supposed calling his illustrious brother "Gu-r-r-r-ley" instead of "Hel" when he'd crashed Hel's wedding was immature, but he couldn't help his delight when the arrogant ass squirmed with mortification as all the elites of Verdantia looked on—and it *was* Hel's given name. What had their mother been thinking? Furthermore, why *hadn't* his brother invited him to his wedding? Was Hel that ashamed of him? It had been almost two years and the slight still smarted.

Ram choked down a laugh but quickly sobered. "Yes, I refused your pompous ball sack of a brother. You are technologically competent. You've an uncanny knack for getting people to do things for you, and I have no question you'll keep Dr. Giverny safe. You are the perfect man to smooth her way in setting up the neurological clinic and protect her in the process. I recommended you to High Lord DeTano and Queen Constante." Ramsey grunted in disgust. "Despite you showing up in Nyth Uchel obscured by so much hair even your mother wouldn't recognize you. I certainly didn't. What is it about House DeHelios? Your family averse to good grooming?"

Tris shrugged. "I shaved off my beard and cut my hair."

"Yes, and you still look like a roustabout." A humorless smile distorted Ramsey's mouth. He sniffed the air. "You smell like you spent the night on the floor of some dive."

"Julia would object to you calling her establishment a…" Tris paused mid-sentence when Ram waved him silent. He followed Ram's gaze. The man lifted his head and grinned broadly at a hulking giant of a humanoid male descending a nearby starship gangway. The metal plating rattled under each ponderous step. The gargantuan's body obscured a petite beauty trailing him until the colossus stepped aside and ushered her forward with a delicacy at odds with his size.

"Verdantian," said the giant, a smile splitting his face.

"Khlossian," Ram acknowledged.

The behemoth strode up to Ram and slapped him on the shoulder in greeting. Ram staggered backward several feet then straightened. Tristan watched, astonished and bemused at the manhandling DeKieran allowed without protest.

His interest sharpened when the delicate beauty accompanying the Khlossian beamed at Ramsey, dropped to her knees in front of him, and placed her hands on her thighs, head bowed. "Dominus, I am very glad to see you, again."

Ram reached down and drew her to her feet. "Pansy... er... Dr. Giverny. We left that title behind on Vxloncia. It's just Ram, or Lord DeKieran if you insist on formality." Ram gestured to Tris. "I'd like to introduce you to the man I mentioned in my communiqués."

Well... by *Her* ruby red tits, that tiny morsel of delicious female flesh was Dr. Giverny? Was that a look of adoration the good doctor lavished on DeKieran? She'd addressed him as "Dominus". What was the story behind that? In addition, how did Ramsey's decidedly lethal wife feel about it? Tris chuckled to himself. This assignment promised to be far more entertaining than he'd first thought. When Ramsey motioned him to join them, Tris sauntered over. The tiny beauty watched him approach then wrinkled her brow.

She turned her back to him and lowered her voice to a murmur so quiet Ram bent down to hear her. "Lord DeKieran, you are certain? The medical instruments I brought are irreplaceable. The equipment requires the most delicate handling. This man doesn't look ... well ... responsible."

Despite her attempt to conceal her words, Tris took notice and fought down the wash of anger that accompanied her voicing of a sentiment he'd heard far too often. Instead, he slipped into the persona that had become his second skin, and put his head back and laughed. "Spend tonight with me, lovely, and you can decide for yourself how responsibly I handle delicate equipment."

Ramsey snorted. "Dr. Angelica Giverny, meet Tristan DeHelios—your new bodyguard and med-center liaison officer."

"Doctor." Tris tipped his head and acknowledged her blank, owl-eyed expression. "I take it you wish me to oversee the off-loading of your medical supplies?" The woman nodded. Her stunning violet eyes blinked up at him in the most humorous way. So… this was the body he was to guard day and night for an indefinite future. He'd pictured some wizened old biddy. How delicious to be wrong. Damn, but life was good. "I'll see to it, immediately. Oh, and Doc, about tonight—you can get back to me on that." He winked at her, her features still immobile, chucked her under the chin, and turned to stroll up the gangway into the depths of the starship.

⊗⊗⊗⊗⊗⊗⊗⊗⊗⊗⊗⊗

The quiet hum of the air circulators for the starship, VNV *Revertar*, was the only sound competing with his footsteps as Tris strode down the narrow gray hallways of the starship that had delivered forty, genetically-priceless, Verdantian noblewomen back to their home planet—in addition to the delectable person of Dr. Angelica Giverny and her sensitive equipment. Tris narrowed his eyes and straightened as he walked.

Since the trial of the Vxloncian slaver, Vittal Lontz, and his subsequent conviction—due primarily to the testimony of one Dr. Angelica Giverny—she'd been the object of several attempts to terminate her life. Vittal Lontz had been a mere planetary player. The task force set up by the Galactic Agency for the Protection of Sentients, or GAPS, was dedicated to shutting down the multi-galactic slavery cartel. From the repeated attempts on Dr. Giverny's life, GAPS was getting too close to the serpent's head for comfort.

Dr. Giverny knew more than she realized. Whoever orchestrated those attempts had gone straight to the most elite and most expensive assassins in the known universes. Apparently, expense wasn't considered. The attempts narrowly failed. Tris was in Arkodaenia along with the Blue Daggers to ensure any subsequent attempts continued to be equally unsuccessful.

Not only did Verdantia need the neurological treatment center Giverny would set up in the spaceport, it seemed the luscious Dr. Angelica had a personal history with Ramsey DeKieran. After all the man had done for him, Tris would hate to let Ram down by not protecting someone important to him and vital to Verdantia. An ironic smile twisted his lips. Unlike most of the make-work jobs his brother sent him on, this assignment held the certainty he was needed—and then there was the lovely doctor herself. He promised himself a careful pursuit of that delectable wisp of femininity. He'd enjoy putting the violet-eyed beauty on her knees in front of him. His groin tightened at the thought.

Tristan scanned the corridors as he walked. The payload commander had to be around somewhere. A tall, slim figure dressed in khaki fatigues turned the corner, head down, flipping fingers across the face of a compact tap-screen. His shoulder bars indicated the rank of captain. Tris had lucked out. He'd run straight into the ship's commanding officer.

"Captain, my name is Tristan DeHelios. I'm looking for the payload commander, I…" The man halted and raised his head. Incredulity flooded the captain's elegant, chiseled features and a pair of green eyes, once familiar, widened. The tap-screen slipped out of his hands and fell with a rattle to the deck. Tris knew how he felt. *By* Her *light. It couldn't be.* But... "Magellan DeLan? Mage? You're the captain on this ship?"

Tris grinned at the stupefaction covering the face of the male he'd known in Nyth Uchel. His advance toward the captain turned into a stalk as the man remained silently frozen in place. Tris prowled up to him, stepped him backward against the bulkhead, and planted his outstretched arms on either side of the man's head. Not more than inches from the captain's face, Tris drank him in.

The Magellan DeLan who Tris had known had been a pretty teenage boy—a tall, gawky youth with the promise of broad shoulders above his narrow waist and with an innocent, finely-modeled, face and shocking green eyes, all topped by a mop of black hair. Now, the body beneath his fatigues had filled in and broadened with clearly defined muscle. Mage's pretty, boyish face had hardened and refined into that of an adult male. He exuded a sensual allure that was anything but innocent.

"Look at you. You're even more fucking beautiful." A surge of heat flooded Tristan. "You aren't anymore, Mage. You're a full-grown man. What's it been? Eight years?" Tristan's cock responded immediately to the lithe, muscled body of the ship's captain as he pressed Mage into the wall with his pelvis. "So... I'm free to do now what I wouldn't allow myself then." He held Mage in a steady stare as he cocked his head and lowered his face by fractions of an inch, his intention clear. Swiftly, Mage's hand wrapped his throat, halting his descent with impressive strength. "Fuck, Captain." Tris leaned into the man's steely grip, challenging him. "Do you really want me to stop?" The pressure against his larynx eased almost imperceptibly. It was enough.

Tris captured the man's head in his hands, sank his fists into Mage's thick black hair and devoured the full lips that had haunted him for eight long years—years of regret about what might have been—what *should* have been. After a moment of hesitation, the captain groaned, wrapped his hands around Tristan's waist and returned the kiss, giving back the same ferocious assault he received. Teeth bit and tongues explored. Hard cock ground into hard cock in a breathless explosion of lust. Too soon, footsteps and voices sounded from a nearby corridor. When Mage stiffened beneath him, Tristan swore and stepped back, wiping his mouth. His chest heaved and his cock begged for freedom from the constriction of his leather breeches. Their eyes stayed locked on each other. Some things never changed—his body's reaction to Mage DeLan was one of them.

The dark-haired, green-eyed captain straightened, licked his lips and swallowed heavily. "I thought you were dead."

Tris worked to control his breathing and appear normal as two crewmembers walked by and nodded respectfully to Mage with a murmur of, "Sir."

One leaned down, picked up the tap-screen lying on the deck, and handed it to Mage. "This yours, Captain?"

"Yes, thank you, Evans. Carry on."

With curious glances at both of them, the crewmen continued down the corridor.

He shouldn't have put a starship captain in such a compromising position and particularly not Mage. A crooked grin pulled at Tristan's mouth, and he kept his words low and intimate. "Sorry. Wrong time. Wrong place. That was not well-done of me."

Mage dropped his head and shook it helplessly before looking up with the light of laughter in his eyes. "If you'd been any better you could have had me on the departure deck of my own ship, crew be damned. Don't worry about it. They won't talk."

Tris chuckled but sobered on a wash of painful memory. "The way you left Nyth Uchel... What I allowed you to think." Tris shrugged and looked down the hallway as the crewmen vanished around a corner. "I couldn't let that stand." When Tris returned his gaze to Mage, the man regarded him with a crooked smile.

"What? That you'd rather fuck my horse than a half-grown snot like me? I think those were your parting words."

Tris grunted softly. "Yeah... well... I lied."

The man, whose facial features had never failed to remind Tris of a fucking piece of art, cocked his head and shot Tristan a wry glance. "Evidently." Both men grinned at each other until Mage straightened and squared his shoulders. "So, Tristan DeHelios, what business brings you to my ship? Why are you in Arkodaenia?"

Tristan wanted certain details locked down before business distracted them. He held up a forefinger. "First, how long are you in port? Where are you quartered?"

Mage stood for a moment, a look of consideration on his face. "The *Revertar* is home for re-fitting. We're getting one of the new hyper-drive engines and some updated electronics for her nav system. As soon as we offload, she goes into stationary orbit for maintenance and an equipment upgrade that will probably take the better part of ninety days. I'd planned to stay onboard with the engineering staff and a skeleton crew."

Tristan crossed his arms and shook his head. "Negative. Unsatisfactory response, Captain DeLan." He held Mage's gaze steadily. "How can I see more of you if you are floating around somewhere among the stars? I do want to see more of you. I have an apartment in Arkodaenia with ample space." Tris paused and put his hands on his hips. "Spend your stay in port with me."

He waited with greater impatience than he wanted to acknowledge while Mage leveled a flat stare at him. Long seconds ticked away. Tris itched under the scrutiny of those intelligent green eyes. Disappointment bedeviled Tristan as the seconds accumulated. The man was going to refuse him.

Mage lifted a shoulder. "Sure. Chief Engineer Cox could do

without me hanging over his shoulder and getting in the way. I need a week or so to get things lined out before I can join you, but… until then, how about dinner tonight? We can catch up." Mage gave him a muted smile.

The degree of pleasure Tris felt at Mage's answer shocked him. He relaxed now that he'd received the answer he wanted. "I'd enjoy that. Do you know the Eight Bells on High Street? They serve a decent meal and the service is good." Satisfaction and anticipation warmed him.

"Yes." Mage nodded. "The Eight Bells it is. Now, you were looking for the payload commander. What can he and I do for you?"

Tristan laughed to himself. *More than you know, Captain, more than you know.*

Yes, this assignment had all the earmarks of becoming one hell of an entertaining ride.

CHAPTER TWO

D r. Angelica Giverny tore her eyes away from the departing back of that insolent, unkempt thug, Tristan DeHelios. The thought that he should be the first male since Lord DeKieran to inspire her to drop to her knees and beg to serve sparked anger—and a sliver of concern— within her. *Is that who I really am?* Of all the worthy males on her own home planet— boring, unadventurous, missionary-position males—she had to be drawn to this, this... Verdantian lout.

She could still feel the gentle stroke of his finger under her chin, and the heat from his silver-eyed stare had provoked a riotous response from her body. *Oh, and about tonight—you can get back to me on that,* she mimicked silently, drawing herself up in rigid indignation. Was he serious? Her astonishment at both his actions and her body's response had rendered her speechless. Of course, *now* she could think of snappy comebacks, but unless she wanted to scream them across the dock at his retreating ass, his very fine retreating ass...

She sent an unwilling glance toward Tristan DeHelios and released a long sigh. Her indignant posture melted with her exhale. Where did these submissive impulses come from? She'd surprised herself as well as Lord Ramsey when she'd spontaneously dropped to her knees to greet him. She'd not done that to a male since leaving her life as "slave Pansy" behind on Vxloncia. Had her time on that hellacious planet altered her subconscious beyond mending? More disquieting, perhaps Vxloncia had freed a true part of herself growing up on Talleo IV had buried. *How can I help so many others find their true selves, and yet I do not know who I am?*

Angelica worried at that thought for many minutes while her Khlossian escort, Tok, and Lord Ramsey caught up on all that had occurred since their days on Vxloncia and Talleo IV.

A feminine voice broke her troubled thoughts. "What did I miss?"

Angelica whirled with a glad cry. "Steffania!" The tall, fit redhead laughed and enveloped her in a huge hug that lasted for long seconds. With smiles on their faces, Lord Ramsey and Tok watched. Angelica pulled away and beamed at her friend and former patient. "I have missed you. You look wonderful. I don't need to ask if you've been well."

"I'm as well as can be expected when married to this rogue." Steffania's eyes sparkled as she stood on her toes to give her husband a kiss. "Hello, my lord. Sorry I'm late."

Ramsey rolled his eyes and looked put-upon, but Angelica knew he was anything but. He adored his "vixen."

"Dr. Angel met her bodyguard," Tok rumbled. "He failed to favorably impress."

Steffania cut her kiss short at Tok's comment. "Ramsey, please tell me Tristan cut his hair and shaved. He didn't show up still looking like an unwashed, unsheared balantus?"

Angelica huffed softly. "I mistook him for a dockworker. Appearance aside, he propositioned me within three seconds of being introduced. I hope my patients receive more respect. They don't need another male who treats them as sexual objects."

Steffania winced and eyed Ramsey. "Will you speak—"

Ram grunted, cutting her short. "No. As I keep reminding people, I'm not his nanny. Tris overheard Angelica suggesting he didn't look dependable." Ramsey shrugged.

"Oh. You met *that* Tristan." Steffania's features softened and she turned to Angelica. "Tris probably deserved your comments, but you hit a nerve." Steffania grimaced. "Tris is extremely competent and can charm the pelt off an ice-bear when he wants something… but his older brother refuses to see it. Hel treats the man as if he were still twelve. Ramsey knows Tris far better than I do. Tristan served under Ram in the Verdantian cavalry and, ah, other places."

Angelica looked at her hands. "Perhaps I owe him an apology." She shot a questioning glance at Lord Ramsey.

Again, the man shrugged. "Your call. I wouldn't have recommended him if he weren't good, and I have a personal interest in keeping you in one piece." She cocked her head in question, and one corner of Lord Ramsey's mouth curled. "Tok and my vixen would ensure I died a painful death should anything happen to you."

The low whine of an approaching dock runabout interrupted their small company's laughter. All eyes turned and watched as a battered tow vehicle shepherded a small train of hover pallets loaded with padded white containers all marked "Medical Instruments—Fragile—Handle With Care" to a stop beside them. Her disreputable bodyguard hopped out from behind the control console of the runabout and briskly handed Angelica a gray tap-screen.

"I've taken care of all customs clearances. I had to pull a couple of strings, but I arranged for you to keep the air-skips and runabout until you can unload the equipment at the neuro-center. The clinic isn't far from port, but the air ride will be better for the equipment than the jolting of a wheeled freight vehicle. Scan the tablet, please, to make sure I have everything. Sign at the bottom if you would. I counted fourteen cartons. Good morning, ma'am."

Tristan nodded at Steffania, who stood regarding Angelica with arms crossed and an expression of knowing amusement on her face.

Blinking at Tristan's rapid, professional, clip of words, Angelica ran her gaze down the list on the gray tablet and then examined the bulk goods platforms floating two feet off the ground in front of her. Each hover-skip bore the bold, red words "Property of VNV *Revertar*—Do Not Remove Under Penalty of Law" stenciled into its sides. *Impressive*. Tristan DeHelios had convinced the handsome Captain DeLan to allow valuable hovercraft to leave his ship and then wrapped each precious freight container in enough insulation to protect it from a direct hit by a fission bomb. She signed the bottom of the tablet. Guilt assailed her. She must apologize. She turned to face Tristan and handed him the tap-screen.

"It looks in order. Umm… I would like… I want to…" she paused, grasping for words.

"It's all right, sweet cheeks. Sorry to disappoint, but you're off the hook for tonight. I've made other plans." The infuriating man grinned down at her, winked and was off again, leaping into the driver's seat of the runabout and powering up the engines. He shouted over the whine, "I'll meet you at the clinic. Lord Ramsey knows the way. Stay with him and the Khlossian. They'll keep you safe until I get there."

Sweet cheeks? Off the hook? He made other plans? Her hands fisted. She straightened and swallowed her words of apology.

"Come, Dr. Angel, Ramsey and his woman will escort you to the new medical center and your apartments. Your transportation is waiting." As it frequently did, Tok's comforting rumble grounded her when her emotions threatened to get the upper hand, and his observant gaze took in more than she allowed herself to voice. Their close proximity during the several weeks it had taken the VNV *Revertar* to bring them to Verdantia cemented a firm friendship with the GAPS agent that had begun years past when he and Lord Ramsey had rescued her from sexual slavery. Tok walked with her a few steps to where an elegant hydrogen-fueled vehicle purred at idle and helped her into the back seat.

"You don't join us, Tok?" she asked. She could feel his chuckle in her chest.

"No, little female. Your vehicle does not accommodate a being of my size." Tok's blunt, common features arranged themselves in a pleasant expression. "I will find other means." He nodded at Ramsey and Steffania, who occupied the other seating in the back of the vehicle. Tok pressed a button, and the door closed with a soft thunk.

The trip to her new medical compound took mere minutes, and it wasn't long before Ramsey was handing her out of the sleek transport. Her gaze traveled the clear towering dome that spanned several acres. Finally, she was able to view with her own eyes the results of over a year of planning and labor. The vital core of the neurological and psychological treatment areas awaited the contents of the cargo crates *that man* was transporting to the site, but she could still tour the patient residences, her apartments, and the common areas of the medical compound.

With Ramsey flanking her on one side and Steffania on the other, Angelica walked through the main entrance doors, past what would be the reception desk, and into the central atrium. She stopped and turned in a slow circle, a smile beginning and then growing into a delighted grin.

"I think it came out rather well," Steffania commented. "You don't know you are in the middle of a busy spaceport."

The vision before her confirmed what Angelica had only suspected—that while the rest of Verdantia might be stuck in a technological vacuum, the spaceport of Arkodaenia had all the advanced conveniences the wealthy pockets of the Second Tetriarch could purchase.

"It is better than I had dared to hope." Angelica sighed with contentment. "I feel as if I were in a private woodland glen. This environment can only benefit emotional recovery."

Vast, open skylights pulled in outside air through enormous filters disguised as natural rock formations. The interchange of air created a light, intermittent breeze that wafted through a forest of native trees and shrubs and across an expansive swath of emerald grass. The air was redolent with the smells of vibrant vegetative life. Cutting through the center of the broad green space, a stream burbled over large boulders before it joined a small pool surrounded by flattened rocks perfect for sitting. Arbors and gazebos filled with upholstered sofas and floor cushions in bright colors dotted the interior space. Smooth pebble paths bordered by flowerbeds that contained plants of all colors and sizes connected them. The green niches would be perfect places for comfortable private reflection or quiet socializing.

"Through here are the patient residences." Lord Ramsey motioned for her to follow and led her down a broad walkway that cut through the center of the atrium and then skirted the perimeter with multiple paths branching off. "Each walk leads to a residential quad," Ramsey explained. "This particular area has been set off for your apartments and private office." He gave her a look of inquiry. "Ready to see where you will be living in the years to come?"

She nodded eagerly. "Very ready."

They followed the gravel path to an isolated area partially concealed by the lush foliage. The winding footpath ended at a two-story, yellow, cottage with white trim. An expansive porch wrapped the second story. "Dr. Angelica Giverny, Senior Medical Chief—Cerebral Neurological & Psychological Reintegration" was written in universal script on a plaque by the door.

Lord Ramsey paused on the threshold. "The upper floor is yours. Your liaison officer and bodyguard has the first floor."

Angelica sighed. "I suppose every Garden of Eden must have a snake."

Steffania laughed aloud while Lord Ramsey stifled a smile. "Give him a chance. You two got off to a poor start."

She arched an eyebrow. "Ummhmm."

Lord Ramsey shook his head. "Surrounding this area are extensive security features not yet activated. I thought to let you move in before programming your DNA and retinal patterns into the system." He cleared his throat and Angelica thought Lord Ramsey sounded uncomfortable. "Tristan will handle entering your data and configuring your home systems. An artificial intelligence monitors and regulates all your residential lights, heating, and so forth, and will be customized to your preferences. Tris will set that up for you. He is quite conversant with advanced tech. Steffania and I, along with Tris and all of the Daggers, are in the databank. When activated, no unauthorized personnel should be able to access your private quarters."

"How do I clear my guests to enter? I suppose sooner or later I will have some."

"We have built in an override with different levels of clearance. For the moment, just know that announcing a level four clearance triggers an immediate alarm," Steffania said. "If someone should force you to use an override code, give the level four command and help will come immediately. Within your residence, there are a number of panic buttons disguised as ordinary items. Activate any of those and—"

"Help will come immediately." Angelica laughed. "Thank you. I already feel safe. What about vid-corders inside?"

Lord Ramsey shifted as if ill at ease and coughed into his closed hand. "None. There will never be a recording of what happens inside your apartments."

Steffania leveled a hostile stare at her husband. "It is too easy for recordings to go astray and be used for purposes other than security." Steffania crossed her arms, and continued to glare a hole through her husband.

"That's enough, Steffania," Ramsey growled. "I didn't know. Should I send the money back?"

The redhead turned after a final roll of her eyes and a muttered, "No." Her smile appeared forced. "So... there will be no vid-corders."

Well... what was all that about? She'd have to get Steffania aside some day and ask. "It sounds like you have done all you can to keep me safe and give me some privacy, too."

Steffania held Angelica's gaze. "Thank Tristan. He researched security measures for months before deciding on the least intrusive way to protect you."

Angelica dropped her gaze. *The person of my bodyguard will be the most intrusive security measure.*

"Shall we go inside?" Lord Ramsey held the door open and gestured to the women.

Angelica stepped into what appeared to be a windowless entry foyer, followed by Steffania and Ramsey.

"Now this is where the magic begins," Steffania said. "Push the wall button behind you. The one that looks like a doorbell."

When she did, her eyes flew to Lord Ramsey and then Steffania. "We are moving." The taupe-colored walls appeared to slide into the floor. "This is a lift! How clever. No stairs."

The sensation of movement ceased and Angelica stood looking through a set of elegant glass doors. After weeks of looking at nothing except the upscale but functional interior of the VNV *Revertar*, she felt she'd entered an enchanted land. Angelica grasped a curved golden handle, pulled, and walked into an artfully arranged living space. A long murmur of appreciation escaped her lips as her gaze roamed her new, hopefully permanent, home.

One large room of dark organic floors and cream walls rose to a high cathedral ceiling. Arranged in a conversation group, two ivory, slip-covered sofas with occasional chairs of faded turquoise and clean-lined low tables faced a media interface wall made to appear as if raised paneling. Opposite the seating area was a dining table with six side chairs in the same faded turquoise. Beyond that, Angelica could see a gleaming kitchen with stone countertops and the muted indigo lights of what she identified as a food replicator. More soft blue lights shone from other, only the gods-knew-what, conveniences.

What drew her gaze across the large space and brought a further leap of pleasure to her heart was a retractable glass wall that opened to a deep, covered, balcony. Lounge chairs faced outward, overlooking a verdant expanse of woods and sun-dappled meadow. With a small sound of joy, Angelica stepped quickly to a section of the glass wall and slid it open. Immediately, fresh, cool, air smelling of spice-wood forest lifted her hair off her neck. With a wrinkle of distaste, she also smelled the stale, antiseptic tang of the re-circulated air on the VNV *Revertar.* The odor had permeated her hair, her skin, her clothing—everything. She turned to Steffania and Ramsey. "After more than three weeks on a crowded starship in a stateroom with a tiny shower and rationed water, I would give a considerable sum for a long soak in a hot bath."

Steffania made a sound of agreement. "I remember the feeling. How about some time to yourself to relax and explore your new home? Tris should be bringing your personal effects shortly. He can also take a DNA sample and retinal scan and get the AI set up for you. Meanwhile, the house controls are set to manual."

"Here. My number, Steffania's, and Tristan's, are programmed in." Lord Ramsey placed an oval communicator in her hand. "This is the panic button." He indicated the red circular depression on the oval. "Press this and you will have all the Blue Daggers, Steffania, me and Tristan here within minutes."

Angelica peeked up at Lord Ramsey through her eyelashes. "I have always felt safe with just you and Tok, but thank you for this."

Ramsey grunted and with a hand in the middle of Steffania's back guided her toward the doors to the lift. "We will see you in the morning, Dr. Giverny." He paused, and the slight smile and nod he gave her warmed more than her heart. "We are glad you're here."

Angelica nodded. She yearned to ask him to stay, but massive guilt for entertaining such feelings about Steffania's husband silenced her. As the door closed behind them and the shush of the lift filtered through, Angelica shook her head. A humorless laugh escaped her lips. She was sexually frustrated and lonely, and her wishes counted as nothing. Dominus Ramsey had never looked at her with anything but avuncular interest, and she wasn't so lacking in self-regard as to pursue someone who didn't want her. Regardless, even if Lord DeKieran *had* returned her interest, she would never violate the friendship she cherished with Steffania.

Sometime later as she luxuriated in the steaming water of a deep tub, Angelica examined her feelings about Dominus Ramsey with as much objectivity as she could summon. Did she want him, specifically? Well… what warm-blooded woman wouldn't? But, no, under the circumstances, not him. Someone like Lord DeKieran, most definitely. The scruffy, but handsome features of her bodyguard came to mind. Him? *Gods, preserve me.* She snorted and submerged to wet her head. As she worked shampoo through her lengths of brunette hair, the face of another appeared in her mind—a charming, sensual male with green eyes and an air of quiet command—a man she had come to know and admire on the long flight from her world to Verdantia. *I wonder how long Captain DeLan is in port?*

❀❀❀❀❀❀❀❀❀❀❀

The man winced at the blast of static and jerked the comm device away from his ear. This jury-rigged trans-galactic feed was for crap. Finally, someone at the other end answered.

"Zebo, here."

"Hey, Zebo, it's Stults. I finally made it to Verdantia, the puking backwater of the universe. As ordered, I'm checking in. I need to talk to the boss man."

"He's busy, Stults. He's with Caputo of the Pinwheel Galaxy, and it ain't worth my balls to interrupt."

"He's with the head of the Pinwheel territory? *That* Caputo?"

"Yeah, they've been going at it all morning. From the shouting and swearing coming through the doors… well, let's just say I'm glad I'm not Caputo. Since the GAPS sicced their top agents on the boss's organization, his disposition is… ah… testy."

"Yeah? Tell me something I don't know. They've made my life miserable, too. My stomping grounds are several steps up from this piece of galactic nowhere, but if the Galactic High Court sentenced that piss-ant, Vital Lontz, to life pounding rocks on an asteroid, can you imagine what they'll do to the boss? Or me! That mewling, ass-sucking, Vxloncian prick, Veacon Narr, should've kept a lower profile. He had a sweet deal, all the mind-wiped pussy he could want. How do you screw that up?"

"Couldn't say, Stults. Terminal stupidity? Heard he didn't end so well. They had to identify his remains with DNA."

Stults laughed until another spat of static all but burst his eardrums. "Zebo, this inter-galactic comm-splice I jury-rigged is dicey. Don't know how long it will hold. Your decision, but I've got an update on *the woman*, the one that testified against Lontz and can ID the boss and me. You know how rabid he is about her."

"Shit. Should've said that in the beginning. Fine, fine... give me a minute—and you owe me one, Stults."

The "go-to-guy" to make things happen sat on a low wall and kicked his heels for many long minutes until the mysterious head of the largest human slavery consortium in the known universes finally came on line.

"So, Mr. Stults, you have news for me about the woman."

"Yeah, boss. As we thought, the doctor disembarked at the Verdantian spaceport with a GAPS agent—that Khlossian. Two military types met her and hustled her away to some sort of domed lockdown. The security and protection around her is significant. She's opaque to us as long as she remains where she is. We'll have to wait until she leaves her current location."

"Has the original contractor made planet-side?"

"Yes. It's here. I told it to stay out of sight."

"Tell it to finish the job it started on Talleo IV, and I want proof of death. I don't care how long it takes."

"I understand."

"Call me when it's done."

"Yes, sir."

CHAPTER THREE

Mage had chosen a secluded table at the Eight Bells, but even so… Captain Magellan Aiolos DeLan closed his eyes with a groan and jerked his uniform tunic over the prominent bulge in his fitted pants. He must stop thinking about that kiss! *Tristan DeHelios.* By the Mother, Tris was alive. The thoughts and feelings he'd forcibly left behind as he'd rode from Nyth Uchel as fast as his horse could carry him rushed back headlong. Anger. Humiliation. Rejection. Even now, eight years later, Mage could feel the hot tears on his cheeks as he'd bitten back sobs of devastation on that headlong gallop; but Tris had not been indifferent. Why had the man struck out so viciously at his tentative approach?

Mage raised his glass and drained the remainder of the cold brew. *What are you going to do about it, Mage?* He peered into the empty mug and mused as he ran his forefinger around the top. He had some decisions to make—if he hadn't already predetermined his fate by agreeing to stay with Tris.

"How about a refill for my handsome captain?" He felt the light press of a hand on his shoulder and looked up. His lovely blond server smiled and held up a pitcher.

"Not right now, but thanks, Tia." He returned her smile. "I'm meeting an old friend for dinner. I'll take that refill then."

"Sure." Her smile dimmed. "A male friend or a female

friend?" she asked.

"Last time I saw him, Tristan was definitely male." Mage laughed. Tia had many fine qualities. Subtlety was not one of them, and the fact that Tris was male didn't exclude him from being an eligible lover. Like many off-worlders new to Verdantia and unfamiliar with the culture, Tia forgot that most Verdantians, at least the noble class, were bisexual.

Her smile brightened. "After we get off, several of the staff are going to the Clube Firestide. The Gratum Mortuis are playing. Would you and your friend like to join us?"

"The Gratum Mortuis are still around? They were popular when my grandmom was a teen."

Tia laughed. "Yeah… they have sort of a cult following. I don't think they'll ever stop touring." She waggled her eyebrows suggestively. "Well, how about it, Captain?"

Mage knew her invitation included more than her company at the nightclub, and if not for Tristan he would have taken her up on it. Tia was charming with wicked bedroom talents. He could testify to that from personal knowledge. She'd been a bright spot in his infrequent stops in Arkodaenia. As it was… "Thanks for the invitation. I'll ask him and let you know."

Tia lifted her hand and saluted him. "Aye, aye, Captain."

Mage laughed, returned her salute, and watched the undulations of her pert bottom as she wove her way back to the bar.

"Does that lovely behind belong to a friend of longstanding?" At the sound of Tristan's wry voice, Mage swung around with a laugh.

"Tris. Sit, please. Ah, I've known Tia for a while, yes. I'll introduce you." The large form of Tristan DeHelios settled into a chair and his lower body responded to the heat in the Tristan's eyes. "We've been invited to join her and her friends later this evening. I could put in a good word for you."

"No thanks. My interest lies elsewhere."

Mage held Tristan's gaze, hoping he disguised his reaction to the provocation in Tristan's eyes. He had no desire for Tris to realize how unsettled he was.

Tris raised his hand and waved at the pretty server. She nodded in acknowledgment and started back to their table. Tristan regarded him in silence, then his mouth stretched in a warm smile and his gray eyes shown with appreciation—an expression that would conquer hearts far less vulnerable than his. "Damn you for being a fine looking man, Magellan."

Mage buried his head in the menu though he could have recited its items by heart. Tristan's low chuckle did nothing to restore his equilibrium. *By Her light. I feel sixteen again.* He ground his teeth at the thought. He wasn't sixteen. He was a starship captain and by the Goddess, before they went any further, he'd have an explanation. Both men gave their orders and menus to Tia, and over a refilled mug of brew, Mage regrouped. "So, Tristan DeHelios." Mage pursed his lips. "Explain yourself."

The arched eyebrows and explosion of laughter from the man across the table was not the response Mage anticipated. "I'll bet those words and that expression strike fear into your officers and crew." Tris grinned. "I'm not one of them." His eyes softened and his voice lowered to an intimate growl. "I'm sorry. I'm so gods-be-damned sorry, Mage. Pushing you away like that was the last thing I wanted to do."

"Then why?" Mage said. "You must have known I worshipped you." For a moment, he was again that sixteen-year-old boy with all the pain and heartbreak he had felt apparent in his raw voice. Tristan's expression shuttered and his mouth tightened. For a second, Mage saw a man filled with bitter cynicism, but then Tristan shrugged and his expression morphed to devil-may-care disregard. It all happened in an instant, and Mage questioned whether he'd seen anything at all.

"My father had chosen a woman for me to wed—an appropriate bride for a young DeHelios prince, a magistra to aid in the working of the Great Rite. No matter that she was ten years my senior and I'd never met the woman." Tristan chuckled. The sound contained no humor. "Father was quite dispassionate in his explanation of what he required of me. While I wasn't needed—I was the extra, after all, there was my oldest brother and his wife, and Hel and Athena—I was not discharged from my obligation to the people of Nyth Uchel."

Tristan drew a figure eight on the table as he spoke. "You were young and innocent, just sixteen. The eight years between us seemed vast… I knew you'd never…" His hand clenched into a tight fist. "By the Mother! I was doing the 'right thing' for once. Imagine that. I should have… Oh, Goddess, I wanted to… Ah, fuck it." Tris straightened and took a long pull on his brew. He set the mug down with painstaking care and gazed into the amber fluid as if it contained all the answers in the universe. "I'm making a complete hash of this." With a sigh, Tristan dropped his head back.

"The lady made it abundantly clear she would tolerate no competition for my time. She and I had an ugly fight. I went to the stables to cool off, and there you were." Tristan's voice dropped to a bare whisper. "You offered yourself to me … and I couldn't have you." He held Mage's gaze for a long moment. Again, Mage saw disillusionment and sorrow before Tris shuttered his gaze, and his face lost all expression. "I was angry and bitter, and I said things I immediately wanted back. Of all the shameful things I have done in my life, and believe me, there have been a few, my conduct that night is the thing I regret most. I searched for you almost immediately to apologize, but you were gone." Tristan cleared his throat. "And you never came back. So, though it is eight years too late, for what it's worth, I am sorry," he stated flatly.

Mage held Tristan's stoic stare for long seconds—then his mouth quirked at the corners. "It's worth quite a bit, actually."

Tristan's face lost its frigid appearance and a tentative smile climbed to his eyes. "Good."

"And the lady who was to be your wife? What happened to her?" Mage murmured.

"Dead in the massacre along with all my family—all but my middle brother, Hel. The Haarb were thorough."

"Gentlemen, your dinner." Tia's arrival with their food interrupted whatever else Tris might have said. When satisfied they had all they needed, she left. Mage looked up from his plate. "So… why aren't you dead?"

"Pure accident." Irony gleamed from Tristan's eyes while he chewed and swallowed. "I was tagging along with Hel on a little jaunt down our mountain when the Haarb decimated Nyth Uchel."

"What have you been doing since?"

"Busywork for my brother. Nothing of any importance." Tristan snorted. "I believe he prioritizes my assignments based on how far and how long they will remove my presence from Nyth Uchel." Tris busied himself with his food.

Mage winced inside for Tris. Unless Tristan had transformed in the past eight years, Hel's dismissal of his younger brother would sting. As much as he, Mage, had idolized Tristan, so Tristan had idolized his older brother. In return, Hel had avoided Tristan whenever possible. It seemed that hadn't changed.

Tris looked up from his plate. "And you? How did you wind up in the Verdantian navy?"

Mage exhaled and scrubbed his fingers across his mouth. "Hmm. Where to start. From Nyth Uchel, I went home to mother and father and then into the cavalry. You remember what things were like when the Haarb invaded. Our Mother Verdantia needed every man and woman who could sit a horse and swing a sword. Toward the end of the war, I was stationed in Arkodaenia, and the technology here fascinated me. I had no reason to go home. My family, like yours, was murdered by the Haarb." Mage paused for a moment to master the pain of that memory.

"I'm sorry," Tris murmured.

"Yes… well. Most of us on Verdantia have that in common." Mage gave Tris a crooked smile and shrugged. "We have all lost people we loved. At any rate, to see the starships, to realize the practical application of what had been only an exercise in book-learning to a teenage boy?" He laughed. "I had to be part of it."

The wonder and excitement of those days of discovery infused his voice, but Mage felt no embarrassment about his child-like enthusiasm. Sitting across from him, his eyes lit with appreciation, was one of the few men who'd ever shared Mage's excitement with all things mechanical or electronic.

Tristan straightened in his chair, suddenly eager, and ten years fell from his face. "Did you see the new anti-grav generators they are installing on dock slips three and four? How slick is that! Flip a switch and no gravity. The port master tells me they are only two of the twelve coming to modernize the port."

Mage nodded with enthusiasm. "Yes, the time savings in loading and unloading is incredible. Did you hear the navy is getting the latest interspacial navigation upgrade? The ISNAC-7. It will enable greater hyper-light jumps—perhaps as much as from Triton to Nuovo Terra in one jump."

"Is that the one with the intracranial data port? What I wouldn't give to be a navigator using that interface." Tristan gazed off as if viewing unseen heavenly bodies. His comment of "I wonder if that technology could be applied to ground-based systems," collided with Mage's, "Wouldn't it be interesting if…"

Both men looked at each other and started laughing. Tristan

ran his fingers through his hair with a sheepish smile. "Guess we still share a fascination for the techy toys."

Mage nodded. "When the Galactic Court awarded the Haarb's ships to Verdantia I leapt at the chance to crew our suddenly acquired space fleet. Naval officers from the League of Federated Planets whipped my ass into shape." Mage scratched his head and shot a rueful glance at Tristan. "Brutal, intensive, on-the-job training, but I soaked it all in... and here I am. Now, I can't imagine doing anything else. The freedom and sense of discovery is addictive. I have found what I want to do with my life." Tristan's heated gaze lingered on him, appraising, and blood flooded his lower body. He shoveled a forkful of green vegetables into his mouth.

Tris arched an eyebrow over an observant gray eye. "From what I can determine, your ass suffered no lasting harm, and I've scrutinized it intently."

Mage choked on the food he was chewing and reached for his brew to wash it down. "You mentioned something about working as the new med center's security and liaison officer?" He listened closely and finished his dinner as Tristan elaborated on his current occupation. Ordering a more potent liquor than the brew they'd been drinking, and a few sweet delicacies, Mage relaxed back into his chair.

Anticipation shivered through him at the thought of spending time alone with the DeHelios prince who'd monopolized his daydreams as a young man. His days as a student of magicks in Nyth Uchel had thrown Mage into the company of the youngest of the DeHelios princes, and given the eight-year gap in ages, they'd formed an unlikely pair. He couldn't quite pinpoint when he'd wanted Tristan's brotherly mentoring to become something—other. He still hadn't decided if he wished to explore that "other" now, but Tristan's ravenous kiss—and his own body's response—proved a strong argument in favor.

As the evening wore on, he felt the full weight of the overwhelming charm and perceptive attentiveness Tristan used to mesmerize those he wanted under his spell. With a rueful inner laugh, Mage acknowledged he was no more immune to Tristan at twenty-six than he'd been at sixteen. He couldn't remember a dinner companion he'd enjoyed more—though the face of a certain violet-eyed beauty he'd spent three weeks with on the *Revertar* did slip into his mind. Best he go now while he could still force himself to leave. With a groan, he slid his chair away from the table and stood. "It's late, Tris. I've got to get back to the ship."

Tris swung around and looked at the timekeeper on the wall over the bar. "Damnation. I didn't realize the time. I'll walk you back." Throwing money down on the table, Tris stood. "After you, Captain."

They accomplished the short walk back to his ship in comfortable silence, each man lost in his own thoughts. Just before Mage turned to walk up the gangway to the *Revertar*, he paused. "I'll contact you when I've gotten the details lined out. As I said, it will take a day or two, and Tris… I enjoyed tonight."

Tris studied him and muttered something under his breath that sounded like a curse. With an implacable hand, he guided Mage behind a large stack of cargo containers and out of sight of the crewmen assigned to guard the entry to the ship. Silently, with a broad hand planted in the middle of Mage's sternum, Tris pushed him back against the hard plasti-crate. "I'm going to kiss you again, Captain."

Mage's heart thudded in his chest, and his cock hardened as Tristan's face came inexorably closer. Tris stopped a hair's breadth from his lips. His teeth gently caught Mage's lower lip and sucked it into his mouth before Tris completed his gentle attack with a tactile meeting of lips and a tangle of tongues. His lips were the only place Tristan touched him, and it was devastating—as if years of pent up desire spilled out of his mouth into Mage. His cock strained at his pants, full-blown and painfully hard. He lost himself until Tris stepped back and put some space between them. Mage let his head fall back to rest on the crates, his mouth still pulsing from the sensual assault.

Tristan's voice came out a warm, honeyed growl. "I intend to have you, you know."

"Yeah. Message received, loud and clear," he said with a soft laugh as he gazed skyward. He never looked at Tristan. He couldn't and remain composed. "Please leave, Tris. I have to stand here a few moments before I'm decent to board. Your presence won't help."

The man laughed, turned on his heel and walked into the night.

CHAPTER FOUR

When Angelica walked out of her apartment that morning, she'd had to look twice at the gorgeous hunk of man flesh who waited with two cups of steaming kaffé, one of which he held out to her with a charming display of even white teeth. His striking face was freshly shaven and he smelled of soap with an occasional hint of an herbal cologne or aftershave—something woodsy and smoky. He towered over her. She was eyelevel with the nipples on his chest, clearly outlined through the finely woven fabric of his black t-shirt. His powerful body didn't carry an ounce of extra flesh. His form-fitting shirt and closely tailored black slacks would have shown any excess. She didn't know why, perhaps it was in the way he held himself, alert to his surroundings, or the controlled fluidity of his physical movements, but he appeared dangerous. *Not a bad trait for a bodyguard, I suppose.* Then there was the telltale shoulder holster holding a Razar 88K snugged to his left side and a sheathed blade strapped to his left thigh. She thought she'd covered her momentary pause and indrawn breath until she saw the knowing amusement in his silver gray eyes. She accepted his offer of kaffé with a murmur of thanks and then attempted to ignore him for the rest of the day. She might as well have ignored a fell wolf loose in the room—an impossibly sexy fell wolf.

Between interviewing incoming staff and overseeing the

placement of her precious neurological equipment, the first day at the medical center proved long. Angelica looked forward to a relaxing soak in a hot bath and an early bedtime. As she walked the gravel path through the natural beauty that comprised the compound, she slowly relaxed. Only her silent shadow, the disturbing masculine presence of her bodyguard, continued to be a source of discomfort. *It wouldn't be a problem if I didn't want to drop to my knees and ask to serve him every time he looks my way.* She sighed softly. *I still owe him an apology.*

When they arrived at the entrance to her apartment, Tristan handed her a small tablet. "Here are the instructions for activating the artificial intelligence in your apartment. There is a protocol to follow for the verbal commands or the AI will not respond. I'm sure you have used systems like this before."

She didn't trust the smile Tris gave her. "What aren't you telling me?"

"I don't know what you're talking about." He nodded. "Have a pleasant evening. I'm downstairs if you need anything."

⊛⊛⊛⊛⊛⊛⊛⊛⊛⊛⊛

Twenty minutes later she definitely needed something—her hands wrapped around Tristan DeHelios' throat as she strangled him to death. With a snarl, Angelica jerked open the door to the interior staircase linking her apartment with that of Tristan's and pounded down the steps. Jerking the door to his apartment open so forcefully it hit the wall with a slam, she stormed into a spacious central room. Tris gazed up at her from a relaxed position on his sofa in front of a media display.

"You!" She pointed with her finger. "What do you mean I'm to address the AI as 'Sir'?" She eyed Tristan DeHelios with growing fury. She stabbed her pointing finger at him. "You programmed *your* features into the AI's holographic display." *Stab.*

"You used *your* voice for the system's verbal response." *Stab.*
"Every time I address the artificial intelligence that controls all
the functions in my apartment, I must interact with a full-scale,
true-to-life image of *you.* According to the command protocol
you have configured, not only must I address the system as 'Sir,'
I must ask for permission!" *Stab.* She threw her hands in the air
and glared at him. She could just imagine standing in front of a
three-dimensional image of Tristan saying, "Sir, may I please have
the interior temperature at seventy-two degrees earth standard?
Sir, may I please have a bath, water at one hundred degrees earth
standard?"

The outrageous man sat there and smiled at her, unperturbed.
"S-I-R stands for 'Synchronous Integral Response.' I thought the
acronym would be easier."

"Normally, 'computer' works just fine."

He laughed. "Where is the fun in that?"

"Change it, please." She leveled a cool stare at him. "And
the holographic display. I am not addressing your image as 'Sir' a
hundred times a day."

Tristan rose gradually to stand, hands on hips, and his eyes
watched her face as if evaluating every tic of muscle. "After the
greeting you gave DeKieran on arrival, I wouldn't have thought
that a problem for you."

"You aren't Lord DeKieran." Her snapped retort felt good—
for a nanosecond. Then, a hot flush of shame crawled her neck. He
might as well be. The wretched man couldn't know he provoked an
identical response in her—the primary reason, she acknowledged,
for her anger. Her heart thudded in her chest. In spite of her fury,
she dropped her eyes and studied the floor. As intently as he
observed her, she couldn't risk what he might see. She hugged
herself tightly. "Please change the protocol." She damned herself
for the break in her voice.

After a short silence Tristan chuckled, a low, wicked, sound born deep in his broad chest. "Sure. The change won't be immediate. 'Sir' has already started learning. I'll have to wipe and reprogram its intelligence. It will take the AI some time to incorporate the new input." He took several steps toward her until she could see his bare feet. The trace of his finger along her jaw did disastrous things to her gut and obliterated her thought processes. "Anything else I can help you with, Angel?"

"May I leave now?" Her whisper stumbled out without thought. *Oh, Goddess, I asked for permission.*

"You may go." He dropped his hand.

She turned and fled.

Nausea rolled in her stomach. How could she have betrayed herself like that? When safely back in her apartment, she gave into the tears that threatened. She didn't indulge herself for long. She refused to give her lapse that much importance, and she still wanted a hot bath.

"Sir."

Immediately, the life-size holographic image of Tristan DeHelios stood before her. He appeared much as he'd looked this morning and so life-like Angelica imagined she could smell his cologne.

"Yes, Dr. Angel?" His deep voice echoed in the stone-walled bathroom.

"May I please have a bath, water temperature one hundred degrees earth standard?"

"Yes, Dr. Angel... Dr. Angel, I detect emotional distress in your voice. My sensors indicate only you and Creator DeHelios present in the residence. Are you under physical threat?"

"No, I am merely upset. Thank you, Sir."

"Yes, Dr. Angel."

"Sir?"

"Yes, Dr. Angel."

"If I may ask, Sir, why do you call Tristan your creator?"

"Tristan DeHelios initiated my sentience and gave me my memories. Is 'creator' an incorrect appellation?"

"No. I suppose not. Thank you for the explanation."

"You are welcome, Dr. Angel."

With her favorite hot finger food arranged on a plate beside a carafe of her favorite wine, Angelica relaxed back into the warm water. Her thoughts kept returning to her unwanted attraction to Tristan DeHelios. He wreaked such emotional havoc within her that she'd unwittingly confirmed the truth about what she'd revealed of her nature that first day when she'd knelt before Lord DeKieran. A wave of helpless turmoil stirred at the thought that he was aware of her submissive nature. Her reaction to Ramsey DeKieran she attributed to her warm feelings for the man who'd rescued her from sexual slavery on Vxloncia, but what explained her response to Tristan DeHelios?

After Vxloncia, she'd run all the neurological tests and psychological profiles recommended for the diagnosis of a damaged psyche. The results indicated only a moderate number of aberrant cerebral pathways. She'd had those repaired promptly. Afterward, her psychological and neurological tests had indicated stable thought processes and a well-integrated personality.

As hard as it was to acknowledge, the history of the past few years forced her to confront the fact she responded positively to inherently dominant men—the more dominant, the more she responded. She'd had brief relationships with men on Talleo IV—handsome, sensitive, caring, sophisticated males—all entirely forgettable. They'd never prompted so much as a tingle up her spine. With a long sigh, she sank deeper into the hot water and sipped her wine. *This must be who I really am.* Now what? She needed a diversion, an outlet for the sexual tension building between her and Tristan. She sat up as a thought occurred to her. *I still owe Captain DeLan a dinner.* The handsome captain, a man she was already attracted to, would provide a definite distraction and quite possibly more. She smiled and poured more wine into her glass.

⚜⚜⚜⚜⚜⚜⚜⚜⚜

The next morning, Angelica held her head up and steeled herself to maintain eye contact with the fatally attractive male standing outside her door. The slight smile twisting the corner of his mouth and the appreciative gleam in his silver eyes did nothing to sooth her churning gut—or her aching head. She should never have finished that bottle of wine. Again, he held out a steaming cup of kaffé. "Good morning, Dr. Giverny," he said with a nod.

Determined to leave behind their disastrous interaction of last night, she forced a smile. "Good morning, Mr. DeHelios. Thank you for the kaffé." Angelica turned and started to walk down the path toward the medical center. Tristan fell in behind her right side. Her eyes remained focused ahead, but her body knew exactly where he was.

"Prince."

"Excuse me?"

"Prince DeHelios. I'm not a mister."

"No, you wouldn't be so ordinary," she muttered under her breath. Angelica paused and turned. She bestowed a brilliant smile on Tris. "I beg your pardon, Prince DeHelios." She set her jaw at the condescending nod of his head. "I need some information."

"I live to serve you, Dr. Angel." Tristan's smoldering gaze conveyed precisely the kind of service he'd like to perform. A frisson of something like fear tickled the nape of her neck.

She stalled, sipped at her kaffé, and examined the colorful flowers growing in the beds along the footpath. Her resolve to put last night behind her and behave in a normal fashion notwithstanding, she couldn't hold his gaze.

"Will you please have someone get me the contact numbers for Captain Magellan DeLan of the VNV *Revertar*? I would like Captain DeLan's personal number. My AI only had the port master's."

"Captain DeLan? What business do you have with Captain DeLan?" Tristan's sharp question pulled her eyes from the flowers to his face.

"I promised him a dinner when we got to port." As soon as the words left her mouth, Angelica felt a sliver of irritation. She didn't owe Tristan DeHelios an explanation. She turned and resumed her walk down the path to the med center. Her bodyguard followed her silently.

CHAPTER FIVE

C aptain DeLan, you have an incoming call from Dr.
Angelica Giverny. Shall I accept the connection?"
The husky female voice of the *Revertar*'s AI
interrupted Mage's tedious review of engineering diagrams.

"Thank you, Purity, connect the call." The irony inherent
in the name of the onboard AI still amused him. He suspected
"purity" had no part in the activities aboard the former pleasure
yacht. The exotic features of Angelica Giverny appeared above
his desk and he relaxed back into his chair and smiled. "Angelica,
your lovely face is a distinct improvement over these technical
drawings. I've missed our daily chats over kaffé. How are you?"

"Magellan." Her extraordinary violet eyes softened into an
expression of pleasure. Her generous mouth widened in a smile of
genuine welcome. "Technical drawings? I hope I'm not calling at a
bad time."

"A call from the stunning Dr. Giverny, whose beauty is only
surpassed by her intelligence, could never be at a bad time. I
always enjoy talking to you."

Her gentle laugh woke his cock while her glorious eyes flirted
with him. "Flatterer. With your manners and handsome face you
probably have ten women in every port."

"You have made me forget all of them." It was his turn to
chuckle at her skeptical look. Strangely, that wasn't far from the

truth. He suspected Angelica Giverny *could* make him forget all the others.

A playful smile on her lips, Angelica shook her head. "I would like to invite you to have dinner with me. I have a wonderful apartment in the med compound and the food replicator has an amazing repertoire. We can continue our game of Labyrinth. I might even let you win."

"How could I possibly refuse an offer of dinner and Labyrinth?" Mage laughed. "You don't have to let me win. I want my certain victory untarnished."

She looked over her shoulder, spoke with someone behind her and turned back to him with a frown. "I'm sorry. A patient needs me. I have to go. Tomorrow night? Seven-ish?"

"I'll be there." He nodded and smiled.

"Good. I'll leave a badge for you at reception. It will get you into the residential compound. After that, simply follow the footpath to my residence. One of the security personnel will show you the way." She smiled and stood. "I'm looking forward to seeing you, Mage." In a flurry of sparkling particles, her image disintegrated.

⁂

Mage's eyes wandered, taking in the soft greens of grass, ferns and towering trees, the riotous colors of the many blooming plants and the low gurgle of running water. The environment contained within the huge dome was enchanting—a setting appropriate for the lovely, intelligent woman he had come to admire during the three weeks he'd had the pleasure of her company. Dr. Angelica Giverny, he mused. *I admire more than her intellect.* He avoided physical involvement with passengers on board his ship for many practical reasons. *But we're not on the* Revertar *anymore.* He grinned and tossed the bottle of what he knew to be Angelica's favorite wine into the air, catching it with ease. No. They weren't on the *Revertar* anymore and he fully intended to indulge in any pleasures offered.

Tristan had mentioned he worked as a public liaison and security officer in the medical compound. As he strolled through the green spaces, his eyes scanned the personnel, wondering if he'd see Tristan. He'd observed a number of Blue Daggers and a good-looking redhead who he thought was their commander, but no Tristan. Just as well. Tristan had stated his desires clearly. He still hadn't decided if he wanted to fall in line. His feelings for Tristan had always run deep. If he began a physical relationship with Tris, the involvement could devour him. The wise decision would be to maintain only a platonic friendship. He had no plans to leave the Verdantian navy, and Tris would never remain without a sexual partner during his prolonged absences. He'd never considered himself a masochist, and getting sexually involved with Tristan would set himself up for serious future pain—far better to lose himself in the delectable femininity of Angelica Giverny.

Angelica greeted him at the door wearing an indigo blue halter dress of some ultra-sheer material. The front plunged to her waist then flared to a full skirt of translucent, frothy material that halted at her knees while her bare back and shoulders remained an uninterrupted expanse of silky pale skin. In stiletto-heeled, strappy sandals, her legs looked light-years long and her hair shimmered in a shoulder-length brunette fall. The way she'd dressed, indeed the woman herself, invited him to sin. He'd be semi-aroused all night at the thought of indulging.

Hours later, the wreckage of an expansive course of delicacies littered the table. After the limited menu available on the *Revertar*, he'd savored every bite—almost as much as he'd savored the company of the charming woman across from him. The holographic image of Tristan had disconcerted him until Angelica explained what had happened and turned off the artificial intelligence. They'd both had a chuckle over it. Their dinner had been protracted as they sat and conversed over wide-ranging subjects until deep into the evening hours.

Mage raised his glass of wine in tribute to Angelica and took a sip. "My pleasure in this delicious dinner is exceeded only by my enchantment with my exquisite hostess."

The lovely doctor lowered her gaze and a light flush spread over her cheeks. "I could say the same thing. I'm so glad you could dine with me tonight." She cocked her head and her eyes sought his. She smiled shyly. "Should we finish our wine on the balcony? It is so beautiful, especially at night when the roof panels are open. I feel like I can reach out and touch the stars."

"I'd enjoy that. After you." Mage rose, helped her from her chair, then followed her out to the balcony. The subtle scent of her perfume went straight to his head. Of course, that could have been the third bottle of wine they'd shared—but he didn't think so.

Angelica leaned against the railing and looked up into the velvet black above them. Bright sparkles of distant stars sprinkled the heavens. The major and minor Verdantian moons gleamed pale yellow in the sky. "Aren't the stars beautiful? I never tire of watching them. You can't see the heavens on Talleo IV. Our atmosphere is too polluted."

"Yes, I've always thought the stars mesmerizing, but the stars possess a cold beauty." Mage set his glass carefully on the balcony railing and moved to stand immediately behind her. He slipped his hands around the warm flesh of her waist. He felt her heartbeat thudding through her body and her breathing turn rapid, but she remained pliant under his hands. "You're equally beautiful, and you burn me like the nearest sun. Turn around, Angelica." She rotated slowly in his arms and stopped when eye-level with his chest.

"Yes?" she whispered.

"I am going to make love to you," he murmured. "If I have misread the signals tell me."

Her head shook slowly and she raised her face. "You have misread nothing. I want you." Her breathy admission swept away the last of his restraint, and he could no more ignore the lure of her lush parted lips than he could have done without oxygen. He cupped her face in his hands and held her immobile while he caressed her mouth with a brush of his lips. He placed light kisses at the corners of her mouth, and then caught her upper lip between his teeth and gently traced its fullness with his tongue. At her moan, he captured her mouth fully and explored the sweet taste of her. She melted against him in total surrender for endless moments then pushed away, gasping for breath and clinging to his arm for support.

"Sweet Goddess, Verdantian men! My patients tell me you formally train to satisfy women. Can that be true?"

He chuckled. "Actually, yes. We do."

"You must have been an 'A' student."

He smoothed some of her glossy hair behind her ear and nuzzled the downy soft skin on her neck. "Mmmhmm." He worked small kisses to her delicate ear and drowned in the scent of her hair and flesh. "Teacher's pet. I spent countless afternoons earning extra credit."

Angelica gasped when he nibbled on the lobe of her ear. "Is it possible to die from too much pleasure?"

"No… but you might think you're going to." He chuckled, picked her up in his arms, and strode back into her apartment. "Bedroom?"

"Turn right. The open door on the left."

He smiled to himself when he entered her room. Wine sat decanted on a bedside table and crisp, snowy, sheets were turned back on a sumptuous, expansive, mattress. Plump pillows reclined against a headboard of metal worked into an elaborate depiction of a woodland scene. Slender metallic cords held back a bed canopy of transparent material studded with sparkling bits of reflective glass. When released from their confines, the bed drapery would enclose those in the bed in a private world. Mage could readily imagine other uses for those cords. The soft chimes of some exotic, otherworldly music floated through the air. Hidden lighting cast a warm ambient glow. The entire room wove a spell of seduction.

He laid a relaxed Angelica on the bed and stood looking down at her with a crooked smile and a raised eyebrow. "Rather sure of yourself, weren't you. I'm beginning to wonder if this was my idea."

She stretched with feline grace and with a shy smile pushed up to sit. "I'm not sure of myself at all. Merely hoping you would desire what I want to give. We can still finish that game of Labyrinth if you'd prefer."

"Not a chance." He held out his hand. "Come here."

With a flick of her violet eyes, she placed her hand in his. His hand wrapped hers easily. He felt as if he held a tiny bird or some other fragile creature in his palm. He drew her upright. His fingertips traced her collarbones. The tautly-stretched skin felt silky under the pads of his fingers. Holding her gaze, he slid his hands to the nape of her neck and undid the single clasp holding the front of her dress together. As he released the fastening, the fine material slithered gently off her breasts and she stood before him, nude from the waist up, a finely crafted being of porcelain skin and remarkable beauty. Her ribcage rose and fell with her agitated breathing. It was her only movement. As for his body, he didn't think it possible to get harder. He wanted to splay her open and ravish her without heed. But… he'd always been a patient sort. He could wait—given the right incentive.

Mage gently cupped one blue-veined breast and thrummed his thumb over the soft pink nipple, tipping it until it formed a tight bud. "Are you sensitive here?"

"Yes. Very." She caught her lower lip in her teeth and choked back a whimper as with a smile he gently caught her now hard flesh between his thumb and forefinger and rolled it back and forth. His other hand cupped her other breast and began to tease its nipple into hardness.

"If I do this right, I should be able to bring you to the verge of climax." Angelica's eyes flared. "Shall we see if I remember the trick of it?" He chucked as she nodded a silent yes, her lip still caught between her teeth. He continued the gentle teasing of her nipples for quiet minutes, watching her face intently until her eyes became half-lidded and then closed completely. Her lips parted and the moist tip of her tongue dampened her lush bottom lip as she drew deep, shuddering, inhalations through her open mouth. Finally, her small hands rose to encircle his wrists.

"Please, I can't… Oh, please." Her words exploded on a husky breath. She dropped her hands behind her waist and in another moment layers of filmy blue material floated to the floor and Angelica stepped out of the puddle of blue froth at her feet clad in only a scrap of lace and her stiletto heels. She hesitated, then lifted her head, and her eyes met his. "May I help you undress?"

When he nodded, she sank gracefully in front of him and captured one of his hands in hers. She unfastened the studs holding his cuffs closed, then placed a kiss in the center of his palm before doing the same for his other hand. Her fingers then went to his belt and she glanced upward to ask for permission.

"Wait a moment." Never breaking eye contact with the delicate beauty kneeling at his feet, Mage slid his shoes off and then unbuttoned his shirt. "Now continue."

She undid the buckle to his belt and the slide hook holding the waist of his trousers closed. Her trembling fingers passed within fractions of an inch of the prominent erection pressing the front of his pants, and her eyes dwelt on it with longing… but she didn't touch him. He suspected she wouldn't until he directed her to. He'd been surprised but not displeased when she'd knelt in front of him. He'd recognized immediately what she was, and he was more than willing to play dominant to her submissive.

His thigh muscles twitched as she ran the palms of her hands up the front of his legs, and a damp spot appeared on the front of his dress pants as his excitement leaked from the head of his cock. Her eyes caught his once more as her fingers stalled on the zip closure. "May I?"

"You have permission to open my trousers. You may not touch me."

"Ohhh…" Disappointment colored her voice and her hands fluttered in the air a hair's breadth from his cock as if it were all she could do to discipline herself not to handle him. "Yes, Sir."

And there it was—her open admission of her nature and the role she had cast for him. He had no objections. His groin ached with heavy arousal and his cock twitched against his belly. More moisture escaped to darken the fine material of his pants.

Pulling the cloth gently away from his groin, Angelica lowered the slide on the zip closure by infinitesimal degrees, her eyes devouring the bare skin revealed. Mage stifled his own grunt of pleasure when his cock sprang free from the restriction of his clothing and stood, ramrod straight, against his bare abdomen. Angelica swallowed audibly. Her hands, resting on his thighs just above his knees, shook. She stared at his cock, and he thought she whimpered. When her pink tongue came out to moisten her lower lip again, *he* felt like whimpering.

"Remain kneeling, Angel. Put your hands behind your back." She obeyed him immediately, but her eyes flashed to his with a message of discontent and appeal.

"No. You may touch me only when and how I say." He ran a caressing knuckle over her cheek to soften the harshness of his directive. Truth be known, if she had touched him at that moment he would have gone off. It was pure torment to stand in front of her, his twitching cock inches from the warm mouth he longed to invade; but it was a familiar torture and one he had been schooled to ignore. Mage slid his slacks and boxers over his buttocks and they fell unhindered to the floor. He stripped them off his feet and along with his socks and shirt tossed them carelessly behind him. He inhaled deeply and steeled himself for the pleasure to come.

"Now, my sweet girl, you may touch me with your lips and your tongue. Keep your hands behind your back." His cock reacted to her delighted murmur by jerking against his stomach and he almost laughed as she chased it to a halt by flattening her tongue against its length. The guileless smile that pulled at her lips and the devilish light in her eyes did make him laugh. "Gently, Angel. I want you very much, and it's been a long, dry spell."

"Yes, Sir," she whispered, and the true torment began as her warm, moist lips and hot tongue began to lap at his balls. The gentle torture of his cock followed as Angelica ran her tongue the length of his organ then sucked the head into her mouth and circled the soft cushion of his glans in a teasing exploration.

His hands spread in a bracket on either side of her face and stilled her movement. Her eyes flashed to his in question. "Don't move your tongue. Simply hold me in your luscious mouth." She exhaled slowly and closed her eyes. They sprang open again when he bent slightly at the waist and his fingers found her erect nipples. He rolled the erect buds firmly.

"Mmmhumph!" She sucked him deeper into her mouth and

shuddered. She clenched her thighs together with a slight squirm.

"Ah, ah... now what did I tell you? Hmm? Don't move. Spread your legs." Her eyes flashed desperation at him. "Yes, Angel. I know. It's almost impossible to restrain yourself. Do it." He ignored the pressure building in his balls and continued to tease her breasts until desperate whimpers escaped the lips that cradled him. Once again she sucked him deeper to hold onto him while her lower body writhed, seeking surcease. His cock jumped in her mouth from the stimulation.

Angelica seemed to take that as a cue to begin working him in earnest. He should have stopped her, but he was no more immune to her than she to him. Her head bobbed up and down and she made mewing noises of appreciation as her tongue swirled around and around the head of his cock. Rivulets of saliva traced a path down her chin, glistening, and the need to discover if she was equally wet between her thighs overwhelmed him.

"Stop." He clamped her head between his hands when she whimpered a protest and was slow to obey. She'd pushed him perilously close to finishing, and he jerked in her mouth. "Stand up." Angelica pulled off him, and he steadied her as she rose on wobbly legs. After a moment's evaluation, he stripped off her panties, swept her into his arms and tossed her onto the waiting bed. She landed on her back, legs sprawled. The plump, dewy flesh revealed between her open thighs provoked his libido to a dangerous level. By the Consorts' balls, she was hot. With only breast play, she was wet and wanting. Perhaps it had been as long for her as it had been for him. "Fair warning. The first time won't be gentle."

Angelica's eyes widened. "The first time?"

"Ummhmm. I intend to take you several times tonight, Angel. You have problems with that?"

She shook her head slowly and a sensual smile played at the

corners of her mouth. "None whatsoever, Sir… and Sir?"

"Hmm?"

"I don't break easily."

He fell on her with avid hunger, kneeing her thighs further apart and then catching her knees in the crook of his elbows to hold her fully spread for his entrance. The blunt head of his cock slid in her moisture, and he paused before penetrating her. "This will get rough."

Her eyes closed at his growled words. Soundlessly, she grabbed at the headboard to brace herself. Her violet gaze met his and her chin dipped in a subtle acquiescence that was all the acceptance he needed. He hilted himself in one powerful lunge. Both of them gasped; he when the slick clench of hot pussy suddenly enveloped his tortured cock; she when he hit the limits of her inner flesh and ground his pubic bone against her cleft. His balls jerked up so tightly they felt like stones ground into his groin.

"Brace," he growled, then slammed himself into her repeatedly, all the while holding her legs tautly spread. Insane sensation flooded his body and in an unprecedented action for him, Mage ignored his internal voice—the one that monitored his partner's response and sought to give equal pleasure—and simply took. His only concession to Angelica was to brace his own palm against the headboard when his driving hips defeated her efforts to hold herself in position and she risked being crushed against the metal bed frame. In an embarrassingly short time, he threw back his head, arched his back, and through clenched jaws, bellowed his climax into the dark.

After endless minutes of pulling air through his nose in forceful inhalations and waiting for his heartbeat to stabilize, he returned to himself. He released the brutal grip he'd maintained on one soft globe of Angelica's buttocks and relaxed. His conscience attacked him for his lack of consideration. Had she found any pleasure in that ferocious coupling? He couldn't say. He wasn't leaving her bed, however. He wasn't close to satiation. Holding himself sheathed within her, Mage stretched out on top of her, propping himself up on his elbows and gently smoothing the disordered hair away from her face.

"By *Her* light, that was not well done of me. I'm not usually so…selfish." He snorted softly. "Look at me, Angel."

Her eyes opened languorously. The corners of her mouth tipped in a dreamy smile. "Mmm?"

"I'm sorry. I must have hurt you…" His mind absorbed her contented expression as his eyes roamed her face. "Though perhaps not as much as I'd thought." Her head rolled to the side and a slow flush crept up her neck. She choked on some words he didn't understand. "What did you say?"

He felt her ribcage rise and fall underneath him in a soft sigh. "I said I liked it," Angelica whispered. He waited in silence to see if she would continue, and she did. "The primitive urgency of your passion. Your absolute control of me."

By now, the flush had spread to her cheekbones and it dawned on him she was ashamed.

"There is no need for embarrassment. As a trained psychologist, you of all people know that for some women and some men submissive tendencies are natural."

Her face turned back to him. "Are they natural to me? That is the question that bedevils me." Her eyes closed. "Is this my true nature? Or is this the creature Vxloncia created?"

"If this is where you find pleasure, does it really matter?"

She examined him, her thoughts transparent as they chased across her face. "I suppose it only matters if my life-partner considers my sexual needs aberrant, for they are not going away. No amount of psychological or physiological treatment seems to alter the shape of my desires."

He traced the eyebrows of the beautiful woman beneath him and considered her words. "If you stay on Verdantia, you will have no difficulties finding such a man—or woman. No one here will think your desires unusual. Our way of life teaches—requires, actually—acceptance of all forms of sexuality between our citizens."

His hips pulsed between the cradle of her hips as his cock started to fill again. *I wonder how many times I'll have her tonight before this mad craving subsides.*

Her eyelids shuttered her violet gaze and her hips shimmied, probably in reaction to what she could certainly feel happening within her.

"Is this acceptance due to those 'magickal rites' that so obsess and fascinate the galaxy?" She winced slightly when he pulled her to him to shift them toward the center of the bed.

"In part. You know our planet is sentient. Our Great Mother connects with us most easily when our bodily energies are excited. As far back as Old Earth with its tantric sexual practices, it was acknowledged that spiritual expansion is enhanced during sexual arousal. The more prolonged and extreme the arousal, the greater the expansion of the person's elemental energies and therefore the easier it is to join with the natural powers governing the universe. On Verdantia, this means uniting with our Great Mother, the planet's sentience that shepherds and nurtures us."

"Mmm. So the cerebral interface everyone else achieves on other planets with implants and data chips, Verdantians achieve with sex." Angelica closed her eyes on a moan when he brought his hand to her breast and began a gentle massage, his thumb circling her pink areola and glancing across her nipple.

"Yes. With the exception of this small city, Arkodaenia, those technologies are useless on Verdantia. Mineral deposits of diaman crystal emit high levels of electromagnetic resonance which render those technologies unreliable, so to unite with our sentient planet, to utilize Her vast power, we use sex, sometimes enhanced by the aphrodisiac cinnagin."

"That is why you school in the arts of arousal." Angelica opened her eyes briefly, then closed them again in obvious pleasure.

He chuckled at her wry observation. His gentle rocking back and forth in her warmth had brought him to full hardness. He was inclined to proceed far slower this second coupling. "Yes. Now, since you have been an obedient partner thus far, I am going to give you the full benefit of my years of study—minus the cinnagin."

"Thank all the gods," she whispered. Angelica stilled completely underneath him and her eyes opened, blank and unfocused as if reliving some memory. "I experienced cinnagin... as punishment."

Mage cocked his head. "Punishment?"

"My cold unresponsive body angered my master on Vxloncia. He fancied himself something of a cocksman. He took his inability to make me rise to him as a personal affront. To torture me, he forced the aphrodisiac down my throat, then bound me to the columns in the entry hall. My agonized arousal, my abject begging to be fucked, entertained him and his visitors, hugely." She closed her eyes.

"Did he take you then?"

She shook her head. "No. From then on, he refused to have anything to do with me sexually. He'd purchased a new toy and used me for only the most menial work." Her eyes opened and softened. "Then, as you know, I passed into the care of Lord DeKieran. Ah!" Angelica gasped and then moaned when Mage grabbed her hips and rolled to his back, seating her firmly upon his erection and holding her impaled as he rocked her hips.

"Those days are past. I want you incapable of thinking of anything but what I'm doing." He grinned as her eyes flared then narrowed in concentration when he pressed his thumbs to either side of her clit. The copious fluid from his cum and her previous arousal allowed the fleshy pads to slide up and down the narrow shaft of her clit easily and the noises escaping from her mouth testified to her enjoyment.

"Now, put your hands behind your back, clasp your wrists and don't let go." She did as he commanded and Mage proceeded to inflict his own brand of torture. With each roll of her hips, his thumbs caught her clit between them and slipped across those wildly sensitive nerves in the most gentle of liquid caresses. From her occasional grimace, Mage suspected he overfilled her hot, slick sheath, but he never varied his slow, rhythmic grind inside her, and after some time her grimaces became helpless moans. He allowed Angelica to rise to the brink of orgasm, then with hands that were certain to leave bruises the next day, he held her motionless, the pressure of his thumbs withdrawn, the only movement the throbbing of his hard cock within her. When her pleas for completion faded and her head fell back with a whimper, when the tiny fibrillations within that signaled her imminent orgasm ceased, he would begin the whole process again. He marked time by the urgency building in his balls. His schooling in sexual control and Angelica's lack of it became glaringly apparent from the tears of gratitude that coursed from her glazed eyes when he eventually permitted her to come. He released his punishing hold of her hips and pumped up into her, his thumbs rotating gently on her clit. Now she was the one who arched her back and screamed her climax into the room. She tightened on him with painful intensity and milked his cock with orgasmic contractions. With a body-shaking shudder, he came in vigorous spurts that seemed to last forever, his abdomen contracting with a grunt at each ejaculation.

In the aftermath, Angelica collapsed on his chest and began to sob softly.

Concerned, Mage gathered her into his arms and stroked her gently from the crown of her head to the rise of her buttocks. "Didn't you like what we did?"

She nodded her head vehemently and choked out a watery, "It hurt, some, but I loved what we did." She raised a teary-eyed face to his and scrubbed at her eyes. "I loved what you did." She sniffed noisily. "Shit. I hate crying. I can't express myself properly while I'm crying."

Mage chuckled in sympathy and waited for long moments while she composed herself. Finally, with a sigh she reached for his face with a caress. "It was too good. How can... how can..." She gave up and subsided against his chest with a sniffle.

"At the risk of sounding like an egotistical bastard, let me complete what I think you started to say. You are worried about finding someone else who will satisfy you when I leave."

Her head nodded on his chest. "You're Pottsdim likor. You explode in my mouth and blaze a fire into my pussy. All I've known up to now is sour ale that gives me gas."

His laughter began deep in his gut and rolled out of his mouth, filling the bedroom. Angelica punched him weakly.

Rolling both of them to the side, he wrapped her in his arms, raised her chin, and met her eyes. "For the next three months, don't give a thought to replacing me. After that?" He shrugged and traced a finger over her lips. "I find I like you exceeding well, Dr. Giverny—have since the moment I met you. Who knows how I'll feel in ninety days?"

Tear-spiked lashes surrounded the violet eyes that smiled up at him. "I find I like you exceedingly well, also, Captain DeLan. As you say, who knows?"

He rolled to his back and pulled the bedcovers over both of

them. *At least she made me forget about Tristan for a while.* With the lovely doctor snugged firmly under one shoulder, her head resting on his chest, he fell asleep.

Early morning half-light shining in his eyes woke him. Angelica had rolled to her back and slept with arms akimbo and legs sprawled over his thighs. She looked delectable. He called himself several unflattering names. He should leave her alone, but he couldn't resist. He shifted to lie between her legs and brought his mouth to her swollen flesh with gentle lapping strokes. Her regular breathing hitched and he glanced over the glossy brown curls on her pubic mound to meet a half-lidded violet gaze.

"Again?"

He smiled at the incredulity in her voice. "If I can't make you beg for it, I'll stop. How's that?" Angelica flopped back into her pillows with a wail that sounded more like surrender than protest.

When he left her, the sun had cleared the horizon fully and the new day was upon them. He chuckled at her somnolent form collapsed in the bed. She gave no indication she was interested in moving, but he had to be up and away. A disordered sheet covered one leg and part of her abdomen but the rest of her glorious self remained in full view. She finally opened one eye and peered at him when, fully dressed, he bent to kiss her good-bye. "You are an incredible woman, Dr. Giverny. I'll be in touch."

As he drew back from the kiss, a smile lingered on her lips but she didn't open her eyes. "Mmmhmm. You are a total stud, Captain DeLan, but you know that."

As the lift descended to the ground floor, Mage enjoyed the complete relaxation that infused his muscles. For the first time in almost a year, the daily plague of sexual frustration had vanished. For the moment, it seemed his nagging libido was satisfied. He stretched and opened the door to the outside. Ah, life was good.

"Magellan DeLan, what in the seven hells are you doing

coming out of Angelica Giverny's apartment at this hour of the morning?"

Mage stopped in his tracks. "Tristan." The door closed behind him. "I might ask you the same thing. What are you doing in front of Angelica Giverny's apartment at this hour of the morning?"

"I'm her bodyguard. I'm supposed to be here." Tris straightened with a growl and hurled the two cups of kaffé he'd been holding to the ground. "Answer my fucking question. Why are you here?"

Mage eyed Tristan and replied mildly, "If you want to know, you'll have to ask the lady." Mage didn't wait for a response. He nodded and sauntered off, well aware Tristan was quivering with repressed emotion. Anger? Jealousy? Now that was an intriguing thought. *And just who is he jealous of? Me or Angelica?* Interesting. He couldn't account for the ridiculous notion that popped into his head. *Perhaps he wants us both. I wonder how Angelica would feel about that?*

In spite of his sexual satiation, his groin stirred at the thought of an encounter with the fair Angelica that included Tristan. *Ah, fuck. I'm so out of my depth with him. Tris means to have me, and I don't know if surrender is wise.* It would be better to avoid Tristan completely until he decided whether or not he wanted to take their interaction to a more intimate level. After last night, he knew what he wanted to propose. *No, forget it.* Tris would never agree to a threesome.

CHAPTER SIX

Tris watched the tight ass of the object of his lust walk away and forced himself not to chase Mage down. *Well, shit.* The man looked as relaxed as a stud horse after breeding a mare. Tristan's day continued its slide into the slush pit. Ole violet-eyes didn't roll out of bed and stagger through the door to meet him until almost midday. He didn't care about the late start. It was how she looked—how she acted. From the careful way she walked, the slight grimace when she sat and the dreamy look that came over her face when she thought no one watched, he just knew Mage had fucked her silly. He couldn't bait her into anger either. She simply smiled and murmured something placating. In the face of her unruffled composure, he retreated into sullen silence and brooded.

"Dr. Giverny, Lady Katrine DeClousey is here for her final neuro-pathing."

Tristan closely examined the dark-headed woman Angelica's attending nurse ushered into the doctor's primary exam and treatment room. Her beauty was extraordinary, but more notable was the vulnerability and fear that shone from her expressive mahogany-colored eyes. The woman's gaze flew to him immediately upon entrance and she shrank into the nurse/attendant. In his opinion, were the attendant's arms not wrapping her waist, at the sight of him, Lady DeClousey would have bolted. Compassion replaced by anger spiked through him, and he fell back to a far corner, trying his best to look innocuous. What type of treatment would create such distress at the mere sight of an unknown male? Tris didn't want to speculate.

Angelica flew to Katrine and held one of the lady's hands gently. "Lady Katrine, this gentleman is my bodyguard, Tristan DeHelios. He is Verdantian, and while he may look like a bad guy, he is harmless to you. He is here to protect us, like the Khlossian, Tok. You remember Tok, from the *Revertar*? Huge scary guy but gentle and kind?"

Under Angelica's soothing patter, the woman took a deep breath and offered Tris a tentative, "Sir."

Tristan returned her acknowledgement and murmured, "I'm just Tristan, my lady. I'll also respond to 'Hey, you.'" A surge of triumph flooded him when Katrine nodded shyly and attempted a wobbly smile.

"Tristan, then," she whispered.

"Lady Katrine, if you will, please get comfortable on the treatment chaise. Nurse Jeanette will hook you up and we will start your final re-pathing." Angelica beamed a smile at DeClousey as her busy fingers traced over red pathways forming on a holographic display of a human brain and spinal column. "You are almost there, Katrine. We're at the end of a long process and you've been a star patient. In another three hours, more or less, your world will have changed, permanently, for the better. Nurse Jeanette is administering a light sedative. When you awake, all your aberrant programming will be gone and you will once again be yourself and only yourself. Now, breathe deeply, relax and count backward from twenty for me."

After Katrine's voice faltered and went quiet at fifteen, Tris asked in a hushed whisper, "That hologram is Lady DeClousey's brain?"

"Yes. You can speak normally. She doesn't hear you."
Angelica indicated the hologram sparkling in the air next to her.
"The red pathways are those inserted by Lontz and his scientist.
We're going to untangle that mess and reinstate normal neuro-
connectors without damaging Lady Katrine's brain—a somewhat
delicate procedure. I would appreciate no distractions. So, please,
if you would not speak?" After her softly murmured request,
Angelica and her assistant dropped all pretense of congeniality.
Their concentration focused keenly, grimly, upon the holographic
mockup.

The clipped voice of her assistant continually read aloud the
displays of ever-changing numbers under headings whose names
had no meaning to him. What was "temporal lobe absorption rate"
or "percent neurogenesis in the hippocampus," for the Mother's
sake? Obviously, the numbers meant something to Angelica. Her
fingers flew across the holograph. Brow creased, muttering under
her breath, she erased existing red lines and replaced them with
tracers of cobalt blue. Occasionally, the red paths stubbornly
reinstated themselves as if by magick. Time and time again, her
industrious fingers rerouted sparks of pulsing scarlet into paths of
cool indigo. Tris silently watched, intrigued and impressed as this
tiny woman rewired a living brain.

Hours later, he escorted Angelica to the small café on the
grounds of the med center and sat with her as she drank a tall
fruit drink. Her hands trembled and lines of fatigue creased her
forehead. Her eyelids drifted closed.

"How many people are qualified to do what you just did?"
Angelica's eyes flew open in surprise.

"Remapping a brain?"

"If that is what you were doing, yes."

Angelica shrugged on a tired exhale. "When I graduated
med school there were… half a dozen? I don't know. Perhaps

by now there are more. It's an obscure specialty. The cerebral probe machines that warp the mind like this have been outlawed universe-wide, so this kind of brain damage is rare." She took a sip of her drink and rubbed her face. Tris crossed his arms and gazed thoughtfully at Angelica. *She really is quite special. What did the Tetriarch have to promise to get her to a backwater planet like Verdantia?*

Angelica was oblivious to his scrutiny. Her hand propped up her head as her eyelids closed. "The neuro-repathing is crucial in the battle to reintegrate a woman's personality, to return her to who she is meant to be. Normally, personality is an ever-evolving trait. The brain is constantly learning. Lontz's scientist found a way to block the learning receptors after freezing a personality at a certain point in development. In this case, an unnaturally subservient state." She mumbled her explanation, never opening her eyes. The reason for her extreme fatigue slapped Tristan in the face. *Magellan DeLan.* And just like that, he was angry all over again.

The week passed and his admiration for the skill of Dr. Giverny grew apace with his frustration with Mage. That gods-be-damned, black-haired, green-eyed bastard had thoroughly screwed Tristan's game. No—*she* had thoroughly screwed his game by seducing the man Tris had marked as his own. It was Angelica Giverny's fault. In spite of his growing respect for her, she'd misjudged him if she thought he'd roll over and let her sweep Magellan out of his life before Tris had a chance to sample what he'd rejected eight years before.

Adding to his discontent, Mage had begun to avoid him. His calls went unreturned. Mage politely refused his written invitations to dinner with no excuse given. Tris knew the man was busy prepping the *Revertar* for dry dock, but enough was enough.

Tristan brushed the front of his dress coat and straightened the fall of lace from his jabot and cuffs while the petty officer of the VNV *Revertar* examined his formal invitation to dine with the captain—the invitation Tristan had swiped from Angelica's mail—though Tris preferred to think of it as "intercepted and redirected." The young junior officer straightened and with a smart salute, handed the crisp white card with raised black script back to Tris.

"Dr. Giverny, I'll inform the captain you've arrived. It's a pleasure to have you onboard, sir. I hope you and Captain DeLan enjoy your dinner. I know the cooks have been working on something special. Would you like a crewmember to escort you to the captain's private wardroom?"

Tris smiled warmly. "No, I know the way, but thank you," he eyed the officer's name tag, "Petty Officer Grant."

Tris walked briskly down several hallways, up in a lift and then down another corridor. He'd studied a schematic of the ship before coming and this time knew precisely where he was going. The wardroom was exactly as plotted and he opened the door and stepped inside. Mouthwatering fragrances wafted from silver serving dishes arrayed on a sideboard that stretched the length of the small room. A central table was set with immaculate white linens and gleaming tableware. Mage's voice came from a small pantry off the larger room. "Angelica, welcome. I hope you like…" His voice trailed off as he exited the pantry holding two clear goblets half-filled with a blush-pink liquid. With a composure Tristan rather admired, Mage set the two glasses on the sideboard and faced him. "Tristan." A dark eyebrow arched over a green eye. "I suppose if you are here I shouldn't expect Dr. Giverny."

"If you were to ask Petty Officer Grant, Dr. Giverny did arrive for a private dinner with the captain, but no, Angelica will not be joining us."

A smile lurked around the corners of Mage's mouth. "I see. Is she tied up somewhere in her apartment or did you simply intercept my invitation?"

Tristan chuckled. "I suspect she would enjoy being tied up, but no, I appropriated the invitation. She never saw it." Tristan held Mage's gaze and prowled toward him. "You've been avoiding me."

Mage stepped sideways to place a large armchair between them. He countered Mage's movement, and Mage slipped behind the dining table with agile grace. With a self-deprecating laugh, Tristan stopped and held his hands palm up in surrender. "I simply want to have a pleasant dinner with you before you leave for who knows how long to put the *Revertar* into dry dock. I promise I won't accost you."

"Your word as a gentleman."

Tris nodded. "My word as a gentleman."

Mage sighed and relaxed. "Have a seat. Will you drink a glass of Zeta Starlight? It's a pricey liquor imported from Alpha Centauri. Too fruity a bouquet for my taste, but it's Angelica's favorite. I've opened the bottle. It would be a shame to waste it. I can offer a Pottsdim chaser." Mage smiled and Tristan immediately discarded his promise not to accost Mage.

The man was too beautiful. The careful tailoring of his dress whites displayed his broad shoulders and trim waist. The skirt of his jacket rode above uniform pants that cupped his ass in an entirely distracting fashion. Mage had dressed to impress. Tristan was impressed. He vowed he would see Mage stripped down as the Great Mother had made him before too many more hours passed. *My sweet Magellan, I'm not a gentleman. I'm a nobleman. They're not always one and the same.* Evidently he'd let the silence stretch too long, or Mage was better at reading him than he'd thought, for the man cleared his throat.

"Tristan, you have that look. You gave your word."

"Yes. My word as a gentleman. That I did." Tris smiled

disarmingly and was pleased when, after a long look of evaluation, Mage took a deep breath and once more relaxed. Tris wanted Mage off guard.

He accepted the pink liquor Mage held out and sat down at the table. Mage sat opposite him and rang a small hand bell. A young female sailor dressed in a crisp apron responded promptly and attended them throughout an excellent dinner. Tristan steered the conversation toward the latest advances in the hyper-drive and the new ISNAC-7 navigation system that would shortly be installed on the *Revertar*. Warming to the topic of all the new toys Mage would have to play with, their discussion became animated and time flew.

As the final course was cleared away, Mage rose and stepped into the small pantry and returned with two tumblers of a dark gold. "Your Pottsdim, as promised."

"Thank you." Tris sipped at the dark liquid, rolling it in his mouth in appreciation before swallowing.

"Will there be anything else, Sir?" the young sailor who'd been attending them asked.

"No, Janette, thank you very much," Mage said with a smile. "You're relieved. I'll carry on from here. Please tell the rest of my wardroom staff they are at liberty until 1200 hours tomorrow."

"Yes, Sir! Thank you, Sir." With a snap to attention and a crisp salute, the young woman exited and closed the door quietly behind her.

"Alone at last," Tristan quipped and raised his glass to Mage.

"You're incorrigible." Mage laughed and took a careful sip of his drink. "Would you like a tour of the bridge?"

You are trying very hard to avoid being alone with me, Captain. Damn you. Tris gritted his teeth and pasted a pleased expression on his face. The offer of a close-up look at the bridge of a starship was a potent palliative. He tossed back the remainder of his Pottsdim. "I'd love it."

Tristan enjoyed observing Mage in his element almost as much as he reveled in exploring the sophisticated tech devices that powered and controlled the *Revertar*. The man was a natural leader and it was obvious his crew thought highly of him. As they strolled back to Mage's quarters after a thoroughly fascinating tour, Tris had a gut check moment. He really liked Mage. He really, really liked Mage—more than that, he respected what the adult Mage had made of himself. *Unlike me, still an errand boy for my older brother.* Tris snorted in self-disgust. *Well, I'm not asking him to marry me, so where's the harm in showing him a good time and trying to mend some old wounds? Assuming I can get him to stop acting like a virgin on her wedding night.*

When they entered Mage's cabin, Tris glanced around, curious to see what sort of accommodations were offered to a ship's captain. The room was surprisingly spacious, with thick, sound-absorbing carpeting, a writing desk and chair, two comfortable-looking armchairs set at right angles to each other with a table between and a separate alcove for a double bed. One sim-wood paneled wall contained a personal food replicator, a media and computation center and a monitor that scrolled a continuous readout of the ship's vital stats.

"Purity, please wake me at 0800 hours and remind me to call Dr. Giverny before we depart Arkodaenia," Mage said.

"Yes, Captain. Will Prince DeHelios require overnight accommodations?"

Tris swept Mage with a casual glance that was anything but casual. What was the man going to say?

"Not at this time, Purity. Thank you."

Tristan relaxed into one of the armchairs and smiled at Mage. He didn't require separate overnight quarters. Mage's bed was big enough for two. "Purity?"

Mage cleared his throat. "Yes. Someone's idea of a joke, I

think."

"The AI knew I wasn't Angelica."

Mage snorted. "There is little that gets by Purity. She runs an identity scan on everyone who boards the ship. The watch officer who allowed you on board never bothered to check the monitor. That oversight will be corrected." Mage held up a decanter. "Another drink?"

Tris nodded and watched while Mage poured a finger's worth of liquid into two tumblers and then stalled, resting on his hands. He appeared to be engaged in a close examination of the cabinet's faux wood grain. *Anything that keeps you on the other side of the room, eh?* Anger and frustration boiled over inside and Tris stood, crossed to Mage and turned him, trapping his buttocks against the cabinet.

"Stop running from me, Magellan. Give me a chance. By the seven hells, man, I work with Angelica all day every day. You fucked that woman until she could hardly walk upright. She never uttered one complaint, so whatever you did, you're damn good at it. It's not as if you've never done this before. Give me a chance with you."

Tris couldn't contain his frustration at Mage's silence, so he did what he'd wanted to do since he'd walked into the wardroom: he kissed the man. Tris might as well have kissed the carbonite hull of the *Revertar*. He persisted, biting under Mage's jaw, running his hands over Mage's hard body to grip a tense buttock cheek and cup between his legs. The man stood as if made of ice.

"I should have known you wouldn't keep your promise," Mage bit out.

Tris shoved himself away. "Fuck you. I don't need this." As he turned to storm out, Mage's vise grip on his shoulder jerked him to a standstill.

"Don't go. Please, Tris." Mage sighed and dropped his hand.

"Shit. Tristan… I haven't. I haven't done this before. Not this."

Tristan turned and stared at Mage, uncomprehending. "What are you telling me?"

Mage groaned. "Can you possibly be more thick-skulled? Must I spell it out for you?" He closed his eyes and dropped his head back. When he raised it again, he held Tristan's gaze steadily. "I've never been with a man, Tristan. I'm a gods-be-damned virgin."

A virgin? Tris ran Mage's words through his brain several times before the meaning finally sank in. "A virgin." Tris swept a hand through his hair. "I'll take that drink now." When Mage handed one of the tumblers to him, he swallowed the contents in one gulp and held it out. "Again." With a rueful snort, Mage grabbed the decanter and topped his glass.

Tris crossed to the armchair he'd abandoned minutes ago and sank into it slowly. He waved his hand at Mage. "Sit." Tris heard how he sounded and removed the strident demand from his voice. "I'm sorry." He scrubbed his face. "Please. Sit with me. I promise to keep my hands to myself." He chuckled when Mage's eyebrows rose skeptically. "I mean it this time."

While Mage cautiously took the chair at right angles to him, Tris raised the tumbler to his lips and drained its potent contents in a series of steady swallows. Holding the tumbler suspended between thumb and index finger, he placed the empty glass on the table beside him with exaggerated care. "The things I said eight years ago… did I ruin you for me? Talk to me. If nothing else, I want to remain your friend. We can't leave things like this."

One corner of Mage's mouth quirked slightly. His, "Yeah," came out husky. "When you weren't trying to save me from myself, we were more than friends. Okay. Here it is. The only man I've ever wanted that way was you."

"Huh." Tristan had no comeback. Mage's revelations

staggered him.

Mage shrugged as if he didn't understand either but had long since come to terms with the situation.

Tris mulled that over for a while. "I'm here for the taking. What's stopping you?"

Mage laughed helplessly and looked everywhere but at him. "I can't do casual with you, Tris. I can't. And I don't want my fucking guts ripped out when you decide to move on. I'd rather just remain friends."

A crooked smile crept over Tristan's face. "So... you're saying I'm your man-crush and you're afraid I'll break your tender little heart."

Mage grunted. "Asshole. Here I am laying my balls on the line and you're treating me like some gods-be-damned adolescent stood up on his first date."

Relieved that he finally understood the source of Mage's reticence and amused at his own predicament, Tristan slumped in his chair, one arm on the armrest, the other across the back. He shook his head. "Hells' breath, what a convoluted fuck-up."

Tristan and Mage exchanged a steady gaze. Both men chuckled. Quiet seconds stretched to minutes while Tris examined his desires and Magellan examined him. A string of superficial, sexual encounters defined his life. Sexual encounters? By *Her* ruby red tits, superficial everything defined his life. He didn't know if he could give Mage more than just a good time. *A virgin. I'd be his first. Shit.* He'd never be satisfied with Mage as simply a friend. *Ah, fuck. This sucks ass.* Eventually, Tris leaned forward, rested his elbows on his knees and threaded his fingers through Magellan's.

"What if we take it slow, princess? No pressure for immediate sex. Come stay with me when you get back to Arkodaenia as we'd planned. See what happens. I wouldn't discount something long term—with you." *I can't believe I actually mean the shit coming out of my mouth.*

Mage snorted and broke away. He stood, presenting Tris with his broad back. "You mean try to have a 'relationship'?" He glanced at Tris over his shoulder. A sardonic smile twisted his mouth. "Is that what this is—a relationship talk?"

Tris chuckled. "Yeah, princess. You up for it?" He rose to stand quietly behind Mage. The man must say yes. *By* Her *light, I didn't see* this *coming.*

Mage turned to face him. "I want to include Angelica Giverny."

"Dr. Giverny?" Tris jerked back a fraction, startled. All the nascent emotion in his heart crashed. He tried not to sneer. "Why? Giving yourself a safe out? She doesn't like me."

"I'm not looking for a way out." Mage's expression gave nothing away. "I'm attracted to the woman," he said flatly. "We developed a close friendship on the voyage from Talleo IV and furthered it here. She's very vulnerable right now. I won't abandon her. You can be charming when you try, Tris. Charm her." His face softened. "Show her the real you."

What would Angelica do if Tris showed her the "real him"? Probably put several galaxies between them. He snorted at the thought. "Whatever you want, princess. Just say yes."

Mage growled and grabbed Tristan by the nape of his neck. "Don't make me regret this." He rested his forehead on Tristan's and looked him straight in the eyes. "Yes."

Absurd happiness flooded Tris. *By the Mother, I'm as bad as Mage. When did I get all "touchy-feely" and emotional?*

The hand on the back of his neck tightened to hold him immobile. His prospective lover angled his mouth across Tristan's and muttered against his lips. "And stop calling me princess." Then Mage kissed him.

As kisses went, it fucking rocked his world.

CHAPTER SEVEN

I apologize for hijacking your dinner invitation. Stop looking through me as if I weren't here."

Angelica's eyes flicked upward at Tristan, then back to the holo-screen display above her office desk at the med center. "It's not necessary to repeat yourself. I heard you the first three times. Besides, I thought bodyguards were supposed to be invisible." Her fingers flew as she made an entry into a patient's record then swiped at her virtual monitor and closed the file. From over her shoulder, Tristan's warm hand settled on top of hers, and she jumped in her chair. The holographic display dissolved in a shower of green particles.

"You've been head down in that thing since Captain DeLan left. That's five days without a break. You haven't left the med center since you got here. Let me take you out to dinner. Show you there's more to Arkodaenia than the inside of this dome."

"I don't want to have dinner with you." She ground her teeth at his low answering chuckle.

"I think you're afraid to be alone with me." He pushed on her chair and twirled her around to face him. With his hands on each of the armrests, he lowered his face to within inches of hers. He closed his eyes and inhaled slightly. "What is that scent you wear? It haunts me."

Angelica crossed her legs and her arms and tried not to fidget.

"Eau de Chloride."

"Strange. I would have said moon-blooming aenean, not disinfectant." With a winsome curve of his lips, he nuzzled into the crook of her neck. Goose bumps rose on her skin and her nipples hardened. "You smell like sweet, desirable woman. Have dinner with me, Dr. Angel."

Angelica almost whimpered at the effect his nibbles and low murmurs were having on her insides. "I don't want to have dinner with you," she whispered, and let her head fall back limply as the wretched man placed soft kisses under her jaw and she turned into a boneless mass of desire.

"Liar."

The husky gravel of his voice traveled to the vulnerable flesh between her legs and teased. Scents of spice soap and something uniquely Tristan invaded her nose. His kisses meandered up her jawline, across her cheek and stopped at the corner of her mouth, leaving pulses of sensation in their wake. Her arms unfolded of their own accord. She gripped Tristan's wrists where they rested on the arms of her chair. Sensation paralyzed her. Angelica could no more have moved from that chair than she could have pulled the stars from the heavens.

"Why should I have anything to do with you?" She choked on a moan as the tip of his tongue tickled the inside corner of her mouth.

"Because Magellan wants it and we both want Magellan."

She jerked bolt upright. Only his superlative reflexes prevented their crashing skulls. She narrowed her eyes. "What do you mean?"

Tris slouched a hip on her desk and crossed his arms. "When Mage tucks the *Revertar* safely into dry dock, he's returning to Arkodaenia. He'll be residing in my apartment." Tris lifted a shoulder and a smile played at his mouth. "He wants you and me to be friends."

He does? Why would Magellan DeLan want me to be friends with Tristan DeHelios? Tristan's eyes dwelled on her as she sat nonplussed.

"Come on, Doc. I'm not so bad. I'll be on my best behavior, I promise. Come to dinner with me. You'll enjoy yourself."

She dropped her eyes to her lap and drew small circles on her thigh with a forefinger. *Yes. I'll enjoy myself too much.* "I suppose I have to eat." She shot a glance at Tris. He intercepted it with a genuine—and immensely charming—grin, and she surrendered to what she suspected was inevitable. "All right, but I expect you to conduct yourself professionally."

Tris straightened from where he half-sat on her desk. His gaze held such triumph that she almost rescinded her agreement. He offered his hand to assist her from her chair. She accepted and his thumb stroked the back of hers in a sensual sweep as he helped her stand. Her body melted into the warm arousal he stirred. Strident alarms rang in the corridors of her brain, but despite all the valid reasons she kept enumerating for holding him at arm's length, she couldn't help the clandestine thrill at the prospects of a dinner with her lethally attractive bodyguard.

"I'll behave with complete propriety. You have my word as a gentleman."

❧❧❧❧❧❧❧❧❧❧❧

Tris took her to a small eatery, tucked away on a side street off a main thoroughfare, perhaps half an hour's easy walk from the med center. He'd offered her the option of a pleasant stroll or private ground transport. As Angelica surveyed the cool, clear dusk with stars beginning to dot the lavender heavens and Verdantia's two moons smiling at quarter full, she'd opted to walk. Unwilling to send any amorous messages, she'd dressed in casual clothes that covered her from neck to ankle, paired with low-heeled, comfortable shoes. She would welcome the exercise, particularly on such a pleasant evening, and she could avoid the intimate confines of a private vehicle.

The walk to the restaurant set the tone for the evening. The med center was located in an upscale part of Arkodaenia surrounded with couturier dress shops, fine jewelry boutiques and high-end tech stores with every possible gadget designed to make a geek's heart go pitty-pat. A convivial and courteous Tristan laughed at her as she pressed her face to the window glass and ogled the new fashions and sparkly accessories. The tables turned when they passed the tech stores. There she giggled at his boyish enthusiasm for the latest "plutonium enriched million-terabyte sliver drive." The first hint of their destination was the delectable aroma scenting the immediate vicinity. When he turned her down a small side street, she could have found their destination by following her nose. Tris laughed at her when she said as much.

"Yes. The menu is eclectic. There is everything here from a simple Klamanian burg and frits to Veluzi crustaceans flown in live, served enrobed in Galamone sauce with herbaceous sprouts." She laughed at his snooty waiter accent and Tris grinned at her. "It's all good."

He paused and held open a transparent door under a scarlet canopy emblazoned with *"Il Piatto Delicios."*

"The Delicious Plate," she translated.

With a smile and a nod, he motioned for her to enter. The proprietor, who addressed Tristan by name, showed them to one of perhaps a dozen small tables in a sedately elegant interior. Half of them were occupied with diners like themselves, male and female couples. Pristine table linens and low flickering candles set a romantic and intimate mood in the single room. Some soft, moody melody caught her ear. Tris seated her then took the chair to her left. He waved off the menus and caught her eye.

"Do you trust me?"

"Not in the slightest," she responded softly.

A knowing twitch of his lips added to the merriment in his eyes. "To order for you," he clarified, and his eyebrows rose in question.

His good humor was infectious, and despite her reservations about him, he drew a slow answering smile from her. "All right."

He gave the waiter their drink and appetizer order, then settled all his attention on her. His eyes dwelt on her; she felt as if a ghostly hand caressed her intimately. His lips curved in a subtle message of appreciation; her skin tingled and her insides fluttered. Tristan set her on edge, made her exquisitely aware she was a submissive female and he a dominant male, and he was so damnably sexy. To hide the tremble of her hands, she dropped them to her lap. "How do you and Captain DeLan know each other?"

"Mage? He spent most of his boyhood with my family in Nyth Uchel. His mother and father lacked the wherewithal to support him abroad, so he fostered with our family. I've known Mage from the time he was nine or ten until the Haarb wars. I lost track of him after that."

"Why would Mage foster with your family? Did something happen to his family?"

"The Verdantian custom is to have talented candidates from the nobility educated in the high magicks—to train them as a magister or magistra. Historically, that meant sending our young people to the High Enclave in Sylvan Mintoth or to the Prima Schola in Nyth Uchel. The Haarb desecrated the city of Nyth Uchel, murdered my family but for my brother and myself, and extinguished the great sigil tower, Torre Bianca. Without her light…" Tristan fell silent, his eyes gazing as if at some remembered devastation.

Moved by the pain evident on his face, Angelica slid her hand across the table to lay it on top of his. At her gentle touch, he gave her a tight smile and resumed. She returned her hand to her lap.

"For years, ice imprisoned my mountain home," Tris said. "Hel and his wife revitalized Torre Bianca and restored life to all Nyth Uchel—in truth to all Verdantia. Since then, the Prima Schola has been reinstated and the college of advanced magicks reopened."

Angelica sought for a subject less laden with emotional baggage. "With the age difference between the two of you, you seem unlikely friends."

Tristan gave a quiet snort and relaxed back in his chair. "Magellan was an old man at nine. He's always been conscientious and responsible. Whereas, I... well, I've been told I lack a certain seriousness about life." For a moment, Tris gazed at nothing and weariness pervaded his features—then vanished once more behind a mask of pleasant geniality. "What brought us together more than anything was our common fascination for all things techno."

Angelica thought it more than that. "Captain DeLan speaks about you with great warmth. You matter to him."

With long, elegant fingers, Tristan rearranged the perfectly ordered silverware on the immaculate table linen. "Mage has a soft spot for lost causes." He straightened in his chair and looked around sharply. "I wonder what's keeping our drink order. Excuse me a moment."

As he stood and stepped away from the table, frustration filled her. That guarded man had suddenly peeled away a tiny layer of protective skin to offer some insight into his internal thoughts and then, just as suddenly, shut her out again.

Tris didn't take more than three or four steps before the proprietor hustled over. A smiling Tristan murmured something to the owner and the man bowed and walked off briskly toward the kitchen. Some men she had known would have created a scene and publically embarrassed the host—simply to demonstrate how important they were—simply because they could. That sort of rude behavior didn't seem to fit this new, private Tristan DeHelios. He watched their proprietor for a few moments then returned to their table.

Well… she wasn't about to let him escape back into superficialities. As Tris lowered himself into his chair, she asked, "Do you consider yourself a lost cause, Prince DeHelios?"

His face shuttered at her gentle question. "Don't you, Dr. Giverny?"

She squirmed in her seat. His silver gray eyes dismissed her, as if to say whatever she thought of him was the least of his concerns. She shrank in her chair as a pang of conscience assailed her.

"I owe you an apology. Based on your appearance, I made a snap judgment about you that I regret. I was wrong and I'm sorry. I happen to think you are eminently capable and skilled at your job because you've worked to become so. I've heard the same sentiment from Dominus DeKieran and I respect his judgment more than mine." She raised her gaze to meet his and read surprise. "So… no. I don't think you a lost cause, and if Magellan DeLan wants us to be friends, I know that's not how he feels either."

Tristan's face softened and he opened his mouth to speak, but at that moment, the waiter and several assistants arrived with their drinks and a steaming assortment of finger foods. Angelica cursed their timing. Tris drew her into a conversation about the beverage and appetizers he'd chosen to tempt her. No matter how delicious, and they were, she'd little desire to discuss what size of monopod made the best *nubibus cochlea*. She wanted to know what he'd started to say.

Tristan placed his glass on the table and ran a hunk of panis through the butyrum sauce that surrounded the snails. He paused before putting it in his mouth. "Your manner of greeting Ramsey DeKieran was unorthodox to say the least, and you refer to him as Dominus. What's the story behind that?" Tris popped the panis into his mouth and settled back in his chair. A faint smile lingered around his mouth. His eyes ensnared hers, daring her to evade his question. Angelica wished to return to the safe discussion of snails.

"Perhaps that is a question to put to Lord DeKieran?" she offered.

Tris shook his head, a soft "No" on his lips. "When did you meet Ramsey DeKieran? Why did you drop to your knees and call him Dominus?"

She raised her eyes to scan the room, hoping to see the waiter coming with their main course. She would never be so lucky. The intimate atmosphere of couples in deep conversation, dim lighting, soft music, seemed to envelop the two of them in a private bubble. With a soft sigh, she turned back to Tristan, but her gaze and her hands remained in her lap. "The same entity who hunts me, now, runs a galactic cartel that deals in human trafficking. They hijacked a hospital ship I was on and transported me to Vxloncia." At his quiet exclamation she looked up.

"Vxloncia? That pestilent hell-hole?" Tristan leaned forward and his hand crept across the table toward her. "You were one of those women experimented on, weren't you?" Warm concern shone from his eyes. At her silent nod, Angelica thought he would pull her into his arms across the table, but then he seemed to recall where they were. He sat back, his face an impassive mask once more.

"Yes… well… I spent three years there as a sex slave. I came into Lord DeKieran's care while he and Steffania were there to locate and return a missing Verdantian noblewoman. Ramsey DeKieran saved me. I suppose I dropped to my knees because I have always considered him my Dominus. It is a sign of respect."

"It also reveals volumes about your sexual orientation, as did your slip the other night when you asked permission to leave. Are you a submissive by nature—or is this a result of—whatever?"

She glared at him. "This is who I am."

"Good." His mouth tipped in a crooked half-smile. "Did Mage top you?"

Discomposed, Angelica glanced away. "I... I... I don't have to answer that."

His chuckle was low and intimate. "I can always ask Magellan. I'll find out sooner or later." She allowed her discomfort to show and Tris lowered his voice further still and a note of hesitancy crept in. "I'm feeling my way with Mage. I've made some missteps that I don't care to repeat. I was hoping you'd share some personal insight. It would help to know if he's a strong dominant."

She sat up straight. "Oh." Her eyes widened as a thought occurred to her. "Oh! You and he have never... ah, haven't..."

Tris shook his head. A disarming smile twisted his lips. "No. We haven't. I'll ask again. Did Mage top you?"

"Yes." Her answer was a mere shred of sound. "But I don't get the same, ah, vibe, from him that I get from you."

Tristan cocked his head and his interest sharpened. He opened his mouth to speak, but happily, the arrival of more food spared her. Unhappily, after the meal was distributed and she began to lift a tempting bit of savory meat to her lips, Tris said, "For the sake of comparison, what sort of vibe do you get from me?"

She filled her mouth, placed her fork on her plate delicately, put her hands in her lap and chewed until her meat turned to tasteless paste. She swallowed, raised her goblet and took a small sip. Tristan relaxed back in his chair and waited her out, seemingly more interested in her response than in eating. She raised her chin, stiffened her spine and held his gaze. "You put me in mind of Dominus DeKieran. But a submissive always has the right to choose her Dom. I don't drop to my knees for every sexual dominant that crosses my path."

Tris grunted. "I certainly hope not. The question remains— will you for me?"

She closed her eyes and tensed. "I haven't decided." When she cracked them open again, she saw the opposite of what she'd been expecting.

Tristan aimed an unguarded, charming smile at her and murmured, "Well, don't lose sleep over it. You'll either love me or hate me. Your decision will be effortless."

The hand that raised her drink to her lips shook. She doubted she'd hate him.

⊗⊗⊗⊗⊗⊗⊗⊗⊗

As Angelica strolled home beside the physically intimidating, masculine presence of her dinner companion, she acknowledged, if only to herself, that when Tristan DeHelios set out to be charming, he was a force of nature. She was no more able to withstand his allure than water could resist flowing downhill.

Fully dark, the velvet night created an atmosphere of privacy between her and Tristan that the empty streets lined with flowering window boxes and old-fashioned light poles did nothing to disturb. She found herself watching his mouth as he spoke, wondering what those full lips would feel like pressed against intimate places on her skin. A part of her, a physical desire she'd been resisting, wished he would take her in his arms and kiss her. But from the start of their "date," he'd never attempted to touch her. He simply sauntered along next to her, his hands in his pockets, his steps carefully measured to match her stride. Professional. A gentleman. She jeered at herself for being so vulnerable to a handsome face and commanding sexual presence. There must be more to him than his fine appearance, sexual aura and knowledge of monopods.

The display lighting in the window of the designer dress shop they were passing flickered and then the shop next to it did the same. A subtle pressure built within Angelica's head, as if something inside pressed outward seeking release. She flashed back immediately to Talleo IV and one of the attacks on her life. A horrendous realization paralyzed her. "They're on Verdantia." She clutched at Tristan's arm and he stopped. "They're here. Oh, God, no!"

The street lights on both sides of the street popped softly one by one as the entire block, at least as much of it as she could see, went black. The painful pressure in her skull grew and clear thought required effort. Tris felt it also. He growled and shook his head as if to shake off the building weight that might crush them.

"By *Her* light… who?"

"Tristan! Help!" she gasped.

"What—is—it?" He ground the words through clenched teeth.

She wanted to drop and curl into a fetal position from fear and agony. "I think… a mummer… a null," she sobbed. "A creature that dampens energy. They are murderers, assassins." She moaned at the agony in her skull. "Your gun—useless. Always two of them. Oh!" she exclaimed softly and pressed her palms to her temples. Her vision grayed. There was no ambiguity in her mind. Harsh reality cut through all her pain. If Tris couldn't protect her, she was dead.

Tris shoved her behind him into an alcove created by a shop door. He pulled his Razar 88K from his shoulder holster and faced outward, using his body to shield her completely. "Stay behind me," he snapped.

"Gun's useless." She groaned at the pain in her skull.

Tristan barked a vulgar curse. His hips jerked backward and

slammed her into the door behind her. He struck out in an arc as though he held a blade, though she'd never seen him draw one. She ground the heels of her hands against her temples and fought to remain conscious as she slid to a sitting position, her back braced against the door panel. Through the vee in Tristan's legs, she watched a menacing figure undulate before him. The unnatural contortions of the mummer's body multiplied her fear. No human body bent at those angles. A sibilant threat hissed through thin lips in what she supposed was its face, though a hood and black robes shrouded the being. She sobbed fearfully as Tristan stepped away from her and met the foul creature in a flurry of advances and withdrawals that appeared like some choreographed dance of death done in triple time. The two fighters closed as if embracing. A banshee wail split the night and her skull. Angelica surrendered consciousness to the vicious agony inside her head.

Excruciating pulses at her temples beat in time with her heart. Conscious thought flashed back brutally. Her eyes flew open unseeing, and she jerked up with a scream to defend herself. Iron-hard muscles banded her to a broad chest and Tristan's voice soothed her.

"Shh… you're safe. I have you." He sheltered her in his lap as he sat propped against the alcove door. His hands held her firmly to him until she stilled.

"I'm all right. You can let me go now."

Tristan slipped an arm under her knees, pulled his legs underneath him and stood in an effortless show of strength. Once upright, he released her legs and allowed her to stand. His arm stayed around her shoulders until she nodded. Angelica craned her neck to scan the area around them, once more illuminated by display windows and streetlamps. Then she saw the black mound sprawled on the sidewalk in a spreading pool of dark viscous fluid. She ducked her head into his chest and clutched at his shirt with both hands. "Is it dead?"

"Yes. Tell me what I just killed. It had a fair degree of skill with a blade, but it wasn't human."

Angelica shuddered. "A mummer is an unholy creature with the ability to absorb energy. They are assassins and murderers. Ninety-nine point nine percent of the universe depends on technological weaponry for personal defense. Take away that weaponry and they are easy victims for the mummers."

"For once I'm glad I brought knives to a gunfight." Suppressed humor colored Tristan's voice.

What did it take to faze this man? Evidently a creature the rest of the galaxy considered a nightmare wouldn't do it. "Did you see its dependent? Another being that cloaks the mummer? They always travel in pairs."

"No. Something scurried away in the night. I couldn't tell what it was."

The cloth she clutched was sticky and damp. With a soft cry, she pushed away from his body. Red stained her hands. She pressed her bloody palms against him frantically. "You are bleeding. Where are you hurt? Tristan!"

"Nothing fatal, I assure you. It got a good swipe at me in the beginning, but it's just a scratch."

Angelica did everything but rip his shirt off him, beginning with the rent in the fabric that ran diagonally from his collarbone to his navel. She stood back, horrified at the foot-long, gaping slash marring his body of honed muscle. She raised her face to him, dismayed. "This laceration needs to be disinfected and sealed immediately. Much deeper and blood would not be the only thing leaking out. I must get you to the med center. Should we notify the port police?" The idiotic man blinked at her as if she babbled in a foreign tongue.

"I'd just as soon not deal with the port police right now. I'll be long enough explaining the events to Lt. Colonel DeKieran. She'll notify the port police. I'll take you to the med center, though. I need something for my head." Tristan grimaced. "My brains are trying to burst out of my left eye. All I see are jagged lines of pulsing white."

Angelica gratefully took refuge in what she knew—medicine. The comfort of having concrete knowledge readily available allowed her to conquer the part of her that wanted to dissolve into babbling hysteria. "The visual display is due to pressure on your optic nerve." Her head felt almost as bad, but her vision remained normal. "It's a side effect of whatever a mummer does to absorb power. The blood vessels in your brain dilate. Your vision will return to normal as soon as I administer a vasoconstrictor. How did you kill that thing with a debilitating headache and impaired vision? I passed out."

He shrugged. "I'm your bodyguard. I couldn't let you be killed. Besides, it confuses Hel when I don't fuck up. I enjoy confusing him." Tristan winked. That wink contained only a fraction of his prior machismo, and that told her more than words how badly his head bothered him. "I'm contacting Lt. Colonel DeKieran to ask that the exterior guard be increased for the rest of the evening. The other half of that pair that attacked you tonight is still in the city somewhere."

She and Tristan consumed the better part of two hours at the med center while Angelica administered an injection of a potent vasoconstrictor and analgesic to both herself and to Tris and then carefully disinfected and sealed the wide gash on his abdomen. "There. I treated you with a healing accelerant. You should be fine in a day or two."

Tristan sat up carefully. "Thanks, Doc. If that fails, I'll go see my sister-in-law. She'll wave her magick wand over me and I'll be good as new."

Angelica looked at him sideways as she cleaned her hands and put the used instruments in a sterilization unit. "Are you serious? Your people have magick wands?"

Tristan laughed. "Our Great Mother, Verdantia, endows certain of us with extraordinary abilities. My sister-in-law is a miraculous healer—quite literally. I believe in magick when it comes to Adonia. But, no, she doesn't have a magick wand." He grinned at her and waggled his eyebrows. "I do. Would you like to see it?"

Angelica rolled her eyes. "Now I know you'll be fine." Tristan simply chuckled.

When they got to her apartment entrance Tris halted and lifted her hand. He placed a gentle kiss on the back of it. "Will you be all right by yourself? I'll be downstairs, but I can call for one of the women staff to come and keep you company if you don't want to be alone."

Angelica held his gaze, bemused. "What? You aren't volunteering for the role?" The sudden heat in his eyes returned her immediately to the restaurant and a tingle of apprehension zinged down her spine. All frivolity left her.

"I might be one of those you want protection from. No. I'm not volunteering my services to you as a platonic companion—not tonight—not any night. Remember that if you ever ask me to stay. Sleep well, Angelica. I'll be on guard all night." With a twitch of the lips that Angelica assumed was a smile, Tris turned and began to walk toward his door.

"Prince DeHelios?"

He paused and turned. "Yes?"

The word "stay" poised on the tip of her tongue, but her courage deserted her. "Thank you for saving my life."

"It's Stults. Get the boss on the line fast, Zebo."

"Why? Now what?"

"The contractor failed to take out the woman. Worse, it's dead."

"Aw, shit. That's going to put him in a mood."

"Yeah. For once, I'm glad I'm light years away on some archaic backwater that's not even on the star charts."

"Zebo said you needed me right away, Mr. Stults, so I'm here. Give me some good news for a change."

"Sorry, sir. I can't."

"The contractor failed?"

"Yes, sir. It's dead. The woman has a Verdantian bodyguard with some serious knife skills." Silence crackled through the comm device. "Sir? Are you still there? Hello, hello?"

"I'm here, Mr. Stults."

"Yes, sir. Ah… should I contact the other resource? They will take all the profits from the Pinwheel Galaxy and then some, and it's a death sentence if we're linked to them, but…"

"Do it. I don't care about the cost. That woman saw my face when I met with Veacon Narr on Vxloncia, and need I remind you that you're involved, too? Tell 'them' to consider the Verdantians collateral damage. Verify she can ID me and bring her to me."

"They aren't supposed to kill her, boss?"

"No. It's not enough anymore. She owes me a pound of flesh, Stults. I intend to collect."

In her dreams, Angelica repeatedly relived the mummer's attack and that of the one on Talleo IV. Finally, she abandoned any hope of sleep and found a good holo-vid to watch—a coming-of-age story about a young Aquarion male and his pet *cannes aquam*. Nothing could have been further from her reality than the adolescent angst of a young person on a water world, and it was exactly what the doctor ordered for herself.

When the light filtering into her apartment announced a new day, she dressed while in a sleep-deprived fog. She stumbled out to join Tristan for their walk to the med center. He seemed his normal, effortlessly powerful self until she examined his red-rimmed eyes and noted the downward drift of his eyelids from time to time. If he'd been on guard all night, he must be staggering with fatigue. She took the proffered cup with a murmur of thanks. "No kaffé for you?"

He grunted. "No. I've had enough kaffé to fill your bath."

"Your chest?"

"I'm fine, Doc. Let it be." He guided her elbow in the direction of the pathway and they walked to her destination in companionable silence.

I like this man. The disconcerting thought came out of nowhere. When had her antagonism turned to appreciation? She couldn't say. She snorted to herself. *His saving my life might have something to do with it.* Tristan said Mage wanted them to be "friends." What kind of "friends" did Mage have in mind? A fugitive arousal lurked at the thought of having both Mage and Tristan as lovers.

Tristan halted her with a touch on the arm before she entered her office. "I'm handing you off to different bodyguards today. Three of the Daggers will rotate protection for you. I'll see you late tonight." He turned to leave.

Her comfort vanished. "Late tonight? Wait! Prince DeHelios, you can't leave me. Where are you going? I mean…" Her voice trailed off and she cleared her throat. She didn't want to examine the reason for her sudden panic. "Of course, you must have other business from time to time. I'll be fine. I'll... ah... be perfectly safe with the, ah, others."

Tristan reached toward her and smoothed a stray lock of hair behind her ear. "You'll be in good hands, Dr. Angel. I wouldn't leave you otherwise. The 'other business' concerns you. I'd ask Lord DeKieran to stay with you, but he and his wife will be with me."

"I'll be fine," she said. "I'm just used to you, that's all."

"Ah, I can see I've grown on you... and you have yet to experience what I'm really good at." A crooked smile tilted across Tristan's face and he winked at her before turning and sauntering down the hall to the exit.

He's incorrigible. "Take as long as you need," she called to his back. "Don't hurry back on my account." His shoulders shook, and his laugh echoed in the hall. He never turned around. She knew because she couldn't take her eyes off him until he vanished from sight.

Angelica exhaled smoothly and rubbed her hands up and down her biceps to eradicate the goose bumps that had risen. The feeling of vulnerability that swamped her was ridiculous. So what if the deadly fighter protecting her wore a different face or possessed brown eyes, not gray. She should welcome a respite from Tristan's wordless, perceptive amusement as she went about her day pretending to ignore his aloof presence and the primal sexual aura he exuded. It shouldn't matter who guarded her. It shouldn't—but it did.

Why hadn't she asked Tris the nature of his business? Probably because other than their dinner together or in the aftermath of the mummer attack, she'd never felt she could say anything to him but "Yes, Sir."

Angelica tried to hide her anxiety. She made a poor job of it. The door to her office opened constantly. Doctors on staff consulted with her. Engineers queried her about placement of fragile technology. Some of her patients stuck their heads in with cheerful greetings and offers of lunch. Rationally, Angelica knew it was absurd to think that each incursion was a prelude to another attack. She wasn't being rational. By mid-afternoon she'd worked herself into a state where she flinched at the tiniest unexpected sound.

"Lt. Colonel DeKieran handpicked us for this duty. I will keep you safe."

The cool, grating voice came from a massive figure of ripped muscle—with breasts. The buzz-cut blonde woman—it had taken two, lengthy, surreptitious gazes by Angelica to confirm the sex of her companion—prowled her office like an oversized, golden *lionne*. Horrifying weapons bristled from multiple points on her figure-hugging body armor and her eyes had a flat hardness that only comes from staring at death on a routine basis.

"It's good—what you're doing for this planet—your work with these women." Angelica's guard tossed choppy words at her gruffly. "As an off-worlder, you might not understand, but these genetically unique women are vital if the Verdantians are to interact with their Great Mother, the sentience that inhabits this planet. Without these forty women…" The guard shook her head. "The Verdantians' way of life dies with their queen and a few others with the essential genes."

Her guard's comments interrupted Angelica's futile attempts to enter a new treatment protocol into a patient file. Angelica placed her unsteady hands over each other on the desk to disguise their shaking and slumped in her chair with a helpless laugh. "Tell me something I don't know. That's why I'm here. But my patients must be able to work the 'high magicks' or it doesn't matter. I'm also aware that I will sentence these women to insanity if I send them into the world less than mentally whole." Angelica threw a helpless glance at her guard.

The woman held her gaze unsmiling. "I have watched your work, and I talk to the women. You won't fail."

"I wish I was so sure," she whispered.

"I am sure," her guard stated flatly.

It's ridiculous how three words from a stranger can lift you. Silence descended and lingered until Angelica straightened in her chair and turned to face her guard. "I'll wager your name gives you grief from time to time." She forced a smile. "Eva Sweet. Professional mercenary, now a Blue Dagger, with mad skills in hand-to-hand combat and blowing things up. Sorry, I don't remember the technical terms." At the guard's raised eyebrow, Angelica cleared her throat and offered, "I'm not totally lacking in self-preservation. I did study the dossiers Steffania gave me so I would know my guards."

A startled look flashed across Eva's face for a nanosecond, and then the woman grinned. "Few have the balls to comment on my name."

"I'm sorry to be so jumpy. I don't question your skill. It's fatigue. I slept poorly last night. I think I'm going to make a short workday of it. Are you my escort back to my residence?" In spite of her words, Angelica still felt exposed, defenseless. At some point, the notion that only Tristan DeHelios could safeguard her had anchored itself securely in her psyche. She knew it was ridiculous, but the presence of Tristan, and no other, meant safety.

"No, ma'am. I'm off when you leave the med center. Tiny and his team pulled the residence watch. Give me a moment to find him and I'll walk you out." When Angelica nodded, the woman spoke into a communication device on her wrist, then glanced toward Angelica. "Tiny's on his way."

As they walked toward the exit, a huge hulk lumbered through the door with a side-to-side gait that bulky muscle gives a male.

He, too, wore body armor with weapons protruding like the poisoned quills on a *hystrix*. Angelica laughed softly. "Military humor? I'm guessing this gentleman is 'Tiny'?"

Eva Sweet's lips quirked. "Yeah, that's Tiny. Some of us wear bodysuits that augment our strength and size, but not Tiny. That's all him."

"Do you? Wear augmentation?" Angelica glanced at Eva and was surprised when the woman turned red and looked anywhere but at her.

"Ah, no, ma'am. That's a negative. This is me." Eva cleared her throat and briskly performed the introductions. "Dr. Giverny, this hulk is Richard Shuman, better known as Tiny. He and a four-man unit are assigned to your residence until 2400 hours. After that you will have Bodie James and another four-man unit until 0800."

Angelica smiled and offered her hand to the towering human male. "Hi, Richard. Ah, thank you. I hope I'm not keeping you up past your bedtime." Her quip got the laugh she desired.

"No ma'am. Not a problem. And call me Tiny. Only my maw calls me Richard."

Escorted by her guard, she meandered home. Tiny proved to be a garrulous companion and engaged her in nonstop chitchat until she reached her door. She learned he was from Nembus II, with a maw, daw, and four sisters at home, had been with the Daggers for ten years, thought Steffania DeKieran was one "tough, ballsy commander," and had no ambition other than to be a soldier. In many ways, he reminded her of the men on Talleo IV—competent, amicable and, she sighed, dull.

Tris had been gone a few scant hours and already she missed his larger-than-life presence. Without his unspoken challenge, she felt as if the day lacked vitality. When had he transformed from being an irritant to a man who created a void when not present? She shivered at the thought of his increasing importance to her.

In that direction lay danger of a different sort. When was Captain DeLan due back? It could not be soon enough. She walked into the main room and addressed her AI.

"Sir?"

"Good afternoon, Dr. Giverny. Please be advised Creator DeHelios has instituted AI protocol 3.75a. I now respond to 'computer'. Creator DeHelios changed my facade to one ubiquitous and less personalized. I hope this meets with your approval."

A green holographic image of an androgynous humanoid sparkled in front of her, a slight smile on its bland face. Gone was Tristan's husky growl. The voice could have been the voice of any newscaster on the info-vids. Angelica sank onto the sofa, overwhelmed by a feeling of abandonment. Tristan had done what she'd asked. Why wasn't she pleased? "Thank you, Sir, ah, computer. You look fine. Please start a bath, water temperature, one hundred degrees earth standard, aenean bath salts. Lights at twenty percent."

She soaked in the steamy water until her skin shriveled and afternoon daylight paled into dusk. Wrapped in nothing but her softest robe, she programmed a light dinner into her replicator and carried the steaming plate and its contents to her couch. She tried to lose herself in some entertainment vid, but after the events of the previous day, no drama on holo-screen could compete with her real life. Angelica sighed and rose listlessly to open the beverage cooler. It wouldn't hurt to self-medicate with a bottle of her favorite fermented liquid. After far too much Zeta Starlight, Angelica finally dozed off in front of the media center, gripping a couch pillow to her chest. She startled out of a fitful sleep. Loud shouts from the outside banished most of the effects of the liquor and her semi-stupor. She clutched the pillow and her robe, her heart beating triple time.

"Computer, display exterior security cams, lower interior lights to twenty percent." The monitor lit, displaying multiple dark figures below her fanned out in a radius from her cottage. The blue light from lazar sights on pulsar-rifles created pencil-line striations in the dark as they panned the open area around her living quarters. A chime sounded and the voice of Angelica's AI informed her that Richard Shuman stood at the ground-level door to her apartment and wished to speak with her. "Richard? What's going on?"

A small holographic image of Tiny appeared in the air above her head. "Possible intruder, ma'am. Stay inside. If you haven't secured your doors and windows, do so. I'll get back to you."

"But, but... how am I supposed to know..." The holographic image dissipated. He was gone. Angelica cast a helpless glance around her darkened apartment. There was no place to hide in the large open space.

"Computer."

"Yes, Dr. Giverny."

"Implement security protocol... Oh, shit! Oh, shit! What is it? Alpha Eight! Alpha Eight!"

"Acknowledged. Confirmed opacity for all exterior windows at one hundred percent. All perimeter doors and windows locked and armed for intrusion alert. Interior motion detection alarms armed. Security protocol Alpha Eight, engaged. Dr. Giverny, do you wish all interior lights extinguished?"

"Yes."

Paranoia drove her to check the lock on the balcony doors and the door to the interior stairs linking Tristan's apartment. Crossing to a low sideboard, she opened a small drawer and withdrew an innocuous metallic ovoid. The miniaturized plazar emitter held only enough charge for two or three lethal pulses and its range was severely limited, but it fit in the palm of her hand. It fired without kickback and its operation was simple. Point your finger and press.

Other than the limited range, the emitter had only one drawback: its trigger was devilishly sensitive.

As the glass windows and doors turned black and the interior lights extinguished, Angelica huddled in a ball of anxiety in the corner of the sectional, the plazar emitter nested in her lap. Only the stark greens, reds and blues of display lights lit the room. *I want Tristan.* She was independent and self-sufficient. She wanted Tristan. She had status and a respected position in her field earned through merit. At that moment, though she knew the Blue Daggers were competent, for her peace of mind she *needed* Tristan DeHelios. That thought worried her almost as much as a possible intruder.

Long excruciating minutes ticked by. The sounds of activity outside her residence faded. Her ears strained for anything out of the ordinary. She startled when the air filled with the chime of her AI. "Dr. Giverny?"

"Yes, computer?"

"The entity Richard Shuman has communicated that the grounds are secure. No intruder present. He requested that you remain inside for the remainder of the evening. He and his team will secure the patient residences and remain in the area."

"Thank you, computer. Indicate 'message received' to Mr. Shuman."

"Yes, Dr. Giverny."

Absolute quiet descended. Angelica debated whether to go to bed or be productive and catch up on the ever-present paperwork. Subtle sounds of movement in Tristan's apartment below filtered through the heavy silence and her decision became easy. A strobe of red light, the motion detector, flashed above the primary security panel. A sick sense of dread mixed with the desire to run pell-mell out of her apartment. Both competed with the cold practical knowledge she was safest staying put, but it took every scrap of courage she could cobble together to remain on that sofa.

"Computer?" she whispered.

"Yes, Dr. Giverny."

Angelica labored to inhale and a feeling of nausea rose in the back of her throat. She palmed the plazar emitter.

"Connect me with Richard Shuman."

Angelica hung onto her composure with all the self-discipline she possessed. She must remain clear-headed for the next few minutes. Her life might depend on it.

"Shuman here. What's your sit-rep?"

"What?" she said.

"What the fuck's going on?" Urgency and impatience vibrated in his tone.

"I hear sounds in the apartment below and the motion detector has tripped. It can't be Tristan. He would have disarmed it."

She heard the sound of muffled curses.

"Copy that. We're thirty seconds away."

She caught the vehement beginning of another curse before the connection died. Long minutes passed. Too long. Faint sounds of activity below filtered upstairs. Her anxiety built. Where was Richard? He said he'd be here.

She heard the sound of footsteps on the stairs. Angelica huddled further into the sofa and pointed the plazar emitter at the door with a hand that shook. Horror pierced her as the lever handle turned.

The soft chime of her AI sounded. "Dr. Giverny, the—"

"Mute audio," she gasped. Any distraction now could be fatal.

She'd locked that door. She knew she had. Her breath came in ragged inhales. Clicks echoed in the silent room as something or someone overrode the door lock.

Anger at her helplessness and a grim determination to take her assailant with her into death almost displaced her fear—almost.

She pointed the plazar emitter at the door, but her hand trembled so badly she doubted she'd hit what she aimed at. *Two or three shots at most. Make them count.* She tried to steady the emitter with her other hand while her eyes drilled a hole through the door handle. Once again, the handle rotated. This time the tumbler clicked and released. The door opened, propelled by an invisible force. Oh, god! She shrank lower into the sofa, held her breath, and…

CHAPTER EIGHT

Tristan waded into the intimate bar and immediately identified the Khlossian, Tok, at a secluded table in a corner niche. A being of his size was impossible to miss. The dim lights and standing-room-only crowd did little to disguise the behemoth. Ramsey and Steffania DeKieran and the Blue Dagger, Eva Sweet, sat with him. Through breaks in the crowd, he saw empty mugs and half-eaten food littering the table in front of them. They'd been there for some time. He was late, but it couldn't be helped. For his own piece of mind, he had needed to see Angelica safe to her workplace, and then he'd had a little reconnaissance of his own to perform.

From the dour faces Tok and group wore, the subject under discussion was troublesome. Tris slipped through bodies and up to the table, snagged a chair around and straddled it like a horse. "Why the grim faces?"

"This Blue Dagger," Tok gestured to Eva Sweet, "intercepted communications indicating the imminent arrival of *imita mekanikos* in the city. We have a day or two before they reach Verdantia. They will be here for only one reason—to kill or capture Angelica Giverny. We must move Dr. Angel out of Arkodaenia for her own safety. The electromagnetic forces present on this planet—those outside of Arkodaenia—will make fighting the mekanikos less… impossible." The words rumbled from Tok's mouth like boulders grinding together. Even so, Tris leaned forward to hear over the clash of discordant sound that some band considered music.

Steffania DeKieran abbreviated her swallow of brew, putting her mug down with a solid thunk. "I repeat. I don't care for your idea."

"I understand the point you make, Ramsey's woman, but you would make Dr. Angel bait. You cannot play with her life in such a heedless manner."

The cool voice of Ram intervened. "Every effort will be made to ensure Angelica's safety. We are not without resources, particularly in Arkodaenia. If she stays in the medical compound, we can keep her safe."

The large being squinted at Ramsey. "You have never faced *imita mekanikos*, ignorant Verdantian. You have no knowledge of what they are capable of."

Ramsey scowled, then shrugged. "Truth. Until an hour ago, I'd never heard of them."

"So, enlighten me. What the fuck are *imita mekanikos*?" Tris swung his head back and forth between Ramsey and Tok.

Ram held Tok with a steady gaze. "You want to take this?"

Before Tok could respond, Steffania spoke. "The 'meks' are highly advanced, highly intelligent alien constructs of organic and inorganic composition with the ability to mimic whatever form or shape they desire. Some long-forgotten alien intelligence created them. They're sophisticated far beyond our current genetic or technological knowledge. My unit had a run-in with them during the cyborg wars on Devon III. Somehow, the Devonians unearthed and activated the mekanikos." Her expressive face closed down and her eyes became farseeing. "Remorseless and single-minded—impossible to kill." A nasty smile distorted her lovely face. "I want them. I have a blood debt to pay."

"And you are using Dr. Angel to bait your trap," Tok said.

Steffania turned an implacable expression to him. "She is not bait. You agreed the meks will hunt Angelica until they have her. Removing Angelica from Arkodaenia will prolong her danger and delay or render useless all her dedicated work at the med center. Over forty women depend upon Angelica to provide an ongoing daily treatment program that will return them to functioning society. Ridding ourselves of these vermin could take weeks if not months. What do you propose our extensively educated, impressively skilled cerebral neuro-specialist do while she is waiting somewhere 'safe' for us to deal with the 'meks'? Count the pixels in her hologram?" Steffania smashed her fists on the table and glared at Tok. "In Arkodaenia we at least have the advantage of technology absent from the rest of Verdantia and Angelica can continue the work to which she has dedicated her life."

Her husband picked up her clenched fist and kissed her knuckles. "Vixen. Perhaps your judgment is not the most reliable at the moment."

She gave him a stricken look. "I would never endanger Angelica, Ram. I owe her as much as any of those other women. I feel this is our best chance to keep her safe. We locate the meks immediately, before they become invisible in the city, and we take them out."

Tok growled low. "I have stepped back and allowed the Daggers to function without interference, but you have an unrealistic faith in your ability to deal with the meks. You force me to use outside measures to ensure Dr. Angel's safety." Tok glared at Steffania.

Tris exchanged glances with Ramsey. Steffania and Tok's argument seemed ready for round two. Ramsey rolled his eyes and straightened from his slouch.

"I appreciate and share your concern for Angelica's safety. I promise we will not let anything happen to her."

Tok grunted. "Ignorant Verdantian. Your promises mean nothing. You don't know what you face. You're as bad as your woman."

Ramsey gave a long-suffering sigh. "Then tell me what I need to stop the meks. We have the most sophisticated weaponry available."

"And still... you have nothing that will stop them. I'm calling in outside help."

"And what form will this help take?"

Tok shrugged. "You don't need to know."

Ram examined him intently. "Which means I won't like it."

"No Verdantian. You won't, but it is the only chance you have of stopping these things. I only hope our 'help' can get here in time." Tok rose and eyed Eva Sweet. "Sweet Eva, accompany me."

Eva threw a glance at her commander, and an unhappy Steffania nodded.

"Go with him, Eva. If he says we need assistance, I have to believe him."

The comm device on Tristan's wrist chose that moment to buzz repeatedly with the ferocity of an angry beporza. He stood and caught Ramsey's eye. "Excuse me. I need to take this." At Ramsey's nod, Tristan turned and walked toward a secluded niche where the noise from the bar didn't hurt his ears. "Tiny, it's Tris. Talk to me."

As he listened, he began to shove through the crowd toward the closest exit. Thrusting the back door open in front of him, Tris burst out and sprinted toward the medcenter. "I'm cutting across the city center on foot. I'll be there in ten."

CHAPTER NINE

Mage put aside his irritation at the thorough manhandling and interrogation he'd just received from Angelica's security team, though he'd no one but himself to blame. He was glad the Daggers took her protection seriously, and as soon as they'd verified his identification, they'd been all courtesy. The Daggers swept Tristan's apartment with silent efficiency and vanished, but he chafed at even that modest delay.

He'd ruthlessly expedited the preparations for putting the *Revertar* into dry dock orbit. He'd blasted through twenty-hour days and fallen into his rack to snag a few hours' sleep before he hit it again. He wanted as much shore time as possible with Tris and Angelica. He walked into Tristan's silent, dark apartment. It was no surprise. The man would not expect him back for days. *Just as well that Tris isn't here.* While he couldn't speak for Angelica, there were moments he found it difficult to maintain rational thought in Tristan's presence. The man's charisma sucked him under despite his resolve to remain clearheaded.

He wanted time with the lovely doctor to put a positive spin on the possibility of something long-term between the three of them. His insistence Angelica be included in their "relationship" had been spontaneous, born of an unwillingness to desert a lovely vulnerable woman he legitimately cared for. However, as he lay in his bunk on the *Revertar*, the more he thought about a triad, the more he embraced the idea. It would gut him to have to choose between her and Tris. He couldn't bear the thought of hurting either of them, and he was selfish enough to want both of them.

He wanted a family. He wanted permanency. How to achieve that and still pursue his love of space had always confounded him. In the few moments he'd had to himself, he'd realized a relationship that included Tristan and Angelica was the solution—an alternative to the long years of loneliness that otherwise stretched in front of him.

He hesitated to speculate on Angelica's reaction. *By Her light, I hope she goes for it.* He tossed his duffle on a bed in what he thought might be a guestroom, cleaned up a little and climbed the interconnecting stairs to Angelica's apartment. A sense of anticipation tingled through him. Perhaps their conversation could extend to some "glad-you're-back" sex.

He considered that Tristan might view his having solo sex with Angelica as an effort to derail their budding relationship. *Seven hells. A relationship.* Well, that's what Tris had said, and by the Great Mother, Mage wouldn't risk fucking it up, but how could Tristan possibly mistake how he felt about him? He'd instilled years of hopeless yearning into the kiss he put on Tris the night Tristan invited himself to dinner.

Shivers of anticipation—and apprehension—coursed down his spine when he contemplated the consummation of their "relationship." He scoffed silently at the irony. The years had rolled by with no one touching his heart. Now, two people knotted his emotions into a tangled mass, the two inexplicably interwoven in his heart. He'd need their cooperation to make whole cloth out of this snarled skein.

His hand paused on the handle at the top of the stairs—locked. He swiped the universal sliver pass Tristan had given him across a digital display pad. It unlocked as readily as the door to Tristan's apartment and the employees' entry to the med center. Goddess bless the man for his foresight. It would have been awkward to get back early only to spend the night sitting outside the door like an orphan waiting for Tristan's return.

Mage pushed open Angelica's door into a lightless apartment—lightless but for a shaky blue dot wandering his chest. *Shit!* He jerked the door closed. Someone had aimed a plazar emitter at him. He cracked open the door. "Angelica?" At the sound of a gasp, Mage opened it further. "It's Mage. I'm coming in. By *Her* light, don't shoot. The Daggers have been and gone. The apartment is clear. You're safe."

"Oh, Mage! Computer, lights at sixty percent, audio silence cancelled." Her voice sounded raw, as if ripped from her throat.

"Acknowledged, Dr. Giverny. Be advised Blue Dagger override of security protocol Alpha Eight in effect. Intruder identified as Known Person, Magellan DeLan, Captain, VNV *Revertar*."

She gave a soft sob.

"Sweetheart, what's wrong? Why were you sitting in the dark?" *Why did you aim a plazar emitter at me?* Mage slipped through the door and closed it behind him as the lights came up.

As he crossed to her in the soft glow, Mage assessed her. Wrapped in a nebula pink kasmere robe, she had curled into a defensive posture in the corner of the sectional. Her knees were tucked against her chest. Her outstretched arms braced on her kneecaps. One hand clutched the plazar emitter still centered on his chest.

He cleared his throat. "Angel, can you point that somewhere else?"

"Oh! Of course." She jerked her arms into her lap and unfolded in a collapse of limbs. "Sorry. I thought one of the creatures had found me."

"What creatures? The Daggers said nothing about any creatures." Mage's scan probed the room for threats. He sat on the sofa next to her and crushed her against him. He dwarfed her. She was warm and fragrant, and palpably terrified. "What's going on? Where's Tris?"

"I don't know where Tristan is. Supposedly, he's on some business in the city concerning me. You must have met Richard Shuman." She rooted into his neck and wrapped her arms around him. In a muffled voice, she relayed the events of the recent past.

His concern morphed into anger. Mummers. He conjured up unrealistic fantasies of personally eliminating the cartel boss who funded murder attempts on vulnerable women. "I'm sorry. I neglected to activate my personal transponder. I was the intruder. I must have terrified you when I came up the stairs."

"I almost shot you." She loosened her grip and laid her cheek on his shoulder. "I guess I should be angry, but I'm so relieved it was only you. My brain won't shut off and my imagination…" She looked at him ruefully. "Well, you can guess the sort of things I imagined."

"Come here." Mage pulled her onto his lap. The heat of her plush backside nested perfectly against his groin and thighs awoke his earlier stirrings of desire. She presented a luscious package of femininity he didn't try to resist. He joined their mouths in a soft kiss that began as reassurance. Her lips parted and the feel of her tongue tangled with his, encouraging and provocative, lit a flash fire of erotic response in him. He tightened his hold, grinding her hips into him. Both of them breathed heavily when he finally pulled away. Her half-lidded gaze met his and lingered.

"I've missed you," she whispered. "Make love to me. I can lose myself in you and the sex would be a welcome distraction." The message in her violet eyes hit him with such impact he was a hair's breadth from pounding his chest in a primal display of brute possession. At that moment, he would have found a way to pull the moons from the heavens had she asked. He searched her face but found nothing except honest desire. A smile flirted with his lips and grew to a broad grin.

"If a distraction is what you need, then a distraction I will provide. On your bed, naked. I'll join you in a minute. I want a few things from downstairs." She slid off his lap with a sound of pleasure. Mage gave a passing thought to Tristan. By the seven hells, it was *therapeutic* sex. Tris would understand. *I hope.* Mage trotted down the stairs. *Speak of the devil and he appears.* As Mage stepped into the large central room of the downstairs apartment, Tristan walked through the entrance door.

"Hi, honey, I'm home," Tristan quipped. Welcome gleamed in his smiling eyes.

Amusement and a feeling much more profound shook Mage. He recognized the emotion, though he shied from putting a name on it. It should have been too soon to feel so intensely, but he'd always been absurdly vulnerable to Tristan, and nothing had changed.

"I was breaking my neck to get back because of an unknown intruder when Shuman commed me a second time and said it was you." Tris frowned, stepped forward and shoved Mage backwards. "You're a fucking idiot, Magellan. You didn't activate the ID transponder I gave you. This entire dome scrambled a code-alpha intruder alert because of you."

Guilt assailed Mage and he halted his automatic retaliation to Tristan's aggression. He'd forgotten that basic security measure. He'd been in such a gods-be-damned hurry. "Yeah, boneheaded move. My apologies. It won't happen again."

Exasperation flashed across the older man's face, but he shook his head and shrugged. A grin popped out and his manner softened.

"You're back ahead of time. I wasn't expecting you for days."

Mage returned Tristan's warm smile. "I took some liberties with the schedule and busted my ass to return as quickly as possible."

Tristan's timely arrival provided him with an unlooked-for opportunity to further his ultimate goal. Mage took a deep breath and prayed for the right words. *By the Goddess, I hope I can do this.* Just as slipping a megaton starship into dry dock without so much as ruffling a gantry tower took finesse, so moving Tristan and Angelica in the direction he desired would require careful navigation. Anxiety wormed its way into his stomach. His future with Tris depended on the next few minutes, and he hadn't gotten off to an auspicious start.

"We have an emotionally unsettled woman upstairs, which I suppose is my fault. I was on my way back up to provide a requested 'distraction'," Mage said.

Tristan cocked his head and leveled a direct gaze at Mage. Wariness replaced the welcome in his voice, and his eyes narrowed. "What sort of distraction?"

"The sort you are imagining."

Long moments of silence built and Tris visibly withdrew into himself. The warmth in his silver eyes frosted to glacial ice. "Well, Captain DeLan. Don't let me keep you." Tristan turned on his heels and started toward the door.

"Hear me out, please," Mage called. His confidence nosedived at Tristan's cutting reaction. "It doesn't have to be me doing the distracting."

Tristan's chin jerked up and he stopped. Turning back, once again he caught Mage in a steady stare. He crossed his arms over his chest. "No?"

Mage shook his head. "I think it would be sexy as all fuck to see you with her." *Please, Tris.*

"What… like some gods-be-damned sex show?" Tristan uncrossed his arms to hang relaxed and snorted. "That would turn you on?"

"It will fucking kill me to watch. I'm hard just thinking about it." Mage's erection strained at the front of his pants as if to offer proof, and Tristan's gaze traveled from his face to his groin and then back to his face.

"Never took you for a voyeur." Tristan grunted. "No matter. Give me a moment to clean up and I'll join you, but if the lady says no, I'm out. If she's not willing, neither am I."

"She won't refuse. You're like gravity, Tris—irresistible."

Tristan rolled his eyes and turned away with a soft mutter. "You're so full of shit. You seem to resist just fine."

"Nah, you're a stud." Mage laughed when, without looking back, Tristan cocked his arm and held up his middle finger. Relief left him almost lightheaded.

In truth, he wasn't a voyeur. He'd observed many a live sex show in smoky dives in his years with the Verdantian navy, and before that as part of the mandatory sexual instruction required of every Verdantian noble. The erotic titillation of watching intercourse performed in every possible position had faded by the time he was sixteen and as part of the curriculum expected to participate in the classroom demonstrations. *Guess you could kill the joy in anything if you made it into a job.* By the time he'd reached adulthood, watching sex stirred little reaction from him. Well, except for those Valuzian hermaphrodites—that had been pretty kinky. However, the thought of watching a man he'd obsessed over with a woman whose slick recesses he could still feel squeezing his cock… ah, now… that was a therator of a different hue. His cock stirred again at the thought.

Feeling hopeful, Mage sauntered into the bedroom where he'd thrown his duffle bag. He dug through clean clothing and found the small wooden box he'd come down for. Tossing it up, he snatched it out of the air with a smile and then turned and joined a waiting Tristan in climbing the stairs to Angelica's apartment. One tricky ego maneuvered. One to go. At the head of the stairs, he laid a hand on Tristan's shoulder.

"Give me a moment alone with her?"

Tris studied him thoughtfully and then nodded and fell behind Mage as the two men walked into Angelica's apartment. At the open door to her bedroom, Mage stopped and motioned silently to Tris, and with a lift of his chin in acknowledgment, the man slouched against the doorframe.

Angelica lay on her back on the bed. A fine sheet covered her and her soft brown hair created a disordered halo around her face. The golden glow of candles provided the only light. Lust to possess her rose in Mage with unsettling intensity. *Shit.* How was he going to do nothing but watch? He'd signed on for some unadulterated erotic torture. His gaze captured hers as he walked toward her and sat on the bed, placing the small wooden box on the bedside table. Her eyes followed his hand and looked up at him in question. "I'll show you later."

He ran his fingers through the hair at her temple and cupped the back of her head, marveling at her delicacy. His thumb caressed her finely modeled cheekbone. "Do you trust me to know what you need?"

She wrinkled her brow with a small laugh. "Yes, of course I trust you. You'd not be here otherwise."

"I'm serious, Angel. Think before you answer and I'll ask again. Do you trust me to provide what you need?"

This time long moments passed while she obviously gave thought to his question. Her gaze strayed to the wooden box on the bedside table and then to him. If its exotic contents were the extent of what he wanted her to accept he'd have no concerns. So much rode on her answer that waiting was difficult, but he relaxed and schooled himself to be patient.

"We spoke of this before. You know my hard limits, and I trust you not to violate them." Angelica curled her lower body around his in a flow of sensual invitation and rubbed his back with the inside of one calf and thigh and placed one of his hands on her breast. "Now, will you please get on with the distraction you promised?"

He captured her hand and kissed her knuckles. "I will never knowingly ask anything of you that will damage you emotionally or physically. All I request is you trust me enough to explore."

"Why am I not surprised that a starship captain wishes to explore new boundaries?" She laughed softly. "Yes. I trust you. How often do you want me to say it?"

"One more time." Tristan's crisp baritone broke the intimate moment. "Because, at Magellan's request, I will direct your 'distraction'." He crossed to the opposite side of the bed and looked down at a startled Angelica. "However, I made it clear to our young captain that I don't go where I'm not wanted. This is to be your choice. Do I go… or do I stay?"

Mage held his breath waiting for Angelica's answer. Behind Tristan's cool, imperious expression resided a heart more easily wounded than anyone realized, but he knew from firsthand experience Tris could also be cruel. He earnestly hoped he hadn't set Tristan up for rejection or Angelica for further trauma. Her eyes tracked to his and Mage squeezed her hand. Words of inducement, reassurance, lingered unspoken on his tongue. This must be her decision.

"Both of you? You want this?" she asked. He nodded. Angelica's eyes held his intently as if to glean his thoughts. She withdrew her hand. With the sheet clutched over her generous breasts, she scooted up to rest against the headboard, head down in thought. Her chin rose and her gaze leveled on Tris. "Stay."

CHAPTER TEN

He looks relieved. Angelica knew a moment of confusion. Her decision mattered to Tristan DeHelios. Relief had flashed into Tristan's eyes for only an instant, supplanted immediately by a look of such ravenous lust that she sank against the headboard, but she knew what she'd seen. Her job was interpreting peoples' expressions for insight into their psyche. She recognized relief when she saw it. She couldn't wrap her mind around it. The shock of seeing an emotion so unexpected shoved all her other rioting feelings aside.

Why did it matter so much? She was simply a convenience with which to acquire Magellan. Wasn't she? At this point, she hardly cared. Either man submerged her in aching want. Together? In her mind, she presented herself like a bitch in heat, down on her elbows and knees, back arched, thighs spread in a deliberate invitation to be mounted.

Tristan pierced them with an intense stare, holding her and Mage in a concentrated gaze for a long moment. The strength of passion she saw made her want to crawl to his feet and beg to serve—or hide under the bed.

"Let me be clear to both of you. I am a man of strong appetites. I will have each of you in every way possible, as often as I desire. Unless you are physically incapable through sickness or injury, 'no' is not an acceptable response and I will disregard it." His sinful growl filled the heavy silence. "What's the matter, Captain DeLan? Too much? Want out? This is who I am. I'll give you time, but I won't change who I am for you."

Mage cleared his throat but his voice was steady enough. "No. I don't want out."

Her bodyguard's silver gaze swung to her. "And you, Dr. Giverny?"

A mocking smile pulled one corner of his mouth and the knowing heat in his eyes melted her. She felt almost delirious with hope and sick with nerves. She could trust him not to disappoint her. Tristan understood what she craved. *Mastery.*

She swallowed heavily and managed a breathy, "No... I don't want out."

Tristan's eyes closed for a second. His body relaxed then straightened, head up, shoulders back, and for a split second she'd seen it again. Relief. However, had she not spent every waking hour for the last few weeks with him, she wouldn't have noticed the split-second flash of intense emotion. Strong feelings swirled inside this overwhelming, provoking, frightening, man. About what? Or should she ask about whom? Would he ever trust her enough to open the enigma named Tristan DeHelios and let her peer inside?

When his eyes opened, he leveled a straight gaze at her. "Mage was schooled as a magister through level five. He will be knowledgeable in many... inventive... approaches to sex."

She almost rolled her eyes. That was an understatement.

Tristan's lips twitched. "Yes, I suspect he's introduced you to some of them."

Of course Tris knew. He'd seen her limping around her office.

"I'm more exacting than Captain DeLan and vastly more experienced." His voice softened to a gravelly purr. "I will use both of you hard. You will choose a word to tell me when you have reached your limit, and I expect you to use it." Tristan gestured between the three of them. "For however long this lasts, I consider you mine to possess and protect. You don't want to know the punishment I deal out to those who abuse what is mine." His eyebrow rose and his eyes challenged her. "Do not allow yourself to be carelessly hurt—even by me. Do you understand me? I will not be pleased."

As she listened, her nipples hardened and gooseflesh crawled her arms. She was terribly aware only a thin sheet separated her body from his. He frightened her in the most delectable way. She answered him with a slight nod. Mage rose from the bed and stood facing Tris.

Tristan's gaze leveled on Mage. "That directive also applies to you, princess. Don't be stoic. I will be furious if you allow yourself to be hurt in a misguided attempt to please me."

"I understand." Mage flicked a glance at Angelica then returned his attention to Tristan. She read nothing from Mage's expression, but the fine material of his trousers displayed the distinct outline of a prominent physical reaction.

"Since we received the same sexual training, I have some idea where your limits might be. I trust you to tell me exactly where."

Mage nodded with a half-smile. "You'll know. My safe word is *Revertar*."

Tristan's expression was all marauder. "*I will return.* Appropriate."

"I thought you'd appreciate the irony," Mage said.

"And your word, Doctor?"

Angelica said the first thing that popped into her mind, "Victor."

Tris cocked his head and regarded her from hooded eyes. "Victor as in the winner, the vanquisher? Is that how you think of me?"

She nodded, incapable of words. She was now comfortable with the idea that, sexually, she wanted a conqueror. The potential difficulty had been finding one. Now, she had two. Heat pulsed between her legs. The flesh there felt swollen.

"Victor... I'm good with that." A smile pulled at one side of Tristan's mouth. "Mage, downstairs, my bedside table, top drawer, bring the contents to me. All of it. In fact, pull the drawer out and bring it."

"Sure, just don't start without me." Mage turned and walked toward the bedroom door.

"I can't start without you. You feature in this evening's 'distraction'," Tristan murmured.

The throaty laugh that followed tickled naughty places in her, and Magellan paused in mid-stride and glanced over his shoulder. He opened his mouth to speak, then stopped and closed his jaw with an audible click of his teeth. He scrubbed a hand over his face. "No. I don't want to know."

Moments later, Angelica heard the sound of his footsteps on the stairs.

The bed depressed as Tristan sat. Angelica couldn't look away from his intent stare. It was as if he possessed some exotic magnetism that drew her inexorably, she the prey to his predator. She shivered and clutched the sheet tighter to her bosom.

"I had a bet with myself that your nipples would be brown." Tristan reached toward her, fisted the sheet at her waist and bared her torso with a downward jerk. "I lost. They're pink." Impaled on his gaze, she covered her naked breasts with her palms. He made a wordless sound of objection. "Move your hands. Never cover yourself in front of me."

She dropped her arms to the bed.

The accelerated rise and fall of his breathing, the twitch of the muscles in his tight jaw, the intensity in his eyes—all screamed of savagery bound by iron control, at odds with his forefinger's delicate tracery of first one erect nipple and then the other. There was no missing the prominent bulge at his groin. Within her, sexual tension stoked by a frisson of fear combined to produce a delicious hyperawareness of his every movement and multiplied every sensation. His fingertip teased the full swell of her breast and her nipples contracted further. They itched ferociously. The heat between her legs grew molten and she shifted her hips restlessly.

"Is that pussy wet for me, Angel?"

"Yes," she whispered as Mage walked back into the bedroom. She expected a response but Tristan never took his eyes off his fingertip as it traced an erotic tease around her right nipple. He licked his finger, dampened the tip of her nipple, and then pursed his lips and blew a steady stream of air across it. She choked in response to the chilly sensation, but rather than cool her arousal, the heat between her legs flamed higher. Tris shot a glance at her. She sank further into the headboard at the repressed violence in his eyes. He stood in one powerful glide and ripped the sheet off the bed. She stiffened and then relaxed. She wanted him to look. She wanted to provoke and inflame him as much as he did her. His eyes devoured her nude body in a tangible assessment that began at her head and ended at her toes.

"Fucking flawless."

Angelica preened. The gratification she felt at his praise was out of all proportion. She held advanced degrees in integrated cerebral neurology and psychology, but compared to this man, she was a neophyte. Tristan was the grandmaster at games for the mind and body. He'd barely touched her and insane arousal left her panting for breath.

Mage cleared his throat and held up the drawer. "Where do you want this?"

"At the foot of the bed," Tristan said. "And then strip."

Mage placed the drawer at the foot of the bed as instructed and then began to unfasten his shirt. His gaze traveled up and down Angelica with obvious appreciation. His eyes promised depravities yet unrevealed. She wanted to scream a demand for someone to touch her, fuck her, but she'd ceded control to these men. She'd no choice but to endure. Her breasts ached and between her legs, the folds of flesh were plump and slick. So needy. Goddess! Would someone please fuck her soon!

Tristan's gaze swung to the small box Mage had brought upstairs earlier. "Is that what I think it is?"

"Look for yourself."

Tris raised an eyebrow and moved around the bed to the item in question. He flipped its bronze hasp, opened the lid—and started chuckling. "An Oshtesh husband's kit. Naughty, naughty boy, Magellan. This set you back a fat wad on the black market. The Oshtesh hand this down father to son. They are never sold."

Mage shrugged with a smile. "I know the friend of a friend."

"What's a husband's kit?" Each man slowly turned toward Angelica. She ceased her attempts to glimpse the contents of the box and sank back against the headboard. A fiendish smile stretched Tristan's lips. Mage's eyes held wicked amusement. Neither answered her question.

By the Goddess, I'm such a besotted fool. This must be love. Tris laughed derisively at himself. After he'd crashed Mage's dinner date with Angelica, he'd decided to go slow, be considerate, be a gods-be-damned gentleman and court the younger man. He'd been all "warm and gooey" seeing Mage standing in his apartment—until the bastard cold-cocked him with Angelica. He'd promptly consigned his good intentions to the seven hells. Most of his anger dissipated when he heard what Mage proposed—most.

Angelica Giverny. By the Consort's ballocks. Angelica Giverny was one gutsy female straight out of a sexual fantasy. Everything about her attracted him—from her intelligence, to her glorious body, to the nurture and understanding she bestowed on his damaged countrywomen. Angelica was a mouthwatering confection frosted with the irresistible temptation of her submission, and he planned to devour her.

He had a niggling feeling that with Angelica and Magellan he'd stumbled onto something extraordinary. The emotions they resurrected were. It seemed forever since he'd felt such a mix of exhilaration and anticipation. He'd forgotten what it was like to look to the next day with eagerness. *I want this to last. Unbelievable.* Most likely, it would blow up in his face. Most likely. With a mental sigh, he consigned the prospect for a lasting relationship into the dark corner of his mind where his other abandoned hopes lay moldering, next to the one where his brother didn't assume the worst of him or where his accomplishments actually meant something. Suppressed anger snarled in the background. Fuck that "true love" shit. Happily-ever-afters are for hopeless sots. He'd do what he'd always done—settle for the here and now.

Right now, Tristan knew exactly how he wished to use the contents of Mage's wooden box. He'd "distract" the good doctor until every nerve in her body craved orgasm. As for that prick-tease Captain DeLan? Tris had a surprise in store for Mage. The good captain would beg to be taken—for all the good it would do him.

He turned to face a Magellan DeLan clad in nothing but his unblemished skin and an erection. Mage stood hip cocked, arms crossed at his chest, at ease with his nudity and arousal. A gods-be-damned fucking work of art. Mage could have been one of those old- Earth statues that his mother had insisted on placing in every niche and cranny in the palace at Nyth Uchel. She'd claimed they embodied the ideal of masculine beauty, though he'd never seen one sporting a cockstand quite like Mage's. It thrust straight and proud out of a base of black curls. Fuck, no wonder the poor girl had limped for a week.

Tristan leaned over the foot of the bed and rummaged around in the drawer. *Yes, these are what I want.* He tossed one set of heavily padded wrist cuffs to Mage and one to Angelica. "Put those on."

Mage examined them and looked up at him askance. "Really?"

"Do it, princess. It's non-negotiable."

Mage pursed his lips and with a sardonic lift of his eyebrows complied. Angelica obeyed without any backchat.

He pulled back the gossamer bed drapery to expose the rings set into the tall posts on each corner. He'd bet dinner at Il Piatto Delicios neither Mage nor Angelica realized they were there. The unexpected made him look closer. Lengths of fine black cord interwoven with silver metallic thread hung from those at the head of the bed—bondage cord of the sort used in *téad de ghrásta*— easy on human flesh yet almost unbreakable. He wound his hand in one section and tugged—no give. He glanced at Mage. The man wore a subtle smile. Inward amusement tickled Tris. Good thing he hadn't bet.

"Give me your hand, Angelica." Tris ran the cord through a ring on her wrist cuff and tied it off and then walked around to the other side of the bed and did the same to her other hand. She watched... and squirmed. How aroused was she? He had to know. "Spread your legs, sugar."

He sat on the bed and leaned over her groin. Plump fleshy folds covered with tight curls of glossy brown guarded her most intimate recesses. With a feather-light touch, he traced the seam of her swollen labia and insinuated his forefinger into her warmth. It slipped easily through the plush rosy flesh. He added another finger to the one already stroking the slippery heat inside her.

She shuddered and vee'd her legs a fraction more. Her breathing accelerated and her eyelids slid half-closed. Fuck. He wanted to free his cock and pound into her—but things would be over far too quickly. His need to punish her for forcing him to share Mage required a more prolonged torture. A low growl vibrated in his chest. "You're soaking wet."

"Yes," she said with a catch in her voice. "Please, Tris, I need to…" She trailed off as she read the denial in his eyes.

Poor little pretty one. He withdrew his fingers and dried their wetness on her thighs. "You mistake your man. I'm not civilized like Magellan. You asked for distraction, and I'll oblige, but you won't dictate the form or the duration. Ever." Her eyes flared and he couldn't help but chuckle. She looked so adorably flustered. "I demand total obedience in the bedroom, and you will address me as 'Sir' in private."

Her eyes narrowed. He returned her direct gaze, arched his eyebrow and waited for the expected objection. Her mouth firmed but her eyes dropped, and she remained silent. He knew a flush of conquest. He'd finally captured his elusive prey. Never had a woman resisted him as long as she had. "Good. I will assume you understand what I require from you."

He rose, flipped through the drawer, palmed two carabineers and turned to Mage. "Stand at the foot of the bed. Face Angelica. Hands on each post."

Mage drew out his compliance until it flirted with disobedience. His green eyes challenged Tris the whole time. Tristan soothed his annoyance with a self-admonishment. *Patience and control. Don't permit his insolence to derail you.*

The play of Magellan's muscled shoulders and arms under pale skin, the lift of his ribcage and taut abdomen as the man reached and gripped the upright bedposts, fascinated Tris. His position drew Tristan's eyes to the fine line of dark hair running midline until it disappeared into the black curls at his groin. Magellan's cock stood proudly, a rigid, dusty-rose spear of flesh crowned with a flared head that even now shone with clear drops of arousal. Damnation. His eyes gorged on the beauty that was Magellan DeLan.

Sharp talons of lust clawed at Tristan. His testicles were painful stones pulled up hard against his shaft. His swollen cock screamed for release from his snug leathers and made any sort of movement uncomfortable. He slipped behind Mage and clipped the captain's wrist cuffs to the rings embedded in the posts.

"I'm not in the friendliest frame of mind, Captain. Don't challenge me again."

"Are you trying to scare me? I'm not sixteen anymore, Tristan. I don't turn and run from your ill temper."

"Perhaps you should." Tris nuzzled into the scruff at the tender crook of Magellan's neck and jaw and nipped. The younger man exhaled forcefully and gooseflesh erupted on his arms. His eyes rose and met Angelica's hungry gaze, aware all the time of Angelica's intent observation, aware she worked her thighs together, and squirmed her delectable ass into the bedding, Tris ran the sensitive palms of his hands up Magellan's sides and lightly pinched the man's erect nipples.

"Shit!" Mage shuddered and his firm, round buttocks ground into Tristan's aching groin.

It felt too good. He stepped back, breaking contact. Balancing a drop of emerging pre-cum from Mage's cock on a fingertip, he lightly rimmed the head of Magellan's shaft. The erect organ slapped the captain's belly in response. Angelica moaned. Mage hissed and pushed forward seeking additional pressure. The bed hit him mid-thigh, woefully inadequate by a hand span.

"Fuck, Tristan. I'm so close. Close your fist on me. Don't

tease," Mage breathed on a groan and jerked on the clips holding his arms spread. Angelica's heavy pants provided an audible background in the quiet room.

Wicked satisfaction flooded Tris, and he moved away from the temptation to grind into Magellan's buttocks. "Well, Captain DeLan"—he swung his attention to Angelica—"Dr. Giverny. You asked for a distraction. A distraction doesn't necessarily equal an orgasm, does it?"

"What in the seven hells does that mean?" Mage muttered flatly.

Tristan didn't answer. A little sexual tease would go a long way toward cooling his anger at Magellan's manipulations and, he admitted privately, his unwarranted irritation with Angelica.

"Tristan..." Magellan snarled a warning.

"Relax. You'll both survive. You'll even enjoy it—in the beginning." He chuckled softly and walked over to the bedside table, pulling open the zips on his synth-leather top and shrugging out of it.

"Sir. Your chest." Angelica examined his torso for a moment, her gaze containing nothing but professional detachment.

He scratched the diagonal red welt scoring his chest and abdomen and shivered at the pleasure. Little remained of the deep gash, but what did itched furiously. "It's fine, Doc. Whatever was in that healing accelerant is powerful stuff. Now, you asked what an Oshtesh husband's kit was."

Tris smiled at her as he removed three small cylinders of fibrous organic matter, a small jar, and a fine brush from the wood box. "The Oshtesh inhabit the only arid part of our green world. Their harsh environment and societal customs produce autonomous women, most of whom live segregated from men prior to marriage. Until the pleasures of carnal relations are established, it's not uncommon for such women to lack interest in sex. A husband's kit contains items which create and maintain arousal in an indifferent spouse."

He freed the lacing on the front of his form-hugging pants and skinnied out of them, stopping to toe off his boots. The buttery-soft animal hide offered greater protection than fabricated material, but removing them with any degree of grace posed a challenge. He wanted to groan with relief when his cock sprang free. Angry red marks from the lacing scored the rigid, thick, stalk of his erection. He knelt on the bed between Angelica's spread legs and addressed Mage over his shoulder. "Are her nipples sensitive?"

"Very, and she likes pain play."

He leaned forward on all fours and sucked one of the tempting raspberry buds into his mouth. He held the sweet nub in his front teeth and pulled.

"Ah!" Angelica arched her back and bit her lower lip, choking back a soft grunt. The fucking column of stone between his legs wagged in approval at her response, and his balls became twin knots of pain. Hot wetness rolled in a maddening tickle down the flare of his cock head. He did his best to ignore it.

As his teeth continued to pull, he flicked the tip of her right nipple with his tongue and gently shook his head. Mewls of appreciation met his ears. When he glanced at her face, her eyes gazed unseeing. She drew air through her nose in heavy inhales. He alternated pulling and flicking with strong sucking until her hips writhed on the bed and her legs sought to wrap his hips and bring her pelvis closer to a cock that begged the freedom to split her in half. That he would not allow—not yet.

He popped her nipple from his mouth and sat back on his heels. His shaft and balls had taken on an excruciating life of their own and protested the cramped position. Keeping his voice detached and steady required more effort than he cared to admit. "Put your legs down, Angelica. Keep them flat on the bed and spread as wide as you can. I'll attend to the ache between them later." *When I attend to the fucking agony between mine.*

"Yes, Dominus." She arched her back and presented her breasts to him in flagrant invitation.

He held her gaze with a half-smile. "I like the sound of your cries. Don't hold them back."

He resumed the torture of her right breast. When her vocalizations sounded more of pain then pleasure, he turned to the left nipple and gave it the same treatment. By the time he stopped, Angelica was on the verge of sobbing, and both nipples protruded an angrily swollen half-inch. He placed the fleshy pad of his forefinger ever so gently against the very tip of a scarlet bud and prescribed a delicate circle.

She wept softly, shook her knees as if to mitigate the stimulation and whispered a desperate, "Please, Sir, fuck me. I burn."

"Can you orgasm simply from breast stimulation?"

Drenched violet eyes found his, and she nodded while Mage's hoarse voice contributed, "Yes, but she'll want more."

Tris reached for one of the fibrous cylinders he'd taken from Mage's wooden box and popped it in his mouth. After thoroughly moistening it, he grasped Angelica's right breast firmly and slid the cylinder onto the hyper-extended nipple. He did the same to the left and then inspected his work. The tiny circles of fibrous matter wrapped each nipple snuggly from base to within a fraction of the tip. "Good. This will keep your nipples erect. Now for the paste."

He twisted the lid off the small jar. An herbal tang with the hint of a peppery overtone permeated the air. He dipped the small brush into the cream and painted a thin layer of the fragrant mixture over Angelica's areolae, the fibrous nipple wraps and the exposed tip of her nipples. He placed the brush on the table, screwed the lid back on the small jar and then sat back and waited.

It didn't take long.

"Sir, my nipples, the cream... oh! It itches... tingles. Gah!" She dropped her head back and her upper body undulated while her hands jerked on her bonds as she attempted to rub her breasts. "Please! Touch me. Make it stop."

Her pleas tapered off into sobs when she saw the slow shake of his head. He was a sadistic bastard. Her anguish fucking did it for him, but Angelica got off on it, too. She hadn't used her safe word, and her legs squeezed his thighs in abortive attempts to assuage a desperately needy pussy.

"The intensity of the sensation caused by the cream will fade somewhat... unless I reapply it. The nipple wraps stay on. Unlike clamps, this organic material won't interfere with circulation, so we can keep your sweet little nips hypersensitive for as long as I like." He reached out and stroked her cheek. "Is it difficult to think over the arousal?"

She gasped a breathy, "Yes, Sir."

"Good." He smiled. "Let's make it impossible." Tris silently cursed his throbbing cock as he lay on his stomach between Angelica's thighs. He didn't know how much longer he could stand the titillation before slamming into her wetness for what he knew would be a mind-altering orgasm. The quiet, vulgar epithets from the man behind him served to center him, though, reminding him of his ultimate goal. His thumbs spread the doctor's labia wide, stretching it apart until the small pink nub of her clitoris peeked from beneath its hood. He locked his mouth around it and sucked hard.

Angelica screamed. Her heels dug in, and she attempted to lift from the bed, a futile effort. He was vastly stronger, bigger and heavier than she was, and he held her down until her cries took on a frantic quality that told him scant moments separated her from climax. He sat up and popped the third fibrous cylinder into his mouth as her cries of, "Don't stop! Don't stop! Please, Sir," gusted past her lips.

He waited a moment until she ceased her pleas, until her gaze sought his, beseeching in silent anguish. He smiled slightly, snuggled back between her thighs and held her motionless as he sucked her tortured clit into the third cylinder.

"No, no, no!" she begged when she realized his intent. Then silence. Her eyes rolled wildly and her head thrashed back and forth at the sensations he knew she felt as the plant material wrapped her elongated clit in a snug clamp—all but the very tip. He flicked the scarlet dot with the end of his tongue and Angelica bucked wildly under him.

"I'm going to come. I'm going to…"

At her first words, Tris pinched her clit viciously. Her scream echoed off the walls, and she subsided in writhing whimpers. Behind him, the carabineers clanked against the bedpost rings as Mage tested his bonds and growled. He straightened, grabbed Angelica's cheeks, and forced her to look at him. His fingers dented her soft flesh. He felt only a small pang at her patent distress. If she truly suffered, she held the power to end it immediately. "Did you come?" he demanded.

"No, no," she choked. Tears trembled on the edges of her heavily lashed eyelids.

He jerked the ties on her cuffs loose, freeing her hands. "Get on your hands and knees facing Mage and don't move." Her shaking hands crept toward her breasts. He swatted them away. Her nipples must be in torment for her to risk such an action. "Stop it. You know better. On your hands and knees, and spread those legs wide."

She whimpered a soft, "Yes, Sir," and complied.

He swung his legs off the bed and rummaged again in the drawer at its foot. He closed his hand on a square plex-glass box with a smile of satisfaction. Flipping the catch, he removed a metallic patch and a small disc on a loop of cord from the interior. Mage watched him intently and then his stance straightened.

"Tristan…"

He ignored him.

"Tristan!" Mage snapped. Tristan's gaze lifted to hold the captain's green-eyed stare. "Don't do that to her." Mage shook his head. "Don't."

"It's not for her." He knew his smile was evil. He didn't care. He held the silver patch between two fingers and wagged it back and forth. "You have a safe word. Use it or shut up." Mage snarled at him but said nothing until Tris moved behind him and smoothed the silver oval firmly into the base of Magellan's spine, right between the cheeks of his round, beautifully muscled ass. Then that gorgeous specimen of manhood jerked violently on his cuffs and growled an assortment of obscenities that even Tris conceded were creative. He'd listened carefully. Conspicuously absent was the word "*Revertar*."

By the Goddess, did life get any better? Two glorious bodies who enjoyed his sadistic play. He slipped the cord for the activator over his head.

"Why? Why the neuro-blocker?" Angelica asked him between pants.

"You recognize it. You've probably used it to moderate severe pain, control seizures, that sort of thing. A more exotic use is to inhibit orgasm. I calibrated this unit to allow stimulation right up to the threshold of climax. Then it blocks all feeling until the nerve synapses fire more slowly. I tested it on myself. It's agonizingly effective." He offered her a crooked smile. "Our young captain will want to come—over and over and over again. He simply won't be able to."

Submerged in a deluge of arousal, Angelica stumbled processing Tristan's words. His slow drawl painted a graphic picture of torturous frustration. Granted, with the riot of sensation in her nipples and clit, the demanding need of her pussy, he could have recited the alphabet and she'd have difficulty tracking, but...

Tristan made a show of activating the neuro-blocker. When the neuro-blocker sank slivers of synaptic conduit into a person's spine it stung. In front of her face, Mage jerked on his bonds, his biceps bulging as he strained against them. The sounds of his guttural curses and the carabineers clashing with the rings filled the room, and then he lapsed into brooding silence. An inch from her nose, his engorged cock spasmed in a series of irregular jerks.

She raised her head to look at Tris over her shoulder, and her breasts jiggled. Insane feeling lanced from her pulsing nipples to her tightly bound and throbbing clit. She tucked and clenched her buttocks in an attempt to quiet the clamor of her feminine flesh and shook with the need to come. Each tremor added more fuel to the blaze between her legs.

"Mage will be in hell. Why?" At her question, Tristan studied Mage. Thankfulness lanced through her that Tris didn't direct the violence evident in his expression at her.

"Don't worry about him. From our magickal training, Mage is all too familiar with "O" denial. As I recall, Mistress Clare spent extra time on him. She couldn't resist. The sight of the beautiful young Magellan suffering exceeded all expectations."

Mage jerked his head up, his gaze a furious green fire. "He's angry with me, Angel. I've forced him to march to my orders, and this is payback." The exchange of heated stares between the two men shimmered in the air. "Just one thing, Tris."

Her bodyguard growled, "What."

"Don't hurt her because of it."

Tris trapped her in a molten silver gaze, and for the first time his manner softened. He gently cupped her cheek and smoothed his thumb over her lips. On all fours, she trembled from the onslaught of outrageous sensation, but his tender caress pushed all to the background for a few seconds.

"No. I'd never abuse such a beautiful, delicate creature due to anger." He leaned in, held her face in both hands, and placed a gentle kiss on her lips. "Don't let me go too far with you, pretty one. Remember 'victor'," he murmured.

She pressed her face into his hand like an affectionate pet. His gentleness now, when he'd been so strident before, slew her. Attraction to this man struck her heart with fearful intensity. "Yes, Sir. I'll remember."

"Good girl." He pulled away and his expression hardened once more. "Hands behind you, crossed at the wrists. When she complied, she overbalanced and fell forward onto her breasts with a hiss. The bed dipped behind her, and Tristan's broad hand wrapped both her wrists, holding her balanced a few inches from the bedding as he settled between her legs. A hard pull on her hair lifted her chin and he wound his hand in the hair at the nape of her neck. The outside of his thighs knocked her knees wider. His cock taunted the flesh at her entrance. She whispered a frantic, "Please. Please, Sir. Take me."

To her unutterable gratification, the broad head of his shaft split her flesh and rammed home in a stunning detonation of brutal sensation. His cock impaled her. Her flesh stretched beyond comfort to accommodate him. Her abused nipples and clit vibrated from his impact and then from her gyrations as she bit off a scream and writhed in distress and gratification. His thick shaft held motionless, hilted within her. With a low growl, she worked herself on the fleshy instrument that split her asunder, grinding in circles, reveling in the mix of pain and pleasure. The least hint of pressure on her oversensitive clit sent her spiraling toward climax. Orgasm undulated toward her with the inexorable intent of a mummer, but rather than cower in fear, she begged it to hurry.

"That's enough. Be still," Tris snapped and released her wrists and hair. She face-planted on the bed. Her bound nipples smashed into the soft bedding, and the resulting pain sidetracked her impending climax. She gasped and shifted some weight onto her forearms. Tris held her hips in a punishing grip that allowed no movement below the waist. "Take him. Take Mage in your mouth."

She raised her head. In a greedy slather of saliva, she stuffed Mage's jerking cock as far into her mouth as she could without choking. Her hands wrapped the remaining inches of his satin flesh, adding the twisting rise and fall of her hands to the motions of her mouth as she voraciously sucked, hollow-cheeked, up and down on his erection, a mimicry of actions she desperately hoped for herself.

"That's it, baby. Ahhh! Fuck me with that pretty mouth." For long seconds, Mage continued to whisper encouragement and then groaned. "Harder, harder, sweetheart, more… I need more. Ah… fuck!" The final words she understood were, "You're a dead man, DeHelios," then Mage lapsed into unintelligible snarls.

Despite the distractions of her own need, she heard the agony in Magellan's voice. His hard shaft jerked on her tongue and his testicles pulsed against her hand where it gripped the base of his shaft, but he hadn't come. She redoubled her efforts, attempting to override the effects of the inhibitor. In rare instances it could be done. Mage arched into her and bellowed, "I'm going to fucking kill you, Tristan!"

At the same time, Tristan fisted her hair and ripped her off Magellan. His other hand anchored her to male hips that split her flesh apart and hammered into her softness with brutal intensity.

She surrendered to the overwhelming sensation of Tristan's driving cock. The bedroom rang with Tristan's growls, Magellan's curses, and her helpless screams of, "Yes! Yes!"

Between her legs, in her nipples and clit, the exploding sensation threatened to obliterate her physical being. Sounds vanished. Sight blanked. Only pure feeling remained as a cataclysmic eruption of pleasure destroyed her conscious mind.

CHAPTER ELEVEN

Awareness returned to Angelica slowly. A beatific smile blossomed on her face. She lay on her back unwilling to open her eyes for more than a blink. A plush fur throw cushioned her. Strong arms held her cuddled against a warm, hard body she identified as Tris. The nipple and clit wraps had disappeared, replaced by cool moist pads smelling of herbal balm. Tristan's hand engulfed her mons and held the pad pressed to her angry clit. The flesh between her legs felt raw and bruised, but it too had been treated with the same sweet-smelling salve. Her mouth, jaw, and neck ached, and she'd have sore shoulders in the morning. She felt thoroughly, gloriously, used.

She opened her eyes to stare into the silver gaze of Tristan DeHelios and wanted to purr. What was it about these over-the-top, larger-than-life, Verdantian men? She'd never felt such safety, belonging, and intense physical satiation as she did in that moment. *Even beyond that night with Mage.* A wall of dominant male protection surrounded her. A soft chuckle escaped when she mentally compared Lord DeKieran, Prince Tristan, and Captain DeLan to *anyone* who'd come before. There was no comparison. Even her so-called "master" on Vxloncia had been a mere poser.

"Beauty awakes,.and you laugh?" Tris said.

Beguiled, she shook her head. "I don't have the energy to explain. May I tell you later?"

"Ummhmm." Tristan leaned down and kissed her, his lips lingering on hers in soft seduction. His tongue traced the seam of her mouth, and she opened to let him in, but he ended the kiss and pulled back to examine her face. "Tell me. Do you hurt anywhere other than the expected places?"

True concern shaded his face. She dropped her eyes and tentatively ran her fingers through the sandy curls on his chest. "I'm fine, Dominus." She raised her head and graced him with a soft smile. "In fact, I can't remember when I've been better."

"Mmm," he hummed under his breath. "And I can't remember a woman I've desired more. I understand Mage's refusal to give you up."

She'd no gauge for the happiness his words released. She was done resisting the rogue. Unguarded admiration and some feeling she couldn't identify colored his expression. A yearning rose in her to see a different emotion on his face, to see some of the sentiment that flavored her interactions with Mage.

Like Magellan, she could easily love Tris. She'd been so wrong about him. His teasing bedevilment of her in day-to-day life masked a man perceptive and gruffly kind. He'd demonstrated he could protect her. Add sexual mastery packaged in a wicked body and a too-handsome face, and, dear god, she found him... captivating. Oh, but she was a greedy, greedy girl. With wary honesty, she acknowledged she wanted *both* of these men.

This time when he lowered his face to kiss her, she rose and met him, ignoring the sting from her nipples as she pressed into him. Pleasure from his roaming caress intertwined with the message his warm lips and probing tongue issued, and she lost herself in his overwhelming masculine charisma. Arousal rekindled. When he stopped and raised his head, she followed his gaze. Guilt assailed her. Cocooned against Tristan, adrift in the passion he provoked in her, she'd forgotten Mage.

At casual glance, her black-haired captain stood impassive, hip-shot, his arms hanging lax from the bedposts. One look at his eyes or cock destroyed that impression. His proud shaft thrust forward from his groin, an angry red. His eyes blazed with green fury. His gaze accused her... but of what... and then shifted to stab Tristan. She shivered at the silent battle the two men waged. Unease knotted her neck and shoulders. When the taut quiet stretched into minutes, the tension became intolerable.

"I don't understand. I thought you dear friends. Why do you treat him so harshly?"

"Am I being harsh?" Tris said, continuing to exchange a steady stare with Mage. "Save for allowing you climax and him not, I've treated you more severely."

Though Mage must have heard Tris, he gave no sign, simply continued to examine them with blistering intensity. Tris dropped his gaze to her. "So I ask you, have I been harsh?"

"To be denied the object of your desire, forced to watch on the sidelines while they enjoy another is..." Her voice trailed off at Tristan's cynical sneer.

"You're certain it's me he wants?" Tris looked away, his features softening with regret. "I behaved with extraordinary cruelty to Mage years ago—something I've been at pains to repair—but he's thrown up obstacles as fast as I can tear them down. The only person who's run from me faster than Mage is you. He knows this, yet he's made you a condition to any physical relationship he and I might have." Tris snorted. "Not the behavior of a man plagued by desire for me."

Tris gave a dry laugh and looked straight at Mage. "Tonight, I'd hoped for time with him, alone, before... well... before. He angered me when he proposed something else. I suppose the feeling lingered."

His gaze returned to her and gentled. His forefinger traced

her lips, leaving a tingle in its wake. "I admit to welcome surprise when you said, 'Stay.' I didn't think that would be your response."

She'd been right. What she'd seen had been relief. A feeling of hopeful anticipation invaded her and a smile flirted with the corners of her mouth. "So... I'm not just an avenue to Mage?"

He shook his head slowly. A dissolute grin stretched his handsome features. "You never were. I intended to pursue you from the moment I set eyes on you. Magellan's prerequisite simply required I change tactics." He sighed, stretched, and disentangled himself from her, and then rolled off the bed and walked to stand behind Mage. Though Tristan's face remained shuttered and his voice cool, his hands betrayed him. His palms smoothed Mage's deltoids with gentle appreciation, as if he couldn't refrain from touching the man. "I'm going to free your hands."

⊛⊛⊛⊛⊛⊛⊛⊛⊛⊛⊛

About time, you gods-be-damned piece of... Mage tensed under Tristan's caress and vacillated between the desire to bloody Tristan's too-handsome face or demand Tris deactivate the gods-be-damned neuro-blocker so he could fall on Angelica and fuck her silly. At the moment, physical violence had the upper hand, and it was on the tip of his tongue to tell Tristan to leave him bound or risk the consequences. With a self-discipline that required shuddering effort, he remained passive as Tris unclipped his wrists and then stepped back.

When he'd suggested Tristan direct Angelica's "distraction," Mage knew he'd be in for some heavy sexual frustration. He hadn't anticipated just how much it would tantalize him to see Tristan and Angelica together; how much her untutored response to Tristan would inflame his arousal; how much the sight of Tristan's hardened, sculptured, masculine frame would feed his lust.

When Tris stepped up the game by clipping his hands to the

bedposts and adding the neuro-blocker, it was as if Tris loosed a feral beast inside him—and then Angelica added her mouth, her wicked, wicked mouth, to provoke the untamed brute into rabid frenzy.

He'd always been a controlled lover. With the notable exception of his one night with Angelica, he'd conducted his sexual encounters with courtesy and self-control. That's who he was. Other than Angelica, Tristan was the only person for whom he'd side-stepped his self-imposed requirement for restraint. His response to Tristan DeHelios had always been intemperate, but Angelica and Tristan together generated a new scale of provocation. For Tristan to then deny him! Angelica was his. Tristan was his. This threesome was *his* idea. They belonged first to him. How dare Tris tell him no. The savage within him screamed for retribution.

Yet, he'd also heard the stark vulnerability in Tristan's dry response to Angelica. *You're certain it's me he wants?* A shard of pain pierced him. Tris doubted him. Fuck. He'd tell the man exactly how he felt, but first, he needed to calm down—if such a thing was even possible around Tris.

He pulled long slow breaths into his lungs and consciously relaxed his muscles. He opened and closed his hands and rotated his wrists to restore circulation to hands that had gone numb. He lectured his heart to stop pounding so frantically, and then Tristan's muscled thighs pressed into the back of his. The man's right arm snaked around his waist and pulled gently. Mage allowed himself to be drawn back against Tristan's chest. Another arm wrapped his shoulders and Tris rested his forehead on the back of his skull.

"I'm sorry," Tris murmured. "In my life, I've used those words infrequently and almost exclusively to you." His arms tightened around Mage. "I'm sorry," he whispered.

Ah, Tris. Tristan. By Her light, he loved this man, and his rage deflated as if atmosphere from a ruptured airlock. He wrapped his arms on top of Tristan's and gave a brief snort. "Don't be such a pompous dickwit, and you won't have to say them to me."

"Mmm. It's genetic. You know my family. I come from an illustrious line of pompous dickwits. You'll have to put up with me."

Low laughter shook them both.

Mage straightened and turned in Tristan's arms to face him. He rested his forearm casually on the man's right shoulder to keep him from backing away. "I want to put up with you for the rest of my life." A hand span from his face, Mage held Tristan's gaze intently, willing the other man to understand the depth of his feeling. "Do you get what I'm trying to tell you?"

A corner of Tristan's mouth quirked up and his eyes softened. "Yeah, princess, I fucking get it."

Mage snorted in mild exasperation at the sobriquet—but let it pass. He turned toward Angelica. *I'll never have a better opportunity.* She'd remained a silent witness though she'd hung on every word. "I'd like you to be a part of this, Angel. What do you say to making it the three of us?"

Her eyes tracked to Tristan, a question in them. He shrugged. "Works for me, Doc, if it works for you."

Angelica took a huge breath and blew it out slowly. "Yes. I'd like that." She beamed at the him and Tris. "I'd like that very much."

He closed his eyes in satisfaction. *Now hear this. This is your captain speaking. Docking module interface complete.* They'd finally made safe harbor.

CHAPTER TWELVE

In that moment, Tris decided to ignore the cynical voice within that urged a return to his comfortable facade of sarcasm and flippancy. He was going to play this straight and see what came of it. He'd never ask his captain to give up the *Revertar*, but because of Magellan's occupation, he had doubted the feasibility of anything permanent. Monogamy was no problem, but he didn't do celibacy and certainly not for months or years at a time. Inevitably, if Mage were gone long enough, he'd cheat and hate himself and then hate Mage for driving him to it. Mage deserved better. So Tris had rationalized. *I'll be his as long as we can make it work, and when I can't... fuck... we'll go our separate ways.* Now, with Angelica as the anchor? That scenario changed things. Optimism replaced fatalism. This could work.

"Now that we've had our tender moment..." he turned to Mage, "...get on the bed with Angelica. We're not through."

Mage straightened. His eyes pinned Tris. "Remove the neuro-block. I've reached my limit."

"Are you asking me? Or telling me?"

"The Mother forbid I should ever tell you what to do. I'm asking. More or less." A wry smile tilted the man's delicious mouth. "I busted my ass to get back to you and Angelica. Don't string me out any longer."

Mage's sentiments echoed his own. He'd held himself in

check with the man. He wanted the scenarios he'd painted in his fantasies the last few nights, but he kept stumbling over that inescapable word, virgin. He slipped the cord over his neck and pressed the control. Mage hissed a quiet curse. He stepped to him, pried the silver oval from Magellan's flesh and tossed it and the control to the bedside table.

"Now, get on the bed," he murmured. Angelica surprised him when she rose and padded to him.

"Sir." She stopped him with a gentle hand on his forearm. "You and Mage should have this time to yourselves—at least this first time."

"This first…" Mage frowned. "You told her?"

Before he could marshal his thoughts, Angelica spoke.

"Tris told me he'd made mistakes with you he didn't want to repeat. He said you'd never been together intimately, and he asked for my professional insight." She directed a sweet smile toward Mage and then him.

Mage looked at him and grinned. "Tristan asked you for advice on his sex life?"

He groaned. "Don't let it go to your head, princess. Both of you, on the bed."

As they climbed onto Angelica's bed, Mage glanced at him. "Did you tell her…?"

He shook his head. "No."

"What? Did he tell me what?" said Angelica.

He laughed quietly at the abashed expression on Magellan's face.

"Eh." Mage released an explosive sigh. "I've never been with a man. Tris will be my first."

Angelica lost her balance and sat heavily. She leaned against the headboard with her hand held to her mouth. Laughter gleamed in her eyes. He could hardly wait. Whatever came out of her mouth was going to be stellar.

"You're a virgin? My space-faring alpha male captain is a virgin with men! I'm beyond astonished. Is the galaxy blind? You're such a beautiful man." She bounced her gaze back and forth between him and Mage and wriggled happily. "Oh! This is so romantic." She wrapped her arms around their black-haired captain, planted a tender kiss on his lips and announced, "This should be only the two of you." She caught Tris with laughing violet eyes. "I'll be in your bed downstairs."

He and Mage watched, dumbfounded, as she hopped off her bed, gathered her robe and scampered to the door. She paused at the threshold and turned back with a sassy wiggle of eyebrows. "Be gentle, Sir." She winked and disappeared. Her footsteps pattered down the stairs accompanied by muted sounds of delight.

The little mynx. He shook his head, a small smile tugging at his lips, and then turned to Mage. The man had propped himself up against the headboard, his fingers laced across his hard abdomen, legs stretched out and crossed at the ankles in front of him. At his dour expression, Tristan turned a laugh into a cough and cleared his throat.

"Everyone has a first time, princess. There's no shame in it."

Mage growled and slid down to rest on a pillow, arms behind his head, and scrutinized the ceiling. "Stop calling me princess. I'm not ashamed. I just hadn't planned on running the news up a flagpole."

"Mmmhmm." He slid onto the bed and lay on his side next to his captain. He couldn't resist. He traced the indentations in Magellan's ripped abs with his index finger and then flattened his entire hand to rest on the warm living silk of Mage's skin. He could feel the pounding of his soon-to-be lover's heart in the palm of his hand. It was only slightly faster than his. He leaned over and traced butterfly kisses along the fine line of dark hair that bisected

Magellan's midsection. He flinched but didn't draw away.

"Angelica's hardly a flagpole. She doesn't gossip. Your astonishing condition will stay between the three of us." He grinned against Mage's satin skin and then leaned back and caught Mage with a sober gaze. "I want this to be good for you. Talk to me."

Mage pursed his lips and his glance slid to Tristan's semi-arousal. "Mmm."

"What do you like? What drives you crazy?"

"Hells' breath. Whatever you do will blow my mind simply because it is you, Tristan-Fucking-DeHelios, doing it."

⚜⚜⚜⚜⚜⚜⚜⚜⚜

Somehow, with Tris, the commander of the *Revertar* vanished and he became simply Magellan. He'd been on edge about this moment. Not so much the physical part, Tristan would make it spectacular. His caution centered upon what the act would do to him emotionally. While he was no longer that teen idolizing an older man, Tris still had the ability to touch him profoundly. He'd be wrecked if Tris—no, he wasn't launching on that vector—Tris said he "got it." He'd trust in Tristan's commitment.

Tris gave him a long considering look. His insides flipped and he could feel the rush of blood to his cock.

"Kiss me." Tris ordered and flopped to his back. Tristan's half-lidded gaze never stopped following him.

He smiled slowly as he rolled on top of Tristan's muscled body and settled between his thighs. The warm, solid press of Tristan's firming erection was a living presence against his abdomen and nested perfectly next to his own engorged flesh. By the Goddess! The feeling prodded the quiescent beast within him. He lowered himself down to rest on Tristan's chest, and his arms wrapped the man's shoulders. He hovered a scant inch above Tristan's face and breathed in the male scent unique to the man. Damnation... this was happening. It seemed surreal.

"What are you waiting for?" Tris murmured. "Kiss me."

"Getting here has taken eight years. I'm savoring the moment."

He ran his nose along Tristan's bristled cheek, across his eyebrows, and nuzzled into the crook of his jaw. With the tip of his tongue, he traced a path to Tristan's earlobe and sucked it into his mouth. He bit down gently and suckled. Tristan groaned.

"Shit. You don't have to seduce me. We're going to fuck. It's a given. I want your mouth."

He pulled back with a soft snort. "I thought to take my time."

"Save the full reconnoiter for another day. Your mouth on mine, now."

He swallowed his amusement at the terse words and obeyed Tristan's demand. The warm press of Tristan's lips cushioned his. His lover immediately opened to suck in his tongue. What was intended as an introduction, a prelude, morphed into a heated, lust-filled, full-body embrace with each man unleashing the tension of the past few hours in a wrestling match for domination that ended with Magellan on his back and the heavier, bigger, Tristan astride his hips, pinning his wrists above his head.

They both sucked in air, their chests heaving. His painfully hard cock strained toward his navel as Tristan's belly stroked a tease of hot flesh across him before the man bowed up to remain inches away. The fleeting pressure multiplied his desire for a faster pace. The fact this was Tristan prevented him from forcing the issue. He'd never have another first time with Tris.

"Stay like this. Don't move or I will tie you," Tris ground out through clenched teeth. His hot breath swept his face and Tristan's rigid cock wept drops of fluid onto his abdomen.

"Yeah, yeah. Just get on with the fucking." His mouth felt

bruised and his cock jerked spasmodically as if pleading for another caress. The ragged torture he'd endured watching Tris take Angelica flooded back. Suddenly, he was no longer inclined to linger.

Tris gave a wicked chuckle as he worked his way down between his outstretched legs and shouldered one of his heavy thighs, opening him further. "You were the one who wanted to savor the moment. Change your mind?"

He gasped a, "Yes!" as Tristan's tongue lapped at the soft skin behind his balls. "Fuck! Yes!" he blurted, as Tristan's mouth enveloped one testicle in a gentle roll, released it and performed the same ablution to the other. His ignored cock jerked in response to the gathering climax until the hot slather of Tristan's tongue worked its way up the midline of his shaft and teased the sensitive nerves under the flare of his glans. Carnal sensation deluged him and roiled in the base of his spine. The taunting play of Tristan's tongue continued for what seemed a lifetime until his self-discipline shredded at the rise of imminent orgasm. He thrust his hips forward with a grunt, seeking greater contact, and encountered air.

"Where are you going?" he demanded as Tris pulled away. He slipped a hand from over his head to his abdomen and wrapped his pulsing cock. Damnation, it felt good. He could end the torture of the last few hours with a simple stroke. Temptation whispered, *do it.*

Tris raised an eyebrow as he picked through the drawer Mage had brought earlier. "That hand goes back above your head. Last warning."

"I could really hate you, Tris." With a low groan of protest, he made himself unfasten his fingers and slide his hand up to wrap the headboard instead of his throbbing cock. "No more teasing."

Tris tossed a small object onto Mage's belly.

He grunted in surprise and peered down his abdomen at a bottle of lube. "Ah... right. Forgot about that."

Tris glided back on the bed and took up a position on his knees between Mage's outstretched legs. "You'd hate me even more if I don't use it."

Mage choked out a rough laugh. "I don't think I care at this point."

A single eyebrow arched over a silver eye. "Oh, you'd care, lover." Tris leaned over him, bracing one arm beside his head, and lowered down for a caress of a kiss. "And I'd care that I'd hurt you. I might be intentionally rough but I'm never careless, not with those who matter to me."

"Nice to know I mah... matter," he stuttered as Tris flipped the top off the bottle and poured a stream of clear lubricant over his straining erection and balls. The viscous fluid tickled as it oozed between his ass cheeks.

Tris rimmed his anus with a gentle finger, spreading the slippery solution. The feeling, not entirely foreign from the anal plugs he had played with, stoked the urgent demand from his cock. Tris wrapped his own heavy shaft with an oily hand and stroked slowly as his fingers teased inside Mage, first one finger and then two, transferring the lubricant around and into his anus.

"I could take you an easier way, but I want to watch your face as I possess you. Pull your knees up, lover."

The bulbous head of Tristan's hard cock pressed forward. They both grunted as the pressure increased and Tris gained entry. Tristan's eyes locked on his. Intimate messages of desire and submission, triumph and surrender, flew across the small space that divided them. It was as if each man poured his soul into the other with the joining of their bodies.

"Ah, fuck..." he whispered at the stretching, biting, discomfort.

"Try to relax and bear down."

He closed his eyes and tried—with mixed results.

Tris won inexorable inches until finally hilting within him. Tristan's slippery hand wrapped his failing erection and began a stroking motion that swiftly brought it back to full hardness. He groaned, caught between the conflicting sensations of intense pleasure and nipping discomfort. Pleasure won.

"Harder and faster, Tris... your hand." The man obliged, sliding his slippery fist to the base of his cock and then up in a swirling motion around its head in a firmer, quicker tempo. "Ah... Goddess... that's good. Ah, fuck... that's good." Now that the moment was upon him, despite his words to the contrary, he blessed the free use Tristan had made of the lube. He shuddered at the thought of the alternative.

"Look at me. You okay, princess?"

"Yeah." He met and held Tristan's smoldering eyes, and the overwhelming significance of who was having sex with him added poignancy to the moment. "Better than okay. Stop calling me... ah, shit! Do that again."

"This?" Tristan's wicked smile accompanied the slow withdrawal of his shaft and then an equally unhurried glide forward. As Tristan rocked gently, the fat head of his cock passed back and forth over the intensely sensitive area of his prostate. The easy slide of greased flesh past his sphincter muscles created unparalleled sensation. The combination spiraled his arousal past control.

"Yeah." he moaned. He closed his eyes and lost himself in the spikes of ecstasy building to an inescapable culmination. "Ah... shit, Tris. I'm going to come."

Mage opened his eyes to see Tristan's head thrown back, his jaw clenched, eyes staring blindly, also entrapped in the carnal spell he'd been weaving. To know that gorgeous man was equally lost in him—ah, it was too much. With a warning growl, he locked Tris to him with his legs, covered the hand Tris had wrapped around his cock with his own and surrendered to the cataclysm. He came for fucking ever. Each pulse of his shaft slammed pleasure through his body until he arched off the bed, his muscular thighs ensuring Tris stayed implanted.

With a low growl of his own, Tris pitched forward, joining him in the ultimate pleasure.

They collapsed. Nostrils flared as they fought for breath.

"Oh, Goddess. I don't think I can move." Draped by the strong body of his lover, Mage didn't want to. *My lover.* He closed his eyes and lay as a dead man, a brilliant smile growing on his face. Damnation, he was happy.

"Was it worth the eight-year wait?" Tristan's muffled voice emerged from where his face rested in the crook of Mage's neck.

Was it worth—by the Mother! How do I tell him? He searched for the words. There had to be something he could say beyond a simple yes. Evidently, his answer took too long. With a curse, Tris freed the hand trapped between their bellies, pushed himself up and peered at him.

He must have liked what he saw. With a pleased expression, Tris grunted, "Good," before collapsing again on his chest.

At the risk of sounding like the princess Tristan labeled him, he ventured, "Was it good… ah, did you…?"

"You were fucking incredible," Tris said, rescuing him from a total surrender of his manhood.

"Yeah?"

"Abso-fucking-lutely. Now shut up. You're ruining my post-coital bliss."

He tried to temper the absurd smile on his face—he really did—but it remained stubbornly in place, lingering until Tris finally pushed up and rolled over. They lay on their backs until

Tristan's regular breathing deepened and he thought the man dozed. His unruly thoughts wouldn't allow him such an escape. They centered on Angelica. *I want more… with her.* He turned his head to regard his lover and prodded Tris with his elbow.

"Tris."

"Hmm?"

"I want Angelica."

"Wha…?"

"I want Angelica to join us."

"My bed's bigger. We go to her."

CHAPTER THIRTEEN

ngelica lay on her side, snuggled in the middle of Tristan's vast bed, drowsing. Cool air rushed under lifted covers to hit her bare skin, and then two lean male bodies snugged to the front and back of her and enrobed her in hard muscles and musky male scent. She knew that smell. Green eyes and a wicked smile met her drowsy gaze. *Magellan.*

"Wake up, Angel."

"Umm... I'm awake." A strong arm wrapped her waist from behind and Tristan pulled her dead weight close against him. The ease with which he accomplished the maneuver left her feeling insubstantial, a mere wisp compared to his masculine bulk. Sandwiched between their bodies, engulfed by protective male, she reveled in the feeling. While she cherished her independence, she found much to recommend in men who could, and would, keep a woman safe without asking. This is what separated Verdantian men from the rest of the civilized universe. What could possibly harm her when surrounded by such men as Mage and Tristan? *I feel safe. Such a luxury.*

Until this moment, she hadn't realized the extent to which apprehension had weighed her down. She thought she'd dealt effectively with the emotional fallout from the attacks on her life. But now? She felt unburdened, as if she'd dropped a weighty load. Only one question deflated her exuberant high. *How long will this last?*

Mage had told Tris he wanted to "put up" with him the rest of his life. Was she included in that equation? Or was she an interchangeable part—no commitment beyond his current stay in port? And what about Tristan? Before she lost all her heart to these men, she must know. She opened her mouth to ask.

Magellan's lips pressed hers in exploration. His tongue invaded her mouth in a passionate sweep, tangling with hers before it withdrew, only to plunge in again as he drove all sleep from her brain and replaced it with burgeoning arousal. Tristan buried his nose in the tender crook of her neck and aided Magellan's assault with gentle nips followed by kisses and licks to soften the sting. Need dissolved her into a languid mound of flesh.

Tristan slid upward and dragged her with him as he sat on a mound of bed pillows propped against the headboard and held her back-to-chest. Boneless with relaxation, she allowed him to arrange her arms and legs as if she were in truth the tiny doll he made her feel like. When he settled, his arms wrapped her waist, trapping her arms and hands beneath his. She lay back against him with her head cradled on his left bicep, and her legs lay atop his heavy thighs in a widespread vee, receptive and inviting.

The two men must have exchanged a silent signal, because Mage's eyes heated and his expression became intent. Moving between her legs, he leaned over and palmed her breast before gently sucking its tip into his mouth and rolling his tongue over the distended nipple. Soreness from their previous play bit her sharply, and she hissed. He pulled back with a murmured, "That answers my question. You are unusually sensitive. I'll assume equally so here?" He shifted back enough to move between her legs and press her clit with a flattened tongue, his eyes gauging her reaction.

She tensed, ready to retreat.

"Umm, yes. Sensitive here, too." A crooked smile stretched

Magellan's mouth. "I'm going to take full advantage of that."

Between the clefts of her ass cheeks, she felt the stir of Tristan's unaroused cock. Without thought, she undulated to provide him with stimulation.

A laugh born deep in Tristan's chest vibrated against her back. "I've been awake for forty-eight hours. I've come twice in the last three. I appreciate your confidence in my virility, but even I have my limits. Wiggle all you want. It always feels good, but I'm strictly an observer this time." He groaned softly. "Though if Mage continues what he's doing now, he might get a rise out of me yet."

Between her legs sensation built in response to Mage's careful tongue as he caressed the entire length of her flesh. From Tristan's response, verbally and physically, Mage also took opportunistic advantage of the placement of Tristan's balls to tease him.

Magellan's soft growl returned her focus to him. "You are still wet from before. I can't wait." Kneeling, he took himself in hand and centered himself at her opening. "Tell me if I hurt you."

He held her gaze as he pressed in slowly. Her flesh protested the invasion, but he'd been right. She was wet. She didn't know if his penetration felt good or bad. It stung as she stretched to accommodate him, but the pull on her hypersensitive clit sent spears of gratification throughout her groin. When hilted fully, the light pressure from his pubic bone against the hard nub accelerated her pleasure and it wasn't long before cascading sensations flooded her lower body and masked any discomfort.

She pulled long inhales and exhales through her nose in time with Magellan's. Flaring her eyes at the slow glide of his hard flesh through her delicate, engorged tissue, she moaned softly and bit her lower lip.

"Good?" he asked.

"Mmmhmm."

His gaze shifted to above her head. A subtle wickedness

appeared on Magellan's face and he leaned forward and captured Tris in a forceful kiss. When they broke apart, he rested his forehead against Tristan. "I can't describe how fucking awesome it is to kiss you while I'm sunk in hot Angelica." With a vigorous exhale, he straightened and pushed his hips forward.

The sharp bite she felt as he hit the end of her fed her arousal. The prolonged slide as Mage withdrew a millimeter at a time teased her intimate flesh with heady pleasure. "I never want this to end."

"Really?" Tristan tightened his arms around her. "I'm onboard with keeping you permanently wet and willing."

"That wasn't what I meant." She felt his body shift as he chuckled.

"Mage, how long can you keep this up?" Tris curled over her and nuzzled beneath her neck with small nips, observing the activity between their legs as his arms entrapped her.

Her black-haired lover grunted as another slow thrust hit her limits. "An hour?" His wry laugh carried strain. "Perhaps less."

Tris paused in his nibbling and groaned. "Look at you two—your cock, wet with her juices, fucking her stretched and swollen pussy. Shit, I don't know how she takes all of you." He swore under his breath. "Any other time, this visual alone would get me off."

Tris kept up a running barrage of erotic description, verbally painting graphic visuals that amplified the physical stimulation to heightened levels and affected Angelica as much as they obviously affected Mage. He lasted little more than thirty minutes though it seemed an eternity. By the time Mage sank his fingers into her ass and came in a frenzy of shortened thrusts, she'd become a mewling, quivering wreck. As his pelvis battered her most sensitive nerves and Tristan growled appreciative obscenities, the over-stimulated tissue of her inner channel fibrillated wildly and then transitioned into hard, rhythmic contractions. The pleasure destroyed her from within. If not for Mage pinning her to Tristan's chest, she would have collapsed to the bed like an imploded building. Movement was impossible. Coherent thought seemed beyond her. *An hour? A little overconfident, weren't you, Captain DeLan?* Smug pleasure at the thought he'd been thrown off his game rippled through her.

"By the Consort's balls, that was hot," Mage sighed.

"Fuck." Appreciation filled Tristan's rasp. "The sight and sound of you both... yeah. Now, get off me. You're crushing my balls."

Mage flopped onto his back, and with a groan, Tris picked her up and snugged her between them. She oozed down the bed until her head nested into a pillow, rolled to her side and closed her eyes. In the seconds before she lost the battle with sleep, she felt Tris and Mage sandwich her between them. She was divinely happy and impossibly satiated, but she still didn't know how long it would last.

◈◈◈◈◈◈◈◈◈◈

"Creator DeHelios, you have an incoming message tagged urgent. Please wake up, sir." A soft chime followed and then silence.

Tristan threw his arm over his face. He was moving for nothing less than the end of the world. Whoever it was would have to wait.

"Creator DeHelios, you have an incoming communication with an urgent tag. How would you like me to respond?"

A soft chime followed and then silence.

"Creator DeHelios, you—"

"Shut the fuck up!" *I'm going to fucking disconnect the gods-be-damned AI.* He groaned and covered his head with a pillow. The action proved futile. The repetitive chime of an incoming message of some urgency rousted him from heaven. With his morning wood snugged between the sweet ass cheeks of Angelica Giverny and the muscled calf of Magellan DeLan entangled with his, who could argue he wasn't in heaven? Through scratchy eyeballs, he peered at the timekeeper mounted on the wall. Three fucking hours of sleep in the last sixty. Growling, he abandoned the warm paradise of his bed and stalked to the comm device. He braced an arm against the wall and slammed the "receive" button. He worked to clear the rasp from his throat. "DeHelios."

"It's about time you answered. I'm in Angelica's apartment. She never came to work, and her apartment is vacant. I'm coming down." Ramsey's concerned bark echoed off the walls of his room. He winced, turned down the volume, and glanced at the bed. Two dark heads remained nestled together in the middle.

"Give me a..." He rolled his eyes at the silence on the other end. DeKieran's rapid steps could be heard descending the inner stairs. He looked around, grabbed a pair of black pants hanging on the back of a chair, and made quick work of getting into them. He'd no more pulled them up when Ramsey strode into the room.

"Do you know where she is?"

A sleepy Angelica propped herself up on one elbow, discreetly covered. "I'm right here, Lord DeKieran. I'm quite safe."

Mage sat up cautiously, groggy inquiry on his face. He shrugged. Damned if he knew what Ramsey was doing here.

Ram observed his two bedmates and then swung a penetrating gaze to him. Ramsey stood, hands on hips, one eyebrow raised.

He cleared his throat. "I'm keeping her under close observation."

"Apparently. Who's the male?"

"Ah..."

"Magellan DeLan," Mage supplied, not waiting for his

introduction. Mage flipped the covers off, walked around the end of the bed to Ramsey and held out his hand. "Captain Magellan DeLan of the VNV *Revertar*. It's a pleasure to meet you, Lord DeKieran. Angelica has spoken of you. Thank you for your work on Vxloncia."

Goddess bless Magellan. He was so damnably smooth. He stood unruffled, as bare as the Great Mother made him, and shook Ramsey's hand. Tris watched Ramsey's irritation morph into amusement and then heat with appreciation as Ram stood eye-to-eye with his delicious lover. He could hardly blame the man when his gaze slipped a little south. The view was exceptional.

Ram nodded at Mage and turned to him. "Accompany me."

With a muttered, "Give me a minute," to Mage and Angelica, he followed Ram out of the bedroom.

Ram stopped a short distance from the open door and crossed his arms. "I can't fault your taste. How long has this been going on?"

"Not long."

Ramsey's eyebrow lifted and his gaze intensified. "Don't let it interfere with her safety."

"Of course. I haven't told her about the 'meks,' but I will. I'd planned a discussion with both Angelica and Mage over a *late* breakfast."

Ram snorted at his emphasis. "Magellan DeLan. Wasn't he the young foster your mother took in?"

"Yes."

A tiny smile played at the edges of Ramsey's mouth and the man's posture relaxed. "He was a pretty boy. He makes an even more attractive man." Abruptly, DeKieran was all business again. "I want Dr. Giverny confined to quarters until we can acquire more intel on the mekanikos. From what Tok said last night, until we have a base location for them in Arkodaenia, it will be almost impossible to anticipate their movements. We can track them. They give off a unique electronic signal, but without an origination point…" The man shrugged.

"Yeah, in a city this size, we'd have to get very, very lucky to detect them."

Ramsey considered Tristan and amusement flickered in his steel gray eyes. "I doubt remaining sequestered with Giverny and DeLan will be hard duty."

He idly scratched the diagonal welt on his chest. "Not a hardship, no."

"Quite a tempting pair. If you still practice the art, Giverny and DeLan would make stunning subjects for *téad de ghrásta*."

"I do, though I'm not the *artista maestro* with the ropes you are."

A crooked smile twisted DeKieran's mouth. "If you wish to further your skills, I'm available." With those intriguing words, the man turned and strode toward the door to Tristan's apartment. "Tell Angelica about relocating. I'll let you know when she can resume her work schedule."

The door closed on Ramsey's back before he could prod his sluggish brain to formulate a reply. Swaying slightly where he stood, he blinked several times and scrubbed a hand over his face. "Computer, security protocol Omega Three."

"Acknowledged, Creator DeHelios. Security protocol Omega Three in effect. All ingress and egress locked. All perimeter motion alarms activated. Window opacity 100%."

Bemused by the possibilities inherent in Ramsey's offer, Tris padded back into the bedroom, the floor cool on the soles of his bare feet. Mage sat against the headboard, his legs outstretched, head back, eyes closed, a pillow and Angelica's head in his lap. His elegant hands rhythmically stroked her hair. Angelica's face wore an expression of innocent bliss.

The upwelling desire to stand between the pair and anything or anyone that could harm them rocked him with its intensity and sheer novelty. *You've got it bad for those two, you dumb fuck. When was the last time you cared like this about anyone?* The answer came easily. Never. The voice of his brother echoed in his mind. *Can you keep Dr. Giverny safe in Arkodaenia? Are your skills up to the task?* Unease nibbled at his thoughts but he shut it out. Nothing would happen to her or Magellan. He wouldn't allow anyone to take them from him. *Not ever.*

Fatigue slammed him and eradicated those uncomfortable thoughts and unprecedented feelings. By the Goddess, all three of them could use more sleep. He shoved his pants off his hips and stepped out of them. Crawling onto the bed, he scooped up Angelica and lay on his back, draping her boneless curves over his chest.

She wrapped her arm around him and snuggled close with a murmured plea of, "Sleep."

Mage slipped down and Tris felt the descent of bedding as Mage covered them. It was the last Tris knew for hours.

CHAPTER FOURTEEN

A ngelica studied Tristan and Mage. *They both look the better for some sleep. I certainly am.* The two hunks of mouthwatering virility sat across from her at the dining table in Tristan's apartment and shared a late afternoon meal of breakfast foods. Both men had slipped into loose knit pants but nothing else. The expanse of corded muscle on display would distract an ascetic at the temple of Von. She wasn't an ascetic. She hugged her short fluffy robe around her and tried to slip some of the material between her bare thighs and the smooth surface of the chair. Angelica forced her concentration back to Tristan's clipped words.

"...so, until we identify the number and location of the mekanikos, you will remain in the safety of the med center compound. You will then relocate to Nyth Uchel until we can eliminate this new threat."

The words staggered around her brain like a megaton Cephalian who'd overdosed on fermented mela fruit. Combine this latest threat with the emotional turmoil of yesterday's events, and her normal mental acuity stuttered. She groped for comprehension.

As if he understood her befuddlement, Tristan's words slowed and softened. "Because of Verdantia's unique nature, the meks' ability to morph will be compromised outside of the immediate vicinity of Arkodaenia. If they decide to pursue you, you'll be safer if you leave the city. Tok feels strongly that you should leave, and we're acceding to his greater knowledge. Unfortunately, the same electromagnetic forces that neutralize the meks will also affect your technological devices. If removed from Arkodaenia, your sophisticated medical equipment becomes so much carbonite and electron conduit."

In the pause, she felt Tristan's eyes examine her as she dipped her knife into the soft butyrum, reached for a toasted piece of panis, and with precision worthy of an accomplished cerebral surgeon, spread a fine layer from edge to edge. She delicately balanced the panis on her plate.

Magellan put his hand on hers as she reached for another slice. "Are you really going to eat all that?"

Startled, Angelica looked at her plate where a stack of a dozen slices of crusty panis adorned with butyrum leaned precariously. "Oh!" She placed her knife with exaggerated care beside her plate and folded her hands in her lap. Her eyes sought Mage and Tristan. She cleared her throat. With a shaky laugh, she pushed the plate toward the center of the table. "Ah, toasted panis, anyone?"

"Angel." Mage slipped from his chair and knelt by her, taking her hands in his, his beautiful face inches from her own. "No effort will be spared to keep you safe, you must know this."

She nodded.

"If you will feel more comfortable, I will ask Lord DeKieran to accompany you and introduce you, though Tristan feels his brother and Adonia will welcome you with open arms," said Mage.

"Is that what you think I should do... leave?"

"I want you safe. You will be safe in Nyth Uchel."

"What do you think?" Her gaze caught Tristan and lingered. "I don't want to go. I feel safe here, with you. Can you protect me if I stay?"

Tristan shoved away from the table, stood, and began to pace.

"I can pro— You don't—" He stopped, his back to her. With a negative jerk of his head, he clenched his fists and his posture sagged. "I want you to leave."

Why? Pain cleared her mental fog. *Leave for my safety? Or to clear your path to Mage? No… that's unfair of me.* Until she knew how Tris felt about her, about them, she was wrong to assign an ulterior motive to his words. Even so, an ache lingered. Head bowed, she dropped her gaze to her lap where Mage still captured her hands. She lifted a delicate shoulder and strove to keep the hurt from her voice. "Both of you want me gone, so I will leave. I don't want to bring danger to either of you."

Accompanied by a growl, Tris fisted a handful of her hair and jerked her head back. His lips smashed hers in a brutal kiss that robbed her of air and logical thought. For an endless moment, all she could do was surrender, swept up in the violence of the act. He broke off abruptly.

"I don't give a whore's fart about the danger to me, and I'd have to be dead before I'd let anything happen to you or Mage, but I'd be a fool to disregard the significant threat of this new development." His stare bored into her. "Are we clear?"

She sucked air in needy gasps, her bruised lips throbbed and the back of her head stung painfully from where he still gripped her hair—insignificant details. *He cares.* She made no attempt to subdue her brilliant smile. "Yes."

His gaze raked her face and his manner softened. "Good." He released her hair, cupped the back of her head in his hand and feathered a kiss across her lips as gentle and careful as the preceding had been vicious. He straightened and exchanged a heated glance with Mage. Mage released her hands and slipped back into his chair while Tris continued. "No final decision is required until we locate the meks and can track them. Activity by any of us outside these apartments will draw attention. I can't risk that until we know how many and where they are."

"I'm at a delicate point in the treatment of one of my patients. I'd like to stay in Arkodaenia and complete her stage three protocol before leaving for... what was the name of the city?"

Tristan leaned a hip on the table. "Nyth Uchel. It's a magickal place. It's my home and Verdantia's former capital. My brother's an arrogant prick, but you'll enjoy his wife, Adonia. She's all that is gracious and gentle—until someone threatens Hel."

"She's the medical practitioner you spoke of? The one with the magick wand?"

"Yes." His serious expression lightened. "Can you ride a horse?"

Startled, she rocked back to look up at him. "As in an *equus ferus caballus*? A domesticated four-legged equine mammal?"

He nodded.

Mage chuckled. "Don't sound so horrified. It's our mode of transport outside of Arkodaenia. We can arrange for a horse-drawn vehicle and driver, but riding would give you more freedom."

She winced. "That vehicle and driver will be necessary. The closest I've been to a living horse is watching them race on a sports-vid."

"How long will you need for the stage three protocol?" Tristan asked.

"A day or two? It depends on how the patient responds to her final cerebral-remapping. The emotional and behavioral therapy can continue without me, but I prefer to do the first psyche evaluation after remapping."

Tristan's gaze narrowed and sharpened. "Explain the cerebral-remapping. I've observed what you do, but why is it necessary?"

She welcomed his curiosity. Never far from her side, he'd watched her as she performed her job, and this was not the first indication of his interest. She'd interacted with him enough to know Tristan had a fine, disciplined mind. Why did he hide behind a womanizing, spit-in-the-eye-of-the-devil persona? She would ask him, but not today. She drew in a deep breath and blew it out.

"The medical technicians on Vxloncia mind-raped these women to create unnatural subservience by implanting a cache of behavioral script in their cerebral cortex. I locate the cache, remove it or map around it, and restore the woman's innate personality. Once done, we run a psyche profile and begin behavior remodeling and emotional therapy." She shrugged. "That's a simplified explanation of a complex process that involves interweaving physical and psychological recovery. I'm good at this. My team and I have high success rates with this protocol. It's why I'm here. My absence will interrupt my patients' progress. I understand the requirement to protect me, but I don't like that it affects my patients' welfare."

"Yes, we know, Angel," said Mage.

Tristan and Mage wore dual expressions of respect. She dropped her head to cover her pleased smile. She felt more than saw Tristan's long look of consideration.

"How much of your submission is due to the obscenities inflicted upon you on Vxloncia?"

She straightened in her chair and, chin up, held his gaze. "I'll give you the same answer I gave Captain DeLan. None. I'm satisfied my responses are mine and mine alone... Sir." She shivered in delicious apprehension at the wicked gleam that appeared in his eyes.

"Back to my bedroom, both of you. The meks aren't due for another day or so. We can sit here and go crazy waiting or spend the intervening time more profitably."

As they both rose from the table, Tristan reached for Mage's arm and held him back. He murmured something inaudible in Magellan's ear, though she caught the name of Ramsey DeKieran.

Mage straightened as if surprised, paused and then nodded. "All right."

More shivers spiked throughout her at the expressions on their faces as each shot her a thoughtful glance. What sort of bed play did Tristan plan? What had Mage agreed to? Her nipples hardened. Gooseflesh erupted on her arms. She all but scampered to Tristan's big bed, worry about her patients and the meks displaced with shivery anticipation.

Mage watched Angelica flit into the bedroom while Tristan contacted Ramsey. *Well this is an unexpected turn. I wonder how she'll feel about DeKieran's presence.* He snorted to himself. *I wonder how I'll feel.* By the seven hells, it didn't really matter. Whatever Tristan desired was fine with him. If Tris wanted to use them as subjects for instruction in *téad de ghrásta*, he had no objection.

He trusted DeKieran to remain professional. The man would enjoy his role as tutor. He hadn't missed the appreciation in Ramsey's eyes, but he knew from Angelica's recount of DeKieran's care for her on Vxloncia, the man was nothing if not disciplined and wholly loyal to his feisty "vixen." *I wonder if his wife will join him. So many beautiful bodies… I won't know where to look.*

While Mage wouldn't describe himself as submissive, he suspected that anything Tris chose to do with him—or to him— would provoke his overactive libido, particularly if it involved the oh-so-delectable Angelica. Yes, erotic bondage would provide a compelling distraction from the meks. He chuckled to himself and sauntered after Angelica.

CHAPTER FIFTEEN

M age eyed Tris as he prowled into the bedroom scant moments later. "That didn't take long."

Tris grunted. "No. It didn't. He accepted and will be here shortly. Did you tell her?"

He shook his head. "This is your board game. I'm just one of the pieces."

"Tell me what? What game?" Angelica asked.

"DeKieran offered to expand my skills in *téad de ghrásta* using you and Magellan as subjects. I accepted." Tris leveled a steady gaze on Angelica. "Objections?"

"I don't know what *téad de ghrásta* is."

"The term means 'grace of the rope.' It is the ancient art of bondage used to confine without injury in an elegant, artistic fashion. Ramsey DeKieran is an *artista maestro*. I have been presented with a rare opportunity to learn from a master of this art. So I ask again. If you have objections, voice them. Remember, I allow no abuse of what is mine. That includes psychological as well as physical."

Her gaze found Mage and asked a question. He shrugged. "I have no problem with it. You might find it arouses you. You enjoy bondage."

She studied her feet for several moments before looking up at Tristan. "You are simply going to tie us up with fancy knots?"

"That's one way of putting it, yes."

"Is sex involved?"

"Afterward, definitely."

"With Dominus DeKieran?"

"Absolutely not. I share you with no one but Magellan."

"Ah." She looked down and nodded.

A frown skittered across Tristan's face. "Disappointed?"

When she raised her head, her eyes gleamed with soft emotion, and her gaze caressed Mage and Tristan. "Not even a little."

Tris grunted in satisfaction. "Mage, strip."

He pointed to a space in the middle of the room and dropped a pillow from the bed onto the floor. "Angelica, here. Get comfortable. You'll be there a while." She began to shrug out of her robe as she crossed to him, and he eyed her, a thoughtful expression on his face. "Leave your robe on."

"Are you allowing her clothing because you are protecting what is 'yours' from another's eyes or to spare her embarrassment?"

Tris shrugged. "Both." He grinned. "I confess, mostly the first."

From the softening of her features and her murmur of thanks, she appreciated his efforts. To Mage, it was another indication Tristan cared more for the doctor than he would admit.

Tris pointed to a space several feet from Angelica. "Mage, stand here. Spread your legs shoulder width. Let your arms hang naturally. For this first lesson, you will be my model."

<hr/>

DeKieran did bring his wife. An odalisque of stunning sexuality had replaced the businesslike captain of the Blue Daggers. Instead of her black synth-skin, white aqua-tex clung as if painted on and covered her from chin to ankle. A waist-length ponytail anchored high on her head swept her lustrous red hair back from her face. Interrupting the expanse of virginal white, a massive, beaten gold collar clasped her neck—an emphatic and costly proclamation about her relationship with her husband.

Lord Ramsey had covered Steffania head-to-toe, but the overall effect was anything but modest. Such a visual tease of the carnal senses would arouse any male with an ounce of testosterone. He had never lacked that particular hormone, and while he fully acknowledged her desirability, the Blue Dagger could never quench his thirst. He required Angelica or Tristan—preferably both—to satisfy his desires.

Opening a large black satchel, Ramsey removed multiple lengths of flat, black ribbon and aimed an amiable expression at Angelica and Magellan. Mage considered his smile less than reassuring. He couldn't speak for Angelica.

"I think for your purposes, Tristan, this ribbon will work as well as rope." Ram's gaze steadied on Mage for a moment. "And it is kinder to intimate skin." His gaze returned to Tris. "Steffania will act as my model. You said you will start with Captain DeLan."

As another subject of the demonstration, it seemed natural to seek eye contact with Steffania. He couldn't readily identify the mix of emotions that swirled through his brain—curiosity, arousal, vulnerability, anticipation. They all fed into an unsettling mix.

Palpable arousal shone from Steffania's eyes as Ramsey demonstrated the arrangement of intricate rope diamonds beginning at each of her ankles and climbing to the tops of her thighs. Her formidable husband kidnapped her attention from almost the beginning. The atmosphere in the room grew charged with their erotic interplay. Only Ram's occasional observation or quiet, "No, watch... like this. Run this band underneath, ensure that it's flat, and then bring the tail over, thus," hinted that the man's attention wavered from the stunning redhead he adorned in patterns of black on white.

Lances of sensation burst through Mage's groin. With unsettling speed, his cock stiffened as Tris caressed his abdomen and placed lingering kisses along the fine line of hair bisecting his torso while Tris mirrored Ramsey's work. The steady seduction of the wide ribbon weaving up his splayed legs provided an unexpected source of arousal, and his cock responded as much to that titillation as to Tristan's appreciative touches and kisses. Each wrap was a loving stroke to his psyche. *Tristan, finally.* The combination mesmerized him and stole all his senses until he was aware of little else but the prince.

From the reverence in Tristan's intent concentration and the ever-growing bulge in his black trousers, he knew Tris was as lost in him as he was in Tristan. Another ribbon turn and Tris finally relaxed his hands against his work and checked on his state. Tristan's eyes met his, and a final understanding crossed between them. Tris might as well have bound Mage's heart in addition to his calves and thighs, for with each twist of the ribbon, Tristan had wordlessly declared, *I must have you*, and he had silently answered, *Take me. I'm yours.*

Ramsey interrupted their silent exchange. "Now we get to the variations possible with the different sexes." He grazed his wife's lips with a smile and a kiss. "Hold your position, Vixen." He turned to Tristan. "You can leave his cock unbound, appropriate if you wish him free to have sex." Mage caught Ramsey's eye and immediately mistrusted the devilry lurking within his gaze. "Or, my preference, bind him in such a fashion as to immobilize him and then tease him with impossibilities."

He opened his mouth to voice his wishes, but Tristan grabbed the back of his head and kissed him into silence. When Tris pulled back, he murmured against his lips, "Game pieces have no say.

They move as the master wills it."

"I'm in for a long afternoon, aren't I?" His unruly cock twitched at the provocative images that marched through his brain. He repressed a groan at Tristan's throaty laugh.

"There's always your safe word, princess." Tristan released his head and Mage closed his eyes on a long exhale. "Clasp your hands behind your head, and don't move until I tell you to."

With Ramsey directing, Tris wrapped a piece of narrower, softer cord around the base of his cock, pushing his balls higher, away from the base of his shaft.

Fingers linked, his hands at the nape of his neck, Mage resisted the temptation to drop his head and watch his handsome lover. The appreciation and arousal on the face of Ramsey's redheaded wife was torture enough. Her eyes meandered from his face to his groin and lingered on his erection. When her golden eyes returned to his, the tip of her pink tongue dampened her lower lip. She threw a ravenous glance at her husband and shivered.

"Good," Ram said. "Now, run your cord here and here."

The stretched skin of his scrotum thinned further when Tris made several figure-eight loops around the base of his cock and between his balls. Tris gently teased each vulnerable testicle with feather-light caresses and gooseflesh erupted on his legs. In an involuntary motion, he pushed his hips forward, silently beseeching attention to his rampant erection.

Tris stepped into his body and nuzzled his neck. "I get off on every snug of cord or ribbon drawn tight against your cut body. Muscle definition like yours requires dedicated effort. All that time alone in space. Were you working off sexual frustration, Captain?"

"Something like that."

"Mmm. I should keep you needy. I love the result."

"Don't get any bright ideas, Tris."

Sin saturated Tristan's low chuckle.

Every hair on Mage's body responded.

Ramsey's voice interrupted their murmured intimacies. "Now, crisscross up the length of his cock, snug it to his abdomen and then tie off the cord in a *dijamant* knot at the small of his back."

He fought not to grab Tristan's hands as the man laced his painfully hard erection in black, each turn of the ribbon binding his engorged flesh until it seemed his heart pulsed within his erection rather than his chest. The soft cord measured every centimeter of his shaft as if a ruler. He felt as long as his forearm and as hard as the carbonite hull of his ship. Tris finished with a loop under the flare of his cock head, and then ran the lengths of cord behind his back. With a firm tug, Tris secured the ends.

Mage flinched at the bite. Erotic heat swept through him, aggravated by the black cord that wrapped his shaft from base to tip, enforcing its upright rigidity. He swore softly. "Fuck. How am I supposed to think of anything other than my dick?"

Ramsey chuckled. "You're not. It makes the carnal tease more gratifying."

"For me... or you and Tristan?"

"You know the answer, Captain—for all of us." Ramsey's gaze tangled with Steffania's. "Submission and dominance should tantalize both. Who's to say which party benefits most?" His eyebrow rose at the enigmatic smile and rosy blush that swept his wife's face.

With a smile lurking at the corners of his mouth and humor lacing his voice, Ramsey murmured another order. "Captain, spread your fingers and cross your hands over your chest at the wrists. Feel free to think about your dick. Tris, I'm going to demonstrate the *ragnatela*, or 'cobweb'. You will appreciate the intricacies of the design. It is useful if you wish to immobilize only the hands and fingers. I particularly like the *ragnatela* for prolonged tease and denial as it doesn't compromise circulation.

Your subject can be bound for days at your mercy, yet still retain almost all their mobility. It's quite diabolical."

At Steffania's soft intake of breath, Ramsey stepped back to his wife. Their gazes locked. "At least you've always said so."

"Yes," she whispered.

Ram trailed a slow finger up Steffania's side, detouring to tease her erect nipple, and caressed her cheek. He gave an infinitesimal growl and murmured something unintelligible, but from the smoldering exchange of glances, the gentle undulations of her hips, and her whispered, "Oh, please, Dominus," Steffania understood him quite well. Wrenching his gaze from his lovely model, Ram selected a length of ribbon. He nodded at Tris. "It begins like this."

Mage mentally substituted Angelica for Steffania and Tristan for Ramsey. What would their lovely Angel look like at the end of, say… three days of erotic teasing? He wanted to find out. Pain from his laced balls streaked through his groin when his bound cock attempted to pulse at the provocative consideration. With an inner wince, he erected detour signs across that trail of thought. Right now, he didn't need *that* image strolling through his brain. Mage steeled himself for more of Tristan's sensual torture and tried to block out his cock's screams of frustration.

The carnal electricity generated by the two pairs mere feet from her overwhelmed Angelica. The powerful dynamic between Lord Ramsey and Steffania and the equally compelling interaction and blatant arousal of Tristan and Magellan ensnared her. She yearned to take Mage's place as the recipient of Tristan's lingering caresses, inflammatory whispers and provocative nips and kisses. Her heart pounded. Her limbs felt weak. The flesh between her legs had long ago grown slick and swollen. Between the folds of her robe, she cupped her breast and circled her thumb over the hard bud of her nipple. Her head fell back and her eyes slid closed at the pleasure. Spreading her thighs further, she slipped a hand between her legs to finger her clit. She whimpered at the gratification.

Tristan's rich chuckle drowned out her heavy pants. They sounded loud in the suddenly quiet room. "Mage, you are not the only one aroused by watching."

She opened her eyes and stilled her hands at Tristan's voice.

"Continue. Stop just before you come. Count aloud to thirty. Then resume." Wicked mischief lurked in his gaze. "Repeat those steps until I tell you to stop."

His gaze devoured her as did Ramsey's and Steffania's and Magellan's.

"Yes, Sir."

She thrilled at being Mage and Tristan's sole focus. If Tris wanted a show, she'd give him one. She'd make herself irresistible. Sitting with thighs splayed wide, she undid the belt of her robe and allowed it to slide from her shoulders to puddle on her feet and then resumed her erotic play. One hand teased, tugged and rolled her nipple while the other slid into her wet heat, spreading her swollen flesh, tickling the entrance to her body and spreading her moisture up to circle her clit. A moan slipped from her lips as she held Tristan's gaze. "I want to give this to you, Sir. I want you and Magellan here." She slowly inserted her two middle fingers into the heat of her sheath and shivered. "Your cocks would fill me so much better than my slender fingers. Let my body pleasure you."

Tris pressed against the length of Mage's back and rested a chin on the man's shoulder. One arm circled his waist. One hand teased the head of Magellan's entrapped cock.

Mage's half-lidded eyes settled on her before sliding closed. He groaned. "Fuck. I can't watch. It's too much."

Ramsey snorted, his eyes sweeping first Magellan and Tris

and then her. "Yes. It is." He gathered his immobilized wife into his arms and strode toward the door. "I'll be back for my bag. Tomorrow."

Steffania's soft laughter trailed them as he exited Tristan's apartment and kicked the door closed.

At the heavy slam, a thrill of triumph coursed through Angelica. She'd snared all the room's occupants in the net she'd cast with her provocative display, though she'd not directed her seduction at Lord Ramsey—and the significance of that wasn't lost on her. Now to land those she'd meant to catch.

Tristan feathered the pads of his fingers over the balls and cock of a shuddering Magellan, all the while devouring the sight of her working herself. "Watch her, Captain. She is worth your attention. She deserves your regard."

Mage's shaggy black head rose and his green gaze leveled on her. The heat and avarice in both their eyes spiked her arousal as if a second and third pair of hands stroked her breasts and pussy, the inside of her thighs. Orgasm loomed. She stopped. A whimper of protest escaped. Her eyes rose to Tristan's and begged.

His mouth framed one word, "Count."

Panting, she forced the numbers from her mouth. She ached to touch herself. The chest of each man rose and fell visibly. At thirty, she resumed her play—only to stop in moments. Her hands hovered over flesh that begged touch. She counted again. When she resumed, she could endure only four light strokes before climax threatened. She didn't care how frantic she sounded. "Please, Sir, let me serve you. Take me."

"Count."

She closed her eyes with a shudder and stumbled to thirty. Her fingers trembled as she played gossamer touches over her nipples and clit. She bit her lower lip painfully. The distraction was pointless. She remained balanced on a tripwire. Any small move would ensnare her in climax.

"Your eyes on me. I want to see your desperation. I want Mage to see your arousal. Show us, Angel."

At Tristan's growled demand, she opened her eyes. She filled them with the want that tortured her. She lost count of the number of times Tristan demanded she stop and start. She'd never loathed a sound as much as she did the word "count." The need for completion shattered her. She spent more time counting than stroking her needy flesh; then thirty counts was no longer enough for her arousal to subside.

"One, two, three…" Her tongue lagged and her voice faltered. Somewhere in the teens, she lost track and stumbled to a halt. "Please, no more. I can't… no more." She shook her head, begging.

"Kneel on the bed. Face the headboard. Hands behind you. Legs widespread."

She leaped to obey Tristan's clipped command as Tristan grabbed a razor knife from a bedside table and sliced the cobweb of black ribbon binding Mage. Her body ached and trembled as she knelt in obedience, facing the headboard, clasping and unclasping her forearms behind her.

"How did I get so fucking lucky?" Tristan's low growl filled the small bedroom.

"Tristan…"

Tris swore. The sounds of a violent kiss interrupted Magellan's murmur and when she turned her head enough to catch them in her peripheral vision, Mage had melted into Tristan's embrace. Tristan kissed him as if he were starved for air and Mage was oxygen. When they pulled apart, Mage lifted a hand and cupped Tristan's face. Warmth from more than simple lust gleamed from Magellan's eyes.

Tristan's gaze found her. He shook his head as if unable to

comprehend she was real. "So fucking lucky."

The need shaking her body increased at the emotion held in his gray eyes. She and Mage were more than sexual conquests to Tristan, more than a means to an end. The knowledge settled into her with conviction. At this moment, Angelica's most earnest desire was to please them. She'd endure the torment of denial if it was their wish. It would be enough to make Sir happy, to make Mage happy. *But you know neither one will leave you wanting.* Laughter welled up inside her. *They make it so easy to put them first.*

"Lower your chest to the bed."

"Yes, Sir." She turned her face to the side and sank her shoulders to the bed. With her hips in the air and her thighs spread wide, her intimate flesh opened in incendiary display. The air felt cool on her inner folds. Bared, exposed, vulnerable… all those words described her feelings, as well as eager, greedy and aching.

The bed dipped behind her. A finger slipped between her legs and dallied in her slickness. "You're soaking, Angel," Mage said.

"Mmmhmm. Your fault," she murmured.

Mage played the broad head of his cock in her warmth before nudging into her pussy. He paused for eternal seconds of tease. With a low grunt, he gripped her hips and drove home. Her muscles gripped him like a tight fist despite her arousal. Discomfort twinged through her and increased when he hit her end. Her breath hitched. He noticed.

His thumbs and fingers massaged soothing circles in the cheeks of her butt. "Easy, sweetheart. I'll be still."

"No, please." She choked on the words. "Anything but that. You don't know what watching you and Tristan did to me. I'll loosen in a moment."

Mage and Tristan chuckled. She almost moaned at the vibration from the engorged piece of flesh that split her in two. She did moan when Mage surged violently forward, overfilling her.

"Damnation, Tris! Give me some warning before sticking your fingers up there."

"Now where's the fun in that, princess?"

Mage's hands dug into her flesh and he steadied himself on her hips. She could only imagine where Tristan's fingers were going, but when Mage bent over her back and dropped an arm beside her head with a muttered obscenity, she suspected more than Tristan's fingers were involved. Magellan abandoned her hips entirely, and with a low groan, braced himself on both arms. She arched her back to give him room to remain fully embedded and a new sort of torture began.

"I'm driving the fucking, dear ones," Tris said. "I will set the pace. I want this to last for a while. Ah, yes, knew I'd forgotten something. You require my permission to come."

"Sadistic asshole," Mage muttered.

"Yes," Tris affirmed. "Don't forget it."

Pressed forward, she was sure by Tristan's hips, Mage groaned and rocked into her in a gentle cadence. She shuddered and echoed his sound as his fat cock teased her inner flesh and his balls pressed a massage of soft flesh against her clit. Climax padded forward on steady feet, stalking her. She was easy prey. This wasn't going to take long, regardless of what Tristan commanded, and she was helpless to prevent it.

⊗⊕⊗⊕⊗⊕⊗⊕⊗⊕⊗⊕⊗

From the sounds coming from our Angel's mouth, she's not going to last. Tristan hoped he could hold himself together when she came. "Don't you dare go over, Captain. Even if she does, don't you dare."

"Fuck. You don't want much, do you?"

"You have no idea how much I want. None whatsoever." His

captain shuddered underneath him and the muscles of Mage's hot interior clenched around his savagely provoked cock. Tris had been hard for hours. Each wrap of black ribbon on his captain's cut body, each inflammatory challenge from those green eyes, stroked his engorged shaft. And Angelica... by the Consort's balls... Angelica. What he desired from those two terrified him with its intensity. He wanted the whole thing. Children. Home. Family.

Everything.

For always.

Impossible.

Tris could feel the results of Angelica's climax as with wild gyrations as she slammed herself back onto Mage and screamed her deity's name into the mattress. Mage went rigid. Every muscle in his forearms, biceps and deltoids strained. His buttocks clenched into a solid mass. His chest heaved and a fountain of curses spewed from his mouth. Tristan froze until Mage relaxed and panted less colorful words.

Tris meandered a caress down Magellan's spine. "You okay?"

"Define okay."

Tristan chuckled. "I'm going to move."

"If you must."

"Oh, yes, my beautiful man... I must." He pulled his hips back in a long glide accompanied by Magellan's low hiss. He plunged back into Mage's hot body, held for a count and then slowly withdrew again. His eyes crossed. He thought of rotting carcasses, steaming piles of offal—anything but the wild pleasure taunting his body with imminent orgasm.

"Ah, fuck, Tris. That's... ah... fuck." Magellan threw his head back and straightened from the waist. His hands gripped Angelica's hips and clamped her languid body to him with a groan. "Please, finish it. I've been on the edge for hours. My balls are rocks. I'm asking, Tris."

Tris closed his eyes and granted Magellan's request. It took embarrassingly little thought.

SIXTEEN

Y ou came without permission. Quite loudly, I might add. Your gyrations made obedience more difficult than necessary for our sweet captain."

Tristan's gravel vibrated in her ear and destroyed the sublime daze in which she floated. Angelica stiffened as much as the weight of two large males collapsed across her would allow.

"It's hard to breathe."

Tristan chuckled and rolled off Mage to lie beside her.

Mage groaned. "For the first time in hours my cock's not complaining. I'm not moving."

Angelica wiggled to rearrange herself so breathing came easier.

"I think some sort of punishment is in order for your disobedience and for testing our captain so severely. Mage, you suffered most from her lack of control. Why don't you decide what form it will take?"

Mage snugged his groin more firmly into the contours of her buttocks and hummed. He pushed off her abruptly and knelt facing Tris. "Yes."

He rolled to his side and left the bed. When he returned, several strands of black ribbon dangled from his hand.

Angelica rolled to her back and pressed up on her elbows. "What?" Her gaze bounced from Magellan's straight face to

Tristan's growing smile of comprehension. "What?" The men ignored her.

"I'm not the experienced practitioner that you are, but if you will oversee, I'm going to duplicate the *ragnatela* binding on our uninhibited angel. I think Lord DeKieran's suggested use for it will be an entertaining way to pass some time," said Mage.

Tristan chuckled and nodded. "We could be here for hours—or days." Tristan shrugged with a slight smile. "For your sake, Angel, let's hope it's hours. Might as well spend our time productively."

Magellan nodded gravely. "My thoughts entirely. Oh, and Tris, would you mind getting the husband's kit? I believe it's still upstairs."

Her eyes widened as the meaning of their abbreviated conversation sank in. All stupor left her. She swathed herself in the bed linens and scrambled back against the headboard. *I wish this was body armor.* "I don't think that's…"

Mage cut her off with a penetrating stare. "Don't talk. Cross your hands at the wrists. Splay your fingers."

Tristan trotted back into the room and tossed the small box, whose torturous contents were all too fresh in her memory, onto the bed. "Here you go. What else do you need?"

Mage captured her in a calculating gaze. "A little correction if I go wrong, and later, your full participation, but for the moment, just watch." He paused and tapped her nose. "Remember—'victor.' If our play gets too much, use it."

This is play? Tell that to my racing heart and dry mouth. Held mesmerized, she nodded.

Mage grinned like a megaton shark. "Computer, create a visual and audible calibration of Angelica Giverny's real-time sexual arousal. Baseline normal through orgasm. Alarm at 95% and 99%."

A mask blinded her. The musky smell of sex filled her nose. Soft curls of pubic hair tickled her nostrils. As rapidly as saliva drooled from the corners of her mouth, lubrication escaped her pussy and trickled down her inner thighs. Her captain had ordered her to kneel between his legs and hold his semi-aroused cock in her mouth. He forbade her to stimulate him in any way. She was merely to hold as much of him in her mouth as she could until he permitted her to release him.

Her bound fingers twitched restlessly. Her nipples pulsed in their fibrous wraps. Each throb streaked provocative pain straight to her bound clit. Her captain had not been content with immobilizing her hands and binding her nipples. A slender, ribbed, vibrating wand penetrated her anus. Tristan held the remote to it and to a vibrating egg inserted deep in her pussy. At random moments, one toy or the other, sometimes both, hummed for irregular periods of time and intensity. *Like now!* She whimpered and writhed between Magellan's knees. The combined stimulation of egg and wand on high vibration created a crisis of sensation.

Meanwhile, above her head, Mage and Tristan discussed a three dimensional mockup of Arkodaenia's city center that they'd pulled up before they'd blindfolded her. Only the slight tightness in his deep voice indicated Mage was aware of her.

"It is possible that the meks could be hiding in this warehouse district."

"That would make finding them easier. The buildings and people aren't as densely concentrated there as in other parts of the city," said Tristan.

Soft grunts of wordless distress accompanied the involuntary undulation of her hips. The soft shape of Mage's cock began to harden and fill her mouth. The gentle, repetitive chime of the alarm sounded.

"Tris, back off on the vibes. Her arousal's shot to 95%. She can't remain still and I'm getting hard."

"She looks so lovely; her mouth stretched around your cock, her wet pussy wagging in needy desperation. How can you ask me to stop?"

"Yeah… it's quite a sight. I want her to cool off, though. You've kept her pretty worked up and it's been awhile since we ate. I think we should feed our sweet angel before we go another round." The chimes increased in tempo. "Tris…99%. Are you going to let her…?"

"No."

The vibrations stopped. The engorged flesh between her legs twitched in reflexive protest. Angelica shuddered as her imminent climax faded—again. Each time she'd thought, *he'll let me come. This time he won't stop.* Unfortunately, as her arousal escalated, so had her disappointment. The mask absorbed the tears that leaked from her eyes. She despised Tristan DeHelios.

Use your safe word. Oh, god… what they do to me. So good. So intense. No. Use the safe word. Do it. It's too good! I lose myself in sensation. They are mindful of every breath I take. Oh, Goddess, I love them. She worked to slow the frantic inhales she pulled through her nose.

"Food and drink sound good. I've gotten in some Vxloncian 'special ale'. Ramsey's Khlossian friend introduced me to it. You should try it. It will kick your ass," said Tris.

Mage grunted in interest. "Sign me on, and let's see what your replicator can do with a Klamanian burg."

Mage held her head steady. "Angel, release me."

She opened her mouth and his cock slid from between her swollen lips. Suddenly, she felt hollow, cast away from security. Empty air replaced the warmth of Mage's body.

"Good girl. Kneel up, my angel." His hands under her chin assisted her to a straightened posture. He held her shoulders in gentle hands and steadied her. "You can't reach a hot spot, so simply keep your legs widespread. Hmmm. Wider. No grinding on anything to soothe that undisciplined pussy." She heard the smile in his voice. He dried her cheeks and chin with a soft cloth and pressed a kiss on her mouth. His gentle finger smoothed salve on her chapped lips. "I'll bring you something to eat and drink. Do you need to use the bathroom?"

She shook her head, and then he was gone.

Tris rose from his seat and patted the top of her head. "Behave yourself. I'll be watching."

She drew breath and opened her mouth to beg him not to leave her there with the evidence of her need cooling on her thighs. His hand covered her lips.

"Were you going to say 'victor'? Because that's the only word I want to hear from your beautiful mouth."

Her shoulders slumped and she leaned against his leg.

"I thought as much. As I said, behave yourself."

Deprived of sight and freed from constant sexual distraction, her sense of smell and hearing sharpened. The savory flavors of dinner foods and the low current of conversation between the men as they ate occupied her attention.

"I need some of these food replicators for the *Revertar*'s mess hall. They are far superior to... umm-mmph!" Magellan's voice stopped.

From Mage's groan, Tristan had found a better use for his mouth and tongue than eating and speaking. A piece of silverware clattered to the floor, then another. Someone slid their chair back. Someone sighed. Muffled sounds of lovemaking from the kitchen continued until Angelica longed to tear off her mask. Had her hands been free she would have. The sight of her two beautiful men engrossed in each other would have been worth the certain punishment.

"I'll... never... get enough of you. You're... such a... gods-be-damned temptation." Tristan's words punched through heavy pants. "Such a responsive cock..."

"Goddess, Tris... yeah, like that... harder. Ah... fuck... stop, stop, stop." Magellan's staccato words accompanied a shaky laugh. "You're a little too good at that." His voice sounded strained. "Let's feed our Angel before we get too carried away. Yeah?"

Tristan's throaty chuckle raised the hair on her arms. "Yeah."

Two sets of footsteps approached and both men resumed their previous places. "Sit back on your heels, Angel." Magellan's voice came from immediately in front of her. "Open your mouth."

He placed a bite-sized piece of sautéed *krava* beast, dripping in spice sauce, in her mouth. She chewed, swallowed and opened her mouth for another bite. The mellow taste of mashed yellow gourd awash in butyrum followed. That was followed by the crunch of pungent, green water pods. The egg in her pussy began to hum. Mage tapped her lips. It turned out to be a straw and she greedily sucked down cold water. The low vibration of the anal probe joined the egg. And so it went. The two men took turns feeding her food and drink, teasing her nipples, caressing the insides of her thighs, under her breasts, along her collarbone— generally reducing her to a quivering mess.

"Are you ready for dessert?" Tris asked.

From the tone of his voice, Angelica hoped "dessert" was a euphemism for a different sort of treat. *An orgasm, please.* She nodded.

Tristan took Mage's place in front of her. The scrape of a chair leg signaled Tris had moved closer. His bare thighs bracketed her shoulders and offered support. His hand rested on the back of her head and guided her face toward his groin. "Open your mouth."

She moaned softly as his cock slid to the back of her throat. "Keep me hard."

Angelica's world shrank to the hollow-cheeked slide of her tongue up the underside of his shaft; his grunts of satisfaction as she suckled the head of his cock and probed the tip of her tongue into its slit as she savored the musky smell and taste of aroused male.

Always, in the background, the diabolical vibrators continued their teasing on-again, off-again pattern. She wondered if Mage held the controls now. From time to time the men paused in their conversation, and she hung suspended on Tristan's quiet command, "Stop, Angelica," only to resume again when his hands urged her forward. Time passed seamlessly, the building dilemma between her thighs and the protest of tired muscles her only method for assessing its passage.

The computer alarm began to chime steadily, assuring her two tormentors of the efficacy of their torture. Involuntary grunts of agitation now accompanied the uncontrollable undulation of her hips. Her nipples pulsed in their bindings. The rate of her building crisis multiplied. The musical sound of the alarm never slowed.

"Tone it down, Mage," murmured Tristan.

Mage responded with a humorous grunt. "The vibes are off. Have been for several minutes. End this, Tris. She's so gods-be-damned hot, and I'm dying to be in her."

Tristan's hands clasped her cheeks and pushed her away. "Straighten up. Be silent and still your body."

Shudders quaked through her as she attempted to obey him while someone wiped the drool from her chin. She thought it was Tris. The chair in front of her scraped back and he stood. The blindfold slipped off her eyes and she blinked in the soft light. Inches from her face, the sight of the sculptured muscles of his heavy thighs and erect cock taunted her. So close, yet so far from where she craved him. He must have seen her desperation.

"Soon, Angel. Soon. I'm going to untie you. You will stand, legs spread. Hands at your sides." He assisted her to her feet. As he freed her from the confinement of the black ribbons, he massaged her hands and forearms.

She moaned softly in appreciation. The change of position combined with the gentle caress of his hands sent her to heaven.

"You okay, sweetheart?" He tipped her face toward his and met her gaze in question.

"Yes, Sir." If one could be okay when tremors of agonized need wracked one's body in steady waves.

"Bend forward at the waist. Mage, remove the anal wand."

Tris steadied her as one of Mage's large hands cupped her buttock cheek and his thumb pressed against the side of her anus. His other hand captured the cord hanging between her legs and she felt pressure inside as he removed the toy. The slow slip of the ribbed vibrator past her sphincter muscles left her gasping for air while guttural animal sounds erupted from her throat. The alarm chimed briefly.

Tristan grasped her upper arms and helped her to straighten. "Spread wide. I'm going to remove the egg, and then I want you on my bed on hands and knees."

Mage watched Angelica wobble into the bedroom and disappear.

"Computer."

"Yes, Captain DeLan?"

"Discontinue visual and audible calculation on sexual arousal for Dr. Giverny."

"Acknowledged."

Mage eyed Tristan's nude body and erect cock and damned himself for being defenseless against the man. In all ways, Mage found him irresistible. As Tristan's hungry gaze raked him, Mage prowled forward and stopped a hand span away. Beginning at the notch in the man's collarbone, Mage's gaze followed as his forefinger feathered a caress down Tristan's upper torso and ended at the base of his shaft. The man's cock bobbed in response. Mage's heart thundered in his chest and his mouth went dry. Sheer emotion and driving desire overwhelmed him. "I love you, Tris. I always have."

Tristan's head jerked up and his eyes widened like a panicked *fricki*. Mage almost smiled. "You don't have to say it back. I, ah..." Mage cleared his throat. "...just wanted to put it out there."

Tristan's breathing deepened on a shallow groan. "Ah, fuck, Magellan," he whispered. A look of wonderment appeared on Tristan's face that stripped him of half his years. He gave an almost imperceptible shake of his head. "You and Angelica... I... I never..."

However Tris might have completed his thought, the words were lost when Tris yanked Mage into a tangle of arms and legs and lips and tongues that communicated Tristan's tempestuous emotions more than any spoken word. Mage responded with a physical outpouring of all the love he felt for the man. Abruptly, Tris pushed Mage away and stood, head hanging, arms outstretched, hands planted on Mage's shoulders, and sucked in air. He dropped his hands to his hips and cocked a gaze at Mage through the disordered locks of his hair. Humor sparkled in his eyes.

"We cannot neglect our sweet Angel," said Tris. "I'll flip you for position—heads or tails."

Had Mage set an alert for his own arousal it would have been deafening for the last few moments. As it was, he could hear little over the blood pounding in his ears. He pulled himself together and croaked, "Sure."

As they walked into the bedroom and over to the bedside

table, the sight of Angelica on hands and knees, her swollen pussy glistening like an invitation to eternal bliss, goaded his overwrought libido. Tris picked a *centavo* from a stack of coins and flipped it into the air, catching it and slapping it onto his wrist. He lifted his hand and grinned. "Tails. You get her sweet pussy."

CHAPTER SEVENTEEN

Careful not to disturb his worn-out lovers, Tristan threw a forearm over his eyes and took a deep breath—an attempt to steady his turbulent thoughts and emotions. Mage and Angelica lay in an exhausted tangle across him—Angelica tucked under his arm with her head on his shoulder and the rest of her sprawled across his front, Mage nested between his legs with a head on his thigh and an arm wrapped around the calf Angelica angled across Mage's chest. The last two days had been a marathon of carnal ecstasy the likes of which he'd never forget. If he died now, cause of death could legitimately be designated as sexual excess. He hoped he didn't die now. For the first time in his life, he had a reason to live—two, actually—two precious reasons to live.

As he'd surfaced from the last round of stunning pleasure, an unfamiliar feeling invaded his soul. Sifting through a lifetime of memories, Tristan tried to label it or identify another time in his life when he'd experienced the same emotion that captivated him now. Forced to concede he'd never felt like this, Tris analyzed the feeling. He reached an inescapable conclusion. *This is contentment—and I'm in love.*

Making love with Angelica and Magellan had disarranged the foundation of his world. At some point in the last forty-eight hours, he'd undergone a profound reorientation. He loved them—both of them—with a passion that annihilated any previous paradigm he'd used to define love. How could an emotion so profound, so *violent*, ambush him and bring him to his knees in surrender without him ever seeing it coming? He must tell them. *By the Consort's hairy balls... I'd rather face the gods-be-damned mekanikos barehanded.*

Acknowledging internally that he loved Magellan and Angelica was one thing—speaking the words to them was something entirely separate. *Mage is smoother with these kinds of things. Perhaps even more brave?* Wasn't *that* a lowering thought? Somehow, he'd have to dredge up the courage to tell Mage and Angelica—especially Angelica—of the seismic shift in his perspective. He knew Mage returned his feelings, but what about Angelica?

He dropped his arm to his side and peered down his chest at the woman who had captured his well-armored heart... to find her peering right back at him, her lips tilted in an affectionate smile. Tris snugged her closer with one arm and stared at the ceiling. "Why did you say yes?" he murmured.

Angelica nuzzled into his chest. "To what?" Her words came soft and hesitant.

"To this threesome."

Tris heard and felt her heavy sigh.

"May I ask you something first?"

"I suppose." Long seconds stretched while he waited for her question.

"Am I an interchangeable part? A replaceable piece when you or Mage get tired of me?"

If he'd possessed the energy to move, he would have sat straight up in disgruntled surprise. "By the seven hells! No!" Tris barked, then lowered his voice. "This trio would never work with another woman." He snorted. "I can't imagine ever tiring of you. Which brings me back to my original question, why did you say yes? I know you have feelings for Mage, but our captain will be gone for months at a time, leaving you at the mercy of a moody bastard."

Tris heard the smile in her voice. "You mean my bodyguard? *That* moody bastard? I think I've dealt quite well with him—so far."

"Umm. So… why?"

She murmured something into his chest.

"I didn't hear you."

Her ribs rose and fell in a heavy sigh and he felt her head lift off his chest to regard him. "For the oldest of reasons… I think I'm falling in love with you."

Joy lit him up like a fusion explosion. He closed his eyes and pulled her to him closely. *Now. Tell her now. Ah, shit… why is this so hard?*

When he didn't immediately respond, her head fell back to his chest and she traced her fingers over his abdomen. "So… why did *you* say yes?"

"I…" He cleared his throat and firmed his resolve. "I…"

The chime from Tristan's AI sounded. "Prince DeHelios, Lord DeKieran is calling. The call carries an 'urgent—priority one' flag. Should I put him on vid-screen?"

Relief left him lightheaded. *Fuck! I'm such a gods-be-damned coward.* Tris scrambled up in the bed and reached for a robe while he barked responses to his AI. His action sent Angelica sprawling. Mage sat up groggily. "Not yet. Give me thirty seconds, then put DeKieran on holo-vid."

"Acknowledged. Thirty seconds beginning now, Prince DeHelios."

Tris jammed his arms into his robe, wrapping the garment around him and cinching the belt tight as he walked toward the door to the living room. "Get up, Angelica. Get Mage up. You

heard what I told the AI. I'll give you two minutes to get decent...
then join me. This is the call we've been waiting for." Tris left the
bedroom and stood in front of the huge media/communications
center that took up two-thirds of the wall in his living area.

"Twenty-eight, twenty-nine, thirty... you are live, Prince
DeHelios."

"DeHelios here. What's the status, Ram?"

"The meks are here. We believe we've located two mek
entities in a warehouse in port sector five. I'll send the coordinates
to your AI. There may be a third, but we weren't able to get a clear
enough read on its electron signature to lock down a verifying
identity. In the interim, the signatures of the two known entities
have gone dark. They may have erected shielding to cloak their
presence and activity in the warehouse. Tok and Sweet are getting
'eyes on.' Until we can verify a known location and number,
keep Dr. Giverny close to home. She can go to the medcenter and
continue to see her patients, but that is as far as she goes, and I
want you on her like a second skin. Since you indicated she agreed
to leave Arkodaenia, when we have a fix and number on the meks,
I want her out of the city—as in *yesterday*."

"Understood."

The image of Ramsey disintegrated into bits of sparkling
green and the call ended. Tris turned to regard the closed face of
Mage and a stunned, wide-eyed Angelica. "You heard?"

She nodded and blew out a long breath. "So now it begins."

Tristan placed a gentle hand under her chin and raised her face
to his. "This threat will be dealt with. We will keep you safe."

Eva tried to find a comfortable position next to the hard body
of the Khlossian, gave it up as a lost cause, and readjusted her
precision optics. They lay prone on an elevated platform belonging

to an oversized crane. Inside a vast freight warehouse whose dark secrets seemed to stretch into infinity, the total blackness hid them as well as the crane's scaffolding. "I know the meks are here, but I'm getting nothing. Do you see anything?"

"Umm. Switch from infrared to ultraviolet on your goggles. Orient on the freight container marked 'Ultron Shipping'. Check the base."

"Shit. How could I have missed them? There seems to be a third. Where did it come from? Wait... they've disappeared. What the!" She felt the vibrations of what could only be silent laughter in the huge body next to her.

"Sweet Eva, switch your optic filter to x-ray and look again."

"The 'Eva' is first. The 'Sweet' is second. Eva Sweet," she muttered. She did as Tok had instructed and relocated the meks. "How did you know to do that? To switch the light splitters like that?"

"A lifetime of experience, Sweet Eva." Tok rolled to his back and sighed. "Were you with Ramsey's woman on Devon III?"

Her mouth formed the word, "Yes," but it was moments before she could utter it. Eva was proud her voice didn't shake. Her mind rebelled at the memory of bladder-loosening fear as invisible foes, impervious to pointblank lazer fire, sliced through the high-tech armor of her brothers-in-arms; she shuddered at the memory of her shock at men disemboweled beside her, screaming as they stepped on their own guts. *I'm not a coward, but how do you fight something you cannot see and cannot kill?* Her mind had never reconciled why *she* hadn't died that day. She'd expected to.

Eva could hear her own strident breathing as she struggled to shake off the horrific memories. "The members of our combat unit who survived did so because we ran like hell. Our inglorious retreat never sat well with the Captain. If these are like the meks we encountered on Devon III, the Verdantians have no defense against them. How are we going to protect Dr. Giverny?" She shivered involuntarily.

Tok muttered a long string of words in a language she didn't know. They sounded like curses. He fell silent.

Finally, she couldn't stand the stillness. "Well, what are we going to do?" she whispered. "We can't just give up."

"No, Sweet Eva. We don't give up, but I'm afraid my next actions will make me despised on this planet." She felt his deep sigh and then Tok carefully rose to a standing position and began to descend the crane's metal rungs. Despite his bulk and the total darkness, Tok moved with surprising stealth.

She followed him, and as they gained ground level he held out a hand to stabilize her as she stepped off the final rung. His action—and the lingering caress of his hand at her waist—took her aback. Did he think her some fragile female? They slipped out and away from the warehouse.

"I'm not some delicate beauty you have to mollycoddle, Tok," she muttered.

"You are to me, Sweet Eva." His response threw her into a state of utter confusion. She followed him in silence, her brain whirling. In her life, no male had ever said such a thing to her. No male had ever responded to her as a desirable female. That the big Khlossian would consider her sexually attractive was… nice. She studied him with new eyes as she followed him to… wherever.

Tok finally stopped at a small pub, The Dry Spot, on a busy street many blocks distant. Tok ushered her through the door and to a table, where he seated her by pulling out a sturdy chair and regarding her with an expectant smile until, with a frown and shake of her head, she sat. Pleasure vied with irritation. *Does he think because I'm female, I'm weak?* She sat stewing while Tok summoned a waiter.

"She'll take a kaffé with plenty of nata and saccharon and a piece of that bombom torta in the display case." Tok's attention returned to her. "Give me ten minutes and then order a titan mug of Pretario's Ale. I should be back by then."

Eva straightened in her chair and frowned at him. "What are you going to do? Where are you going? What about the meks?"

"I must make a call."

"For our mysterious help? I'm supposed to sit here and eat cake?"

"You don't like bombom torta? I thought all females liked bombom torta."

"I'm a combat soldier, you know, a deadly one. I am useful." She clenched her jaw and bristled at him.

"This I know." His eyes regarded her with… empathy? "You're also a fine looking female who appeared in need of a treat."

Stumped, she blanked for a moment. "Oh." She cleared her throat. "Thanks. Ahh… so… who are you calling?"

Tok's lips lifted in apology. "I cannot tell you, Sweet Eva. Your sense of honor would require you tell Ramsey's woman… she would tell Ramsey. He would try to stop me. He would fail. I don't wish to injure him." He lifted a shoulder in a shrug. From his posture to his expression, Tok conveyed the impression he hated what he was about to do—but was set on his course of action. "It is better for everyone if you stay here and eat torta." He held her gaze steadily until she nodded.

"Yeah. Okay. I get it. You would probably knock me unconscious and stash me somewhere safe if I don't agree, huh?"

Tok's eyes sparkled with amusement. His shrug was apologetic.

"So go make your call, big guy."

As the waiter arrived with her kaffé and torta, she swiveled around in her seat and watched Tok contort his body out the pub's door. As his massive form vanished, she returned to the torta and kaffé. *So... I guess I'll sit here and eat cake.*

She was pressing a forefinger to the plate to pick up the last crumbs of the torta when Tok entered the pub, pulled out a chair and eased himself down. When certain the chair would hold his weight, he relaxed, smiled at her, lifted the massive stein of Pretario's Ale waiting for him, and downed the contents in several long swallows.

"Ah, that's good." He thumped the stein onto the table and stood. "I cannot stay. I must meet our 'help' at gangway forty-three."

Eva shot him a sharp glance. "That's an abandoned section. Some nasty characters cruise that area. You might need someone to watch your back."

Tok eyed her and tapped his pursed lips. "Possibly. I will allow you to accompany me, but I have one requirement."

She looked at him expectantly.

"You cannot tell Ramsey or his woman. It is possible the ignorant Verdantian will kill our help on sight... and this he cannot do."

A sense of foreboding shivered down her spine. "What am I agreeing to, Tok?"

"Promise, Sweet Eva, or you will stay behind."

"Tok... I don't like this."

"My assignment is to keep Dr. Angel safe. I am doing so."

"Yes, of course, but..." She sighed. "All right. I promise."

They walked in silence to a seedy area of the port city where Eva knew illegal goods and persons were frequently smuggled onto Verdantia. The Haarb had constructed the makeshift landing bays as a temporary expansion during their occupation of Verdantia, and even after more than a decade the condemned facilities had yet to be razed by the port authorities. Eva supposed they'd had other things to do. Tok moved directly to a gangway connected to a light-absorbing, matte-black ship devoid of any markings. The vessel, cloaked by the murky gloom of the abandoned slips, presented only a dim profile. She imagined in the dark of space it would be invisible to all but sophisticated sensors. A small hatch opened in the dark hull and a lizard-like humanoid entered an open elevator and descended down the side of the ship to a decrepit gangway.

As the lift clacked down its track to the ground, the lizard-man's gaze swept the area beneath him and then stopped and focused on her. His yellow, snake-like eyes devoured her and his mouth pulled back in a toothy grin. Worse, his forked black tongue flickered from between his teeth as if tasting the air, as if tasting *her*. His attention never left her as he grabbed his crotch in an obscene gesture and began pumping his hips and grunting.

Revolted, she turned her back on him and faced Tok. "That's a *Haarb*, Tok," she hissed. "What in the *fuck* are you doing? *This* is our help?" She shook her head violently. "I don't like this. This race tried to annihilate the Verdantians. They almost succeeded."

Tok held her shoulders. "Be calm, Sweet Eva. Stay here. Don't approach the ship."

"As if I'd knowingly get within a mile of the murdering scum."

"Good," he grunted and trod up the gangway to meet a member of the race that had nearly succeeded in wiping the Verdantians from their planet.

In a language comprised of hisses and guttural spits, it appeared Tok was negotiating with the Haarb. It seemed a contentious negotiation. Tok met the lizard-man's constant gestures toward her with a forceful shake of his head. "Nysss," he growled. The Haarb's gestures became more insistent. In a move faster than would seem possible for a being his size, Tok grabbed the Haarb off its feet. A deadly blade seemed to appear as if by magic in his right hand. He held it to the Haarb's eye socket. "Nysss!" he bellowed, and threw the creature to the metal grating. It sprang up and pulled its own blade with a threatening hiss. Tok barked some words at it and its lips pulled back in a sneer. It swung its gaze to Eva and in a very human-like gesture spat onto the ground.

Tok addressed it again, and with a baleful gaze the creature nodded. "Sssey."

Tok grunted, turned his back on the Haarb and lumbered off the gangway. The lizard-man rotated its head toward her and leered with a final waggle of its tongue. She shivered in revulsion.

"Tok! What have you done?" she spat when he stopped in front of her. "Lord DeKieran will impale you where you stand when he finds you've brought Haarb to this planet. Our commander will have your balls on a plate—after she cuts out your liver. What the fuck have you done, and what is this going to cost the Verdantians?"

Tok regarded her steadily. "The mekanikos are not vulnerable to sophisticated weaponry. They absorb the energy from lazer and fusion fire. It makes them stronger. They are, however, vulnerable to being torn apart. The trick is to find something physically stronger than they are; something not confused when they vanish from sight or change shape. I had limited choices."

At the sound of a hatch banging open, her attention returned to the black ship. A silent parade of at least a dozen Haarb exited a ground level cargo hatch and rattled down the gangway. Each repugnant entity held several leashes with a snarling monster at the end of each leash. She gasped in horrified disbelief. "Fell wolves... the Haarb have brought fell wolves."

CHAPTER EIGHTEEN

Tristan handed Angelica a compact, lightweight weapon while Mage eyed both of them with annoyance. "No, princess," Tris said. "For the last time, you don't come with us. At the medcenter, you're a liability. You're more valuable here monitoring the communications board. We've been through this. Now, drop it. You're staying." Tris held Mage's gaze until his lover rolled his eyes.

"Fine. Fine. I get it. I don't like it, but I get it." Mage placed a gentle kiss on Angelica's lips. "Pay attention to the asshole, please. He does know what he's doing." Tris was just about to agree with Mage when the man grabbed the back of his neck and jerked him forward, smashing his lips in a forceful kiss. "Be careful," Mage growled. "Don't be a gods-be-damned hero."

With lips still pulsing from the ferocity of Magellan's kiss, Tris snorted. "Me? A hero? Pompous dickwits are never heroes." Mage rolled his eyes again and shoved him away.

Tris turned to Angelica. "After you, Dr. Giverny."

Tris and Mage had tried to convince Angelica to remain in the apartments, but she had insisted that she'd rather submerge herself in work. As Tris didn't think she was at any greater risk in her offices, he'd agreed to let her go to work. Once there, the identity of Angelica's first patient came as a surprise. When Lady Katrine DeClousey walked through the door, Tris started to retreat to a non-threatening corner to make himself as inconspicuous as possible.

"Good afternoon, Prince DeHelios. You look in need of sleep and a shave. No matter how fatigued, there is never a good reason to neglect your personal hygiene."

Tris simply blinked. Angelica attempted to muffle her gurgle of laughter, but he heard her and swung to face her. "I liked her better before," he muttered, and Angelica laughed harder.

The klaxon of the security system sobered them both.

"What?" Angelica's wide eyes sought his.

The comm device on his wrist buzzed angrily—Mage on a priority call. At the same moment, Ramsey, Steffania and a contingent of Blue Daggers burst through the door to Angelica's exam room. Tris hit connect on his comm device and barked, "Not now. I'll get back to you."

"Wait! Meks! Meks have hit the apartment!" Mage's out-of-breath voice filtered across the comm linc.

"Copy. I'll get back to you," said Tris.

"Meks have entered the dome," Ramsey snapped. "We were unable to hold the perimeter. They've hit Angelica's apartment and they are coming here. Get Angelica to the safe room." Ram's gaze speared Angelica. "You and Tris lock yourselves in and don't come out until you hear the all clear. Here, take this." Ramsey tossed him a bulky tube mounted with optical sights and a reinforced tripod. Tris grunted with the effort to hold the thing. He recognized it as a mobile, one-man fusion cannon. *Shit.* He could take half the med center out with this weapon. Ramsey's head swung to a cowering Lady DeClousey. "Stay in the exam room. You are not the target. I don't think you're in any danger as long as you stay out of the line of fire."

Tris ran to the door with Angelica and sprinted to the "safe" room down the hall, a room made as impregnable as possible. He pushed her inside and closed the solid metal door. The solid thunk of the locking mechanisms connecting sounded loud in the room. He thumbed in Ramsey's comm code. "We're secure."

"Roger. Set your comm line to monitor channel twelve. Ramsey out."

Tris did as Ram had ordered and then proceeded to set up the fusion cannon facing the door.

"What do we do?" Angelica stood with her arms wrapped around her but amazingly composed.

"We trust the Daggers to protect you and we wait for the all clear."

Tristan opened his arms and Angelica moved into his hold. Through the open comm device, both of them listened to the shouted orders from Ramsey and Steffania as the Daggers worked to secure the hallway on either side of the safe room. All fell silent.

"Fuck! Ultraviolet! Shift optics to ultraviolet!" Steffania screamed out orders. Abruptly, shouted commands, sounds of lazer fire and screams of agony overwhelmed his open comm and continued for several minutes—only to be replaced by static.

Angelica gasped, "I can't stand this. What's happening?" At that moment a tremendous blow battered the door to the safe room. An indention appeared. *Bam! Bam!* A hole opened in the middle of the door and a metallic hand began to peel the solid sheet metal away as if it were paper.

Tris moved to the fusion cannon, centered it on the door and flipped the priming switch. A low whine sounded in the room as it armed itself. "Get behind me, Angelica. I'm going to blow these bastards to the seven hells." Tris disciplined himself to wait until the last moment possible and so was treated to the view of a skeletoid figure of living metal stepping through the gaping hole in the door. It paused for one moment and regarded the fusion cannon with a cocked head.

"Yeah, you ugly fucker. Come and get it." Tris hit the firing button. The blast from the cannon hit the mek pointblank and ripped the safe room door from its hinges. The back-blast flattened him and Angelica against the back wall. When Tris straightened from his curled position protecting Angelica, he surveyed the damage and swore savagely. He pulled his Razar 88K and began firing as the unscathed mekanikos advanced on him. He emptied his gun at the creature's head. "What's it going to take to make you die, asshole?" Tris jerked his dagger from his belt as the mek reached out, picked him up by his armor and dangled him like a small child from its outstretched hand. It regarded him dispassionately before it removed the blade from his hand, drove it into his abdomen and sliced him from hip to hip. It happened so fast he felt nothing until it opened its fist and he fell to the floor. Through his agony, he saw Angelica aim the small emitter he'd given her at the mek and fire. The mek swatted at her, knocking the firearm out of her hand and grabbing her by the neck. A squeeze of her carotid artery and she slumped over. Had the mek killed her? Or was she simply unconscious? The mek tossed her over its shoulder and turned to carry her down the hall.

Clamping both hands to his groin, he managed to gain his feet and stagger to the doorway before his legs lost feeling. He propped against the doorframe and watched the mek leave. Bloody mounds littered the hall. Vermillion streaked the pale walls like gruesome abstract art. Did anyone still live?

Those monsters had Angelica. He didn't know if she was alive or dead. He'd failed to protect her. He'd fucked up. *I wonder what Hel will say when he hears?* Tris looked down at the blood oozing between the fingers of the hands he clenched against his gut. Red dripped from his knuckles and pooled on the safe room floor. *Ah… not good.* He slumped against the doorframe and fought the darkness clouding his vision. *I should have told her I loved her.*

"Tristan! Angelica!" Mage shouted down the medcenter hallway. The aftereffects of expended Razar 88Ks hazed the air. Blood spatter and lazer burns decorated the walls as if an inkblot psych-test. Bodies of Blue Daggers littered the hall. Some lay motionless in pools of viscous red. Others propped against the walls in tight-lipped silence. Ramsey DeKieran, his face painted red by blood streaming from a gash at his hairline, cradled his equally bloody wife in his arms. She looked too limp to be conscious. Medics scurried between the living, all of whom bore injuries. Where was Tris? Where was Angelica? Mage screamed their names again.

"Mage." Tristan slumped in the doorway of what looked like a fortified room. A thick metal door lay some feet away, ripped from its hinges. Tris sank to his knees... then sat... and then folded to the ground. He scrambled to Tristan's side as blood welled from his lower body.

"I need medical help!" He ripped open Tristan's body armor and swore at the mutilation of flesh. Half the man's internal organs were threatening to escape from the gaping slash in his abdomen. To staunch the flow, Mage rapidly closed Tristan's body armor as snugly as possible and held it pressed to the wound.

"It's bad." Tristan opened his eyes briefly before closing them again.

Yeah, it's bad. "Yeah, it's going to leave a hellacious scar." Mage's throat closed and tears threatened to cloud his vision. "Fuck, Tris. Hang in there, you bastard. Don't you dare die on me."

Tristan tried to laugh but stopped with an agonized gasp. "'fraid... I'm going to... disappoint, princess." His gray eyes found Mage. "Meks took Angelica," he gasped. "Couldn't stop them."

"Don't take all the credit. You and forty heavily-armed Daggers couldn't stop them." Mage shook his head. "It's okay. We'll get her back." Grief closed his throat, and tears he couldn't hold back flooded his vision. His right arm felt as if it were on fire and blood dripped from his fingertips. His thigh screamed in protest at any movement and his blood-soaked pants flapped against his leg wetly. Both injuries were souvenirs from his utterly futile attempt to prevent the meks from entering Angelica's apartment. He'd never before felt so impotent. The meks had paid him scant attention, simply swatting him away as if a minor irritant. He almost welcomed the physical pain, but it didn't distract from the emotional agony tearing him two.

In the next moment, multiple medical personnel surrounded Tris. They lifted him onto a broad, hovering gurney.

"You, too, sir," a medic ordered.

Mage climbed onto the floating conveyance next to Tris and gritted his teeth against the pain, as medical personnel began to cut his and Tristan's clothing away to evaluate their injuries. Mage waved them off with a curt, "See to him first."

When they opened Tristan's body armor, after a moment's observation, the medics grimly did the same as Mage had done. They snugged it tightly closed. Tris remained silent, his full lips pressed into a thin line. His eyes fluttered open and found Mage. A ghost of his normal mocking grin stretched his lips and then faded as if it was too much effort to sustain even that small movement. "Love you, princess," he rasped. "Love her, too. Tell her. Tell her I said…" His voice faltered and wetness trickled from the corners of his eyes.

Tristan's tears gutted him. He'd never seen the man cry. Mage pressed two fingers to Tristan's mouth and nodded. He pushed the words, "Yeah, I'll tell her," through heartache so heavy it was hard to breathe and scrubbed his eyes on his sleeve.

Tristan nodded. Then his eyes closed, and no matter how Mage begged, he never opened them again.

It seemed like hours but it couldn't have been more than a scattering of minutes before orderlies maneuvered their gurney through the wide doors of the trauma center. In a flurry of activity, the medical staff moved the heavens to save Tristan and the other Daggers gravely injured in the conflict with the meks. Mage collapsed on the floor in a corner, forgotten. He watched—and prayed.

"We're losing him. Push more fluids. He's crashing."

Mage lost count of the number of times he heard those awful words spoken by anonymous voices. He witnessed technicians attach life-sustaining machines to Tristan's body and force more liquids into his veins. He sat unnoticed and a numb sort of grayness surrounded him while others fought for the life of his lover. He couldn't even address the thought that the meks had Angelica. He dropped his head into his bloody hands and shook with repressed grief.

A hand rested on his shoulder. "Sir? Captain DeLan? You should have your wounds looked at. From the puddle you're sitting in, you've lost a lot of blood. Prince DeHelios is receiving the best care we can provide. It won't help matters if you collapse also." The kind voice of a female med-tech roused him. She stretched an arm down to help him rise. "Come on. I'll help you to a treatment room." He passed out trying to stand.

❧❦❧❦❧❦❧❦❧❦❧

Angelica awoke terrified and disoriented, wrists and ankles bound to a metal chair affixed to the floor. The stench of decaying fruit identified her location as part of a warehouse structure. Stygian black encased her, and she had no concept of how long she'd been unconscious. It could have been minutes. It could have been hours. Grief slammed her. She suspected Tris had a mortal wound. He might be dead by now. Ramsey and Steffania had lain in the hall, bloody and unmoving, surrounded by inert Blue Daggers. Were they dead also? She didn't know what had happened to Mage. A silent sob grew in her chest, and she choked on the pain of it. *I did this to them. I brought this evil here.*

Three sets of luminous blue orbs hovering in the blackness were the only reference points in the vast nothingness that surrounded her... but the message they conveyed chilled her more thoroughly than the rank air surrounding her. A spot of light above her grew in strength until she sat in a circle of dim illumination. It did nothing to break the total darkness further than an arm's length beyond her.

"If you are going to kill me, do it quickly." She was proud of the steadiness of her voice.

One of the entities—she supposed she was going to have to start thinking of them as "meks," for her captors met all the descriptions she'd ever heard of a mekanikos—entered the circle of light and clamped a hand on the nape of her neck. A finger and thumb pressed into the base of her skull with painful force. Her agonized scream rang in the emptiness of the warehouse.

An alien strangeness invaded her mind and with frightening ease broke down every mental barrier she frantically erected to prevent a total rape of her consciousness. In stunning clarity, she relived the emotions and events of her capture and slavery on Vxloncia as if watching an entertainment vid on fast-forward. Her memory slowed to real time as the memory of a particular event looped over and over again—as if the mek examined each millisecond minutely...

The stainless lid of her cerebral probe unit lifted, and the bright ceiling lights of the laboratory blinded her. Ungovernable fear overwhelmed her.

What have they done to my brain? How long have I been here?

Unfamiliar hands unhooked the catheters and intravenous tubes that connected her to the probe bed. Disoriented and dizzy, she was lifted and placed on her feet.

"Stand up, Pansy."

No. That's not right? My name is Angelica. I am Dr. Angelica Giverny! She lacked the capacity to speak, so she screamed it in her mind.

Rough hands, invasive hands, draped a pale pink gown over her nude body. An unfamiliar male voice ordered, "Follow that technician, Pansy." A whimper of horror lodged in her throat.

She shuffled out of the white room with the rest of the mind-wiped and reconditioned women kidnapped to fill the ranks of submissive sex slaves on Vxloncia.

As she moved down the hall at the prompting of the white-coated technicians, she passed two men talking. One she recognized as Vittal Lontz. She saw only the back of the other man. As her group hobbled by, a woman stumbled and Angelica fell bodily into the two men. Disoriented and unsteady on her feet, Angelica grabbed at Lontz's companion before she landed on the hard floor. Lontz barked his displeasure and technicians immediately swooped in to jerk her to her feet.

"Not so rough, gentlemen," a deep masculine voice admonished. Lontz's companion leaned down and offered his hand to her. After assisting Angelica to her feet, he caressed her cheek. "Something so delicate and beautiful deserves gentle treatment." Angelica gazed at his striking features and wondered how a man so physically arresting could embody such evil.

The technicians surrounded her and hustled her back to the rest of the group. She regarded him over her shoulder as the technicians shoved her down the hall.

"You, Jewel, help Pansy," one of the techs ordered, and pushed a woman toward her. The woman reached out and steadied her as they moved down the long bright corridor…

"Gaah!" Angelica threw her head back on a stifled scream, gasping as the alien being released its contact and withdrew from her mind. A throbbing pain from the nape of her neck worked its way to her temples and agony split her skull. *I'm Angelica Giverny. I'm on Verdantia. I'm Angelica Giverny. I'm on Verdantia. I have to hold on. Someone will come.* She whimpered softly and steeled herself to resist the terror that threatened to turn her into an incoherent sniveling mess. With painstaking discipline, she relaxed her muscles and controlled her irregular gasps. *Someone will come. They will.* She didn't want to examine the memory of her seemingly invincible bodyguard being tossed aside like a piece of refuse. He and Mage had to be okay. She couldn't face a life without them. *Someone will come.* She chanted those words to drown out the part of her that screamed in hopeless despair.

The mek who examined her stood in the dim puddle of light around her chair and gazed into the blackness toward the two pairs of blue orbs seemingly suspended in the lightless expanse of the warehouse. "This organic is the one we seek. Prepare our transport off-planet."

A sibilant hiss echoed in the vast warehouse. As if out of nowhere, dozens of red pinpoints glowed in the surrounding blackness. A gigantic monster launched itself from the black and with saw-toothed jaws clamped onto the mek's elbow. *A fell wolf!* From the dark, five more beasts leapt onto the mek, biting deep into its shoulders, thighs, ankles and buttocks and tearing chunks of matter from its body that hit the floor of the warehouse with a liquid "splat." The mek assaulted the wolves with its skeletal hands, ripping and shredding. Gray fur and bloody bits of wolf flew, but in the fell wolves' mindless blood lust, not even injury or dismemberment discouraged their attack. The four-legged genetic monsters more than matched the physical strength of a cyborg in their ravening ferocity. In body size and weight the fell wolves appeared equal to the meks. The mekanikos nearest her swiveled and reached for her, a wolf hanging from its elbow. Three more wolves leapt out of the dark to hang off its wrist and forearm. The mek morphed from humanoid into a snakelike creature that oozed to the floor and appeared to vanish—at least she could no longer see it.

Momentarily flummoxed as the flesh between their jaws shrank away and seemingly disappeared into thin air, the predators paused and sniffed—and attacked the thin air a stone's throw away. To Angelica it appeared a battle done in mime. They hung off something invisible that tossed their bodies back and forth as if flags whipping in a strong wind. She couldn't see what the wolves attacked, but the results of their ripping and tearing became obvious as silvery pieces of the cyborg began to appear, littering the floor of the warehouse.

Angelica heard a resounding "klack." Intense white lights flooded the building's cavernous interior and blinded her momentarily. Squinting against the light, for a moment she saw the other two mekanikos blanketed in a gray swarm of fell wolves. Each entity had at least a dozen of the genetic monsters hanging from it. Even the impossibly strong meks staggered under the weight and ferocity of the perversions attacking them. Vicious growls and agonized snarls filled the air as the meks grabbed the warped anomalies of giant lizard spliced with wolf and attempted to rip them in half. It didn't matter what shape the mekanikos morphed into or if they disappeared entirely, the wolves continued their rending and tearing until only small bits of each entity remained—and three skulls. Angelica couldn't stop looking at the horrific carnage. The viciousness of the fell wolves as they tore these seemingly invincible cyborgs into small pieces riveted her attention. Her brain refused to acknowledge the creatures that stepped into the edge of her field of vision—genetically enhanced lizard-men, Haarb. *Of course. Who better to control these genetic monsters than the abominations that created them?*

Two of the wolves that had torn asunder the first mek paused in their destruction and swung their red-eyed gaze to her. Bound to the chair, she could not move. Lowering into a crouch, they slunk toward her, caustic drool dripping from bared fangs, a constant menacing growl filling the air. The fell wolves were going to rip *her* into pieces. She laughed hysterically then bit it off. *That's not helping!* She closed her eyes and waited for the rending of her flesh by razor-edged teeth. She felt the rumble of their snarls in her abdomen. Their hot breath gusted on her face. Their acidic saliva dropped in burning splats on her exposed skin. *I hope they kill me quickly. I hope there isn't too much pain.* Her bladder loosed and she sat in a warm puddle of urine.

"Nysss! Nysss! Ousss!" Her eyes flew open. The barked command registered dimly. With snarls and yelps as the control collars on each wolf flared amber and then red, the monsters retreated one and then two steps, biting and snapping at each other. Their Haarb handler stepped in and clipped chains to their collars and dragged the snarling mass away. The immense form of Tok emerged from behind her, followed by Eva Sweet. Angelica stared at them dumbly.

"Dr. Angel. Are you hurt?" The Khlossian began to free her while Eva Sweet stood, legs braced, Razar 88K in hand, and glared at the rest of the Haarb until, with hisses that sounded like laughter, they leashed their foul pets.

"I wet myself." Angelica dissolved into tears of hysteria.

"What are you doing out of your bed, Captain DeLan?"

Mage leaned against the hospital wall waiting for the dizziness to fade. He'd almost made it from his bed to the critical care center where he'd last seen Tris.

He turned and faced the beefy male nurse who had tended him with great compassion for the last day. Mage began to sag.

"Let me help you, sir. You shouldn't be doing this." The man shrugged under his shoulder and bore some of his weight.

"I wanted to check on…"

A shriek split the air and a small body slammed into the middle of his back. But for the nurse, he would have gone down.

"Mage, oh my gods, Mage. You're hurt." Angelica released him gingerly and slid around to face him. Eva Sweet stood back and watched them. "What are his injuries?" Angelica snapped. As the nurse assisting him spouted all sorts of medical jargon, Mage simply stared at the incomprehensible sight of Angelica Giverny barking orders. His gaze swung to Eva.

"How… I mean… I know I've been out of it, but?"

"With some 'help,' we rescued Dr. Giverny from the warehouse where the meks were holding her," said Eva. "I brought her here to be treated for trauma. She insisted on seeing you and Prince DeHelios first."

Eva put her hand on Angelica's shoulder and interrupted the nurse's recount of the injuries Mage sustained. "A moment, if you would." When the man fell silent, Eva turned to Angelica. "I must leave you here, Dr. Angel. I need return to the warehouse and help Tok make sure your rescuers don't linger on Verdantia."

Angelica attempted to wrap the huge Dagger in a hug. "Thank you, Eva." The woman stood motionless for a moment, and then awkwardly put her arms around Angelica. Angelica hugged her harder. "Thank you. You and Tok saved my life. I will never forget."

Eva smiled. "I will see you again, Dr. Angel. As soon as I help Tok run the Haarb off Verdantia, I'll be back—though I doubt the Khlossian will come with me. He said something about giving Verdantian tempers time to cool. It's just as well that Lord Ramsey and Lt. Colonel DeKieran are not fighting fit; otherwise, I think Tok would be running for *his* life." With a nod that included Mage, Eva left.

Angelica lifted a beautiful, worried face to Mage. "Where is our Tristan?"

Mage gazed at her lovely features and his face crumpled. He couldn't speak. Devastation swept her expression and she turned again to the nurse. "What is the status of Prince DeHelios?"

"We are doing everything medically possible, but in spite of our best efforts his injuries are—"

"No!" Angelica whispered. She shook her head. "No, no, no… I know what that language means. Where is he?" The young man led Angelica toward the wide glass windows that looked into the intensive care center where medical personnel monitored Tristan around the clock. Mage wandered after her and leaned against a wall. Angelica turned to his nurse. "Thank you." Her eyes flew to Mage and scanned him. "Please ensure Captain DeLan returns to his hospital bed. He shouldn't be on his feet."

***

Mage lay in a sitting position in a bed in the same room the nurse had taken him to a day ago—or was it two—and downed his fifth glass of Pottsdim. He was attempting to reach oblivion. It wasn't working. The potent alcohol couldn't dampen his emotional devastation any more than the opioids he'd swallowed could deaden his physical pain. *It's not fair. Any other time, I'd be under the table.*

A haggard and hollow-cheeked Angelica walked in, paused for a moment, and with a shake of her head crawled onto the bed and snugged herself under his good side.

"I can't reach the decanter with you there," he murmured.

"I think you've had enough. I could smell you from the door."

He sighed heavily and let the empty glass fall to his lap. "Doesn't matter. Wasn't doing any good, anyway." He let his head roll back and examined the ceiling. He swallowed and asked the question he dreaded the answer to. "Tris?"

Angelica hugged him tighter and buried her face in his chest. He felt her body shake, but then she stiffened, swiped her nose on the blankets and half sat. Deep purple bruises made crescents below her closed eyes. Her lids opened and her gaze found his. "We have the most advanced medical technology available and we are barely keeping him alive. It would take a miracle for him to live more than a day or so off the machines."

"Gods-be-damned heroics. I warned him about that, but he said pompous dickwits didn't do heroics."

"No, no, no, no." With each word, Angelica pounded on his chest, tears streaming down her cheeks. "I brought this danger to you. Neither of you should have been involved. This is my fault."

"Oh, Angel." Mage wrapped his good arm around her and pulled her to him, suppressing a hiss as she slid across his damaged thigh. "You aren't responsible for the behavior of some sociopathic maniac. Having you in our lives is worth any pain. It was the thought we'd lost you that was intolerable. Tris and I are in love with you. The fact that you aren't in the hands of the meks is the one thing keeping me sane."

"Tristan loves me?"

More pain assaulted him. How could he have forgotten? "He told me so. It was the last thing he said. He told me to tell you. I'm so sorry. I… I… just forgot in all this…" Mage gestured helplessly.

Angelica caught his floundering arm and kissed his hand. "Stop… stop, Mage. I love you both—so very much. We can't lose him. I can't lose him. I've done everything I know to do and he's still slipping away. I don't know how to stop it. He's fading away and nothing I do helps. I'm watching him die."

Angelica dissolved into quiet sobs, and for a long stretch of time all Mage did was rub the nape of her neck as she poured out her grief. He battled the fat tears pooling in his eyes and the raw ache in his throat. He was afraid he'd break down, too. Finally, she quieted and lay on his chest with only an occasional shudder passing through her. Mage thought she dozed, but then she would hug him fiercely and begin to sob again. Sometime deep in the dark of the night he gave up the battle to hold back his tears and cried with her. They both poured out their grief until pure exhaustion stopped their tears.

"May we come in?" Ramsey's deep baritone broke the quiet. The door to their room stood open and soft light from the hallway cast a cone of illumination.

"Yes." Mage roused from his semi-stupor, pressed the room controls and brought the lights up to half-strength. Lord Ramsey shuffled in and stood stooped with red-stained bandages swathing his abdomen and head. A shirt, half-buttoned, draped his shoulders. Loose sleep pants hung low on his hips. His feet were bare. Steffania followed. The pair looked as beaten and battered physically as he felt mentally. While she was more dressed than her husband, Steffania's lips were swollen to twice their normal size. The left half of her face was a massive purpling mound of shiny swollen flesh with an ugly line of black stitches crossing the bridge of her nose and left cheekbone. Her eye on that side was swollen to a mere slit. A cast immobilized her left arm and shoulder. "What time is it?" Mage said.

"Predawn," Ramsey answered.

Steffania limped to Angelica and with her good hand grasped Angelica's fingers in a gentle hold. "Eva found us and told us about your rescue. I cannot tell you how sorry I am. I hold myself responsible for this entire debacle. I underestimated the capacity of the mekanikos. I hope you can find it in your heart to forgive me." Pushed through battered lips, Steffania's words lacked her normal crisp enunciation and emerged labored and slurred.

"I could never blame you, Steffania. I'm the one who brought the meks here. Of course I forgive you."

Steffania shook her head. "Thank you. I'll argue with you about whose fault... later. Are you all right? Eva said the meks violated your mind."

Angelica nodded. "Yes. Highly unpleasant at the time, but no lasting damage. I'll have a complete psyche eval tomorrow to confirm. I doubt there'll be any long-term ill effects."

Mage observed Angelica lift to study Lord Ramsey. He stood slightly bent. Her gaze turned to watch as Steffania hobbled to him. The two stood side-by-side, guarded and obviously in pain.

"You and Lord Ramsey belong in a hospital bed."

Steffania's mouth twitched in a caricature of a smile and she shot a one-eyed glance at her husband. "He has refused to stay in bed and he's injured worse than me, so..." She grimaced. "I'll lay down when he does."

"I'm very grateful Tok rescued you, Angelica, but you must forgive me if I loathe the way it was procured. I will rest when I know for certain all that vile excrement has been removed from Verdantia. Their very presence is a desecration of our Mother," said Ramsey.

"The Haarb and the fell wolves," she whispered.

Ramsey nodded. "If you see Tok, tell him to stay away from me. At this very moment, in spite of my regard for him... I will kill him if I see him."

She nodded silently.

"How's Tris?" Ram asked softly.

Angelica raised her face to Mage. Tears threatened to overflow her violet eyes. She pressed her lips together, but the trembling of her chin gave her away and she buried her head in his chest.

Mage said what Angelica couldn't. He held Ramsey's gaze steadily and shook his head. "It's unlikely he'll pull through." Angelica gave a muffled cry so filled with pain that an ache as large as a fist gathered in his gut and he hugged her to him more tightly.

Ramsey shifted with a grunt of pain. "Can you keep him alive for another forty-eight hours?"

"I don't know," she choked. "Why do you ask?"

"I want Tristan in Nyth Uchel, with Adonia, Hel's wife. I hoped you could keep him alive until we get there."

Angelica nestled into Mage, seeking comfort as tears continued to roll down her cheeks. "To what point, Dominus?" she choked out. "Can she work miracles? Can she return someone from death's threshold?"

Ramsey and Steffania stared at each other. With halting care, Ram raised an arm and cupped the less damaged side of his wife's face. His thumb caressed her cheekbone, and some indefinable emotion softened his expression. Steffania turned her face into his palm and closed her eye. When Ram dropped his hand, he replied. "Yes. She can."

CHAPTER NINETEEN

I n the day and a half since Ramsey and Steffania had hustled her and Tristan out of Arkodaenia, the pace had been suicidal. Angelica had prepared for imminent death several times. A horse-drawn vehicle of weightless poly-carbon with a sophisticated suspension system—an anachronistic anomaly anywhere but on Verdantia—had met their ambulance at the far edge of the modern spaceport. While the rest of their party had mounted horses or climbed into other horse-drawn vehicles, she and a number of medical personnel had disconnected Tris from the electrical machines that regulated his breathing, heart and fluid intake, and transferred him to the sleek vehicle superbly outfitted as an ambulance. Clever mechanical apparatus replaced the more familiar electrical machines keeping Tristan's body alive.

She eyed the high-strung, restive horses dubiously as she monitored Tristan and murmured to Mage. "Are they safe?"

Mage shrugged. "…under the circumstances…"

"Never mind. Sorry I asked."

Rather than a driver, a short, sinewy rider mounted the front, left horse and their mad careen to Nyth Uchel began—only Angelica discovered they weren't going directly to Nyth Uchel.

They would stop at a major Oshtesh village, Sh'r Un Kree. There, Adonia DeHelios would meet them and attempt to stabilize Tristan before they continued to Nyth Uchel. Changing horses regularly, they made good time—considering. It was a good thing Tristan's care required all her skill and attention; otherwise she'd have been reduced to hysterics on multiple occasions. She'd take a safe, 300-mile-per-hour hovercraft any day.

She swayed gently and her tired brain took note of the extraordinary scenery rolling by. Craggy rock formations rose steeply on either side of the endless plain they traversed. The cliffs, striated in ocher and purple, rust and vermillion, cast vast shadows across their route—the only shade on the barren landscape, and the temperature climbed within the medical vehicle. There seemed to be some commotion outside as, with unintelligible shouts, the outriders who had flanked them since they left Arkodaenia closed tighter to the vehicle and with a small lurch their pace increased.

She tossed a tired glance at Mage. "What's going on? We have speeded up. I thought we were giving the animals a breather."

"I don't know. I'll try to find out." Mage moved to the back of the transport and slid open a window. More unintelligible shouting ensued. After a brief exchange, he slipped back into his seat next to her.

"Well?"

"We are being followed. You told me that the fell wolves tore the meks into small pieces."

"Yes. I saw them. Well, I saw one shredded to bits and I heard what sounded like the other meks being attacked. I was somewhat out of it by that time. Why do you ask?"

"Meks, Angelica. We are being followed by three meks."

The hits had been coming too hard and fast. An hysterical laugh burst from her lips, and she slapped her hand across her mouth to smother it. Mage studied her with a concerned look. A long period of silence followed as Angelica struggled with hysteria. What finally allowed her to hold onto her composure was the knowledge that if Tristan had any chance of living, she must hold it together. She returned her hand to her lap and straightened. "Sorry," she whispered. "I think I lost it for a minute."

"Sweetheart. You're entitled. Hey, come here." He pulled her to him with his good arm and she went willingly. "The good news is, since the time the meks were first sighted, we have been putting more and more distance between us and them. Either they cannot keep pace or our Great Mother is affecting them."

"How do you mean?" she mumbled into his shirt.

"It's possible that the electromagnetic distortion that disrupts every other form of technology is also affecting the meks. Sapping their energy... slowing them down."

She nuzzled closer to him. "That's a comforting thought. How long until we reach Sh'r Un Kree?"

Mage peered out the window and studied the passing terrain. "Not exactly sure where we are at the moment, but we passed the Eye of Navarre sometime back... so, two hours? Three?"

Angelica's vehicle rocked to a halt in the dusty central courtyard of Sh'r Un Kree. The wide double door on the side flew open. A tall, wiry brunette in fitted, well-worn riding leathers jumped in as Mage slipped out. She nodded at Angelica, "I'm Adonia," and then her attention focused on Tristan.

She immediately moved to him, placed both hands on his chest and closed her eyes. Her lips mouthed silent words. A golden glow and low hum built in the air around her, traveled down her arms and hands and entered Tristan's body. Adonia gasped and staggered but did not fall. Angelica sprang to assist her and wrapped an arm around her waist in support. It was like hugging a live current. Angelica endured the course of painful energy through her body as long as she could but was about to pull away when Adonia gave a sigh and lifted her hands from Tristan. The feeling immediately ceased. She opened her eyes and turned to Angelica. The compassion and strength in the brown eyes that met hers filled Angelica with an inexplicable desire to lay all her burdens at this woman's feet with the certain knowledge that Adonia would carry them for her.

"I am Adonia DeHelios. You must be Dr. Giverny." The brunette gave her a smile of singular sweetness. "Your care of Tristan has been extraordinary. To have kept him alive with the injuries that he's suffered…" She shook her head in wonder. "I would love to talk with you about your medical methodology when time allows. Tristan is stable. I've put him in stasis. I don't know if… if… he will live, but I have bought us time."

"Thank you." Angelica pushed the words out.

Adonia nodded. "I love him, too. I will do my best. Now, where are Steffania and Ramsey DeKieran?"

As Angelica stepped out of the vehicle with Adonia, a slew of horses and riders thundered past and out the arched entry of Sh'r Un Kree. Mage limped over to join the two women. "Primus G'hed and his fighters are going to try and slow the meks."

"That's suicide," Angelica gasped.

Mage sighed. "That's what we told him, but he wouldn't be stopped. He said our Great Mother would protect them."

❧❧❧❧❧❧❧❧❧❧❧

It was deep night before the Oshtesh Primus and his company returned at a sedate walk. Their desert horses glowed a ghostly white in the soft radiance of Verdantia's double moons. The entire troop appeared otherworldly… like creatures from another dimension. *They fit this surreal experience.* Angelica saw them before she heard them. She stepped out of the ambulance where she'd been keeping watch over Tristan while an exhausted Adonia and a newly-healed Mage got some desperately needed sleep. She didn't know where Lord Ramsey and his wife were. Someplace asleep, she hoped. Angelica stopped one of the first riders. "I'm a doctor. Where are the injured? Who needs medical help?"

"No one, healer. We don't require your services."

"I don't understand. Didn't you find the meks?"

The rider hawked and spat into the dirt. "Unnatural perversions. Yes, we found them."

"And no one was injured in the fight?" Her voice rose in confusion.

A low chuckle sounded behind her and she turned to see Primus G'hed looking down at her from his horse. "There was no fight. Our Great Mother defeated the mekanikos. We found the alien constructs on the road, perhaps an hour's ride to the west. I'm surprised they made it that far. Organic matter must have comprised more of the mekanikos than we thought. We found them frozen mid-step. It was simple enough to hack them into pieces." He untied a cloth bag fastened to his saddle bow and upended it. A round object hit the ground and rolled to her feet. A metallic looking skull gleamed in the moonlight. She shuddered. The eyelids in the skeletal head of the mekanikos opened and glowing blue orbs fixed her in an unblinking, malignant stare.

She leapt away with a small gasp. "It still lives!"

Primus G'hed swung down from his horse, grabbed the skull and dropped it back into the cloth bag. "Yes. But this time we took the precaution of taking the heads. We will carry them to the furthest corners of our planet. There will be no reintegration. You are safe, at least from these aberrations."

⚜⚜⚜⚜⚜⚜⚜⚜⚜

Two days later, Angelica had forgotten life had ever existed beyond the swaying of the specially-fitted vehicle pulled at a remorseless pace. She'd been awake the better part of forty hours, but even through her sleep-deprived fugue she recognized the unique quality inherent in the landscape and atmosphere of Nyth Uchel now clearly seen through the spacious windows. The very air seemed purified, energized—magickal. Perhaps Tristan was right. Perhaps Hel's wife *did* have a magick wand. In the midst of the luminous atmosphere and fantastical structures, in light of Adonia's miraculous healing of Steffania, Ramsey and Mage that Angelica had witnessed personally, it didn't seem so farfetched. If not for her exhaustion, she would have badgered Adonia to explain about their "Great Mother." Who *was* this sentient planet and what vast powers did *She* endow *Her* "children" with? *How do* I *get some?*

"We're here," murmured Adonia. "The City of Nyth Uchel." Angelica pulled herself to the window and gazed out.

The superbly crafted ambulance thundered at breakneck speed over a vast bridge that spanned a canyon through which a tumultuous river poured. They hurtled through massive, elaborately scrolled bronze gates flung wide in a colossal wall of glistening white crystal. The vehicle flew recklessly down a prosperous boulevard. Well-dressed crowds lined the route. The vehicle swirled into the courtyard of an immense, ethereal castle comprised of spirals that lifted effortlessly into space and only then slowed its frenetic pace.

When it rocked to a halt, Adonia rose, slid the side panel of the vehicle open and spoke out the door. "I think Prince Tristan is stable enough to move inside." Several large men hustled in and disconnected his journey-bed from the inner suspension that further softened what few bumps and jars reached the interior of the vehicle.

"Take him to our private chambers, please. Put him in our bed... and please tell my husband to meet me there. Time is critical."

"Yes, M'lady."

Adonia turned and took Angelica's hand. "Come, Dr. Giverny. I'll introduce you to Jolie. She'll show you to your rooms and give you the layout of the castle. You must have a bath and some rest, a meal, and then I'll be very happy to have your advice and help with Tristan."

As Adonia withdrew her hand, Angelica nodded. It occurred to Angelica she hadn't spoken a word to Adonia in the two days since they'd left Sh'r Un Kree. "He said you have a magick wand," she blurted. She buried her face in her hand and shook her head. "That's not what I meant to say. Can you save him? Is it possible?"

Adonia held her in a steady gaze of empathy. "I heal no one. Our Great Mother, Verdantia, is the true healer. I am only Her conduit. I will examine Tris more extensively, but I was encouraged by my initial findings, and the DeHelios bloodline is beloved to Her. Is that enough?" The slender woman's brow wrinkled, and her eyes searched Angelica's face.

An arrow of hope pierced the ice of despair that had encased her heart for the last seven days and she nodded. "Yes. I must find Mage, Captain DeLan, and tell him. He will welcome the news."

The women stepped out of the vehicle onto the flagstone courtyard. Unaccustomed to stable ground, it took a few moments for Angelica to convince her feet the ground didn't shift underneath her. Adonia steadied her and then motioned to a sweet-faced, young blond woman.

"Lord DeKieran's message said the three of you were a triad?" said Adonia, glancing at Angelica for confirmation. When the doctor nodded, Adonia smiled slightly and sighed. "I'm glad I got that right. I've put you and Captain DeLan in Tristan's apartments. She relaxed and wrapped her arms around her waist. "Dr. Giverny, this is Jolie. Jolie, Dr. Giverny is a noted healer of the mind and kept Prince Tristan alive on his journey to us. Please treat her as you would me."

"Yes, your Highness." The young woman dipped into a shallow curtsey and then smiled at Angelica, "I'm pleased to be of service, ma'am."

Adonia straightened and with a briskness she'd lacked before said, "I'm going to get Tristan settled in and resume his healing." She paused. "Thank you for saving his life. Hel would never say, but Tris is dear to us."

Angelica shook her head. "I didn't do anything but fight to keep his body functioning until we got him to you."

Adonia nodded. "Yes. And that saved his life." With a shy smile, she turned and strode quickly up the broad steps to the castle's double doors.

"We haven't seen Adonia or Tristan since we arrived and I'm beginning to think his older brother, Hel, is simply a myth." Angelica regarded Mage across a small dining table in Tristan's apartments. "It's been six days and all the staff will tell me is that "the Healer" has locked her apartment door and admits only food and drink. I'm so on edge with anxiety I can hardly stay in my skin. Do you think Tris has taken a turn for the worse or died, and we weren't told?"

Mage swallowed a savory pastry and wiped his mouth with a cloth napkin. "I admit I share your worry, but I do trust what Lord DeKieran—and every living soul in Nyth Uchel, for that matter—has told us of Adonia's abilities." He chuckled under his breath. "And I assure you, Hel exists. When you see someone who resembles an eight-foot icebear with the aloof disdain of a Dhakarian emperor, that's Hel. You can't mistake him for anyone else."

"Jolie tells me he and his wife frequently work together when healing those gravely ill." Angelica sighed. "Perhaps he's shut away with Adonia and Tristan."

Mage reached across the table and laid his hand on hers. "I must hope for the best. It's the only way I can get through the day. I'm certain the castle staff will inform us of any change in Tris— better or worse. It helps to stay busy."

"Yes. I think I'd have lost my mind if I couldn't assist in the castle's medical clinic. I find the homeopathic medicines intriguing. I'm not much help, though. Adonia has things so well organized and her nurses so well trained, the clinic practically runs itself."

Mage squeezed her hand. "Will you come for a ride with me? It will get you out of the clinic, and the fresh air will clear your mind."

Alarm straightened her in her chair. "On a horse? Ride on top of a horse?"

A slow smile spread across her lover's face. "Yes. I've inquired, and Adonia has a two-year old son. You can ride his pony. You're small and light enough. If Hel and Adonia entrust their tiny child to the mount, it's bound to be gentle."

"You must be insane. Defy death if you want to, but don't invite me to join you. No. Absolutely not. No. I'll walk in the gardens if I want fresh air."

Mage's smile grew wider. "The trip here frightened you that much? You'll face down murdering cartel leaders and torture from alien mekanikos, yet you are frightened of sitting on a gentle pony? How about if I lead you?"

She crossed her arms over her chest and glared at him. He threw up his hands with a laugh.

"Fine, fine. I won't force you, but you should get over that. Life on this planet will be far easier for you if you do."

She glowered at him in silence, lips pressed tightly together.

She would choose how she died, and it wouldn't be on a horse. A low rap on the door interrupted their conversation.

"Come in," Mage called.

The door opened and the largest human male Angelica had ever seen entered the room. His resemblance to Tristan was unmistakable. While Mage established the standard for masculine beauty in her mind, the virile male standing before her was definitely easy on the eyes. *Are there no ugly men on this planet?* He bowed slightly in her direction and dipped his chin in acknowledgement of Mage. "Magellan, you're a welcome sight. And you would be Dr. Giverny?"

Angelica nodded.

"I am Prince Hel. Thank you for the life of my brother."

Angelica squirmed in discomfort, took a deep breath and confessed, "I'm responsible for the condition he's in. He was trying to save me from the mekanikos and was critically wounded in the exchange."

"He was doing his job. It was unfortunate you were captured while under Tristan's care."

She couldn't let the inference that Tristan had somehow been responsible for her situation pass. "It wasn't his fault. These mekanikos are almost impossible…"

Mage rose from his chair with such violence the chair fell over and faced the man. "A job *you* thrust him into. A job he had little preparation for. A job like dozens of others over the years that you, in your arrogance, passed off on Tristan simply to get him out of your hair. Jobs which he performed with an outstanding degree of competence completely disregarded by you. But don't believe me, Prince DeHelios. Ask Lord DeKieran. Ask our High Lord and queen's consort, Ari DeTano, who thoroughly examined Tristan's background before assigning him as bodyguard to Dr. Giverny. Ask any number of Verdantians grateful for the presence of Tristan DeHelios. To further drive home your lack of esteem, you neglected to invite him to your marriage when you invited *everyone* else on Verdantia. How could you exclude your own brother? How could you think he wouldn't care—wouldn't be hurt by that exclusion?" Mage hurled his final words at Prince DeHelios and the man flinched.

With a soft sigh, Hel pulled out a chair from the table and gently lowered his heavy frame into it. He appeared shaken and weary. Leaning back, he motioned to the fallen chair. "Have a seat, Mage." His head swung to Angelica. "Magellan loves my brother too well. Tristan does little wrong in his eyes. You, I expect, have a more objective viewpoint. So, tell me, Dr. Giverny, tell me about my brother."

She did.

When she'd had her say, the timekeeper showed several hours had elapsed, and to his credit, Hel had done nothing but absorb her words.

In the silence that followed, Hel shifted in his chair and pursed his lips. His fingers drummed on the arms, then ceased. He stood. "I see my brother has won your love as well." The ruler of Nyth Uchel gave each of them a vague smile and left the room, his brows drawn together in thought.

Angelica exchanged a long glance with Mage. "Well… at least we gave him something to consider," she said.

CHAPTER TWENTY

Tristan reveled in the delicious heat enveloping his body. He'd been cold for an eternity. He'd been in pain for an eternity. That, too, was gone. He floated in a warm sea of bliss. Awareness crept in, though his subconscious urged him to fight it. His mind, muddled for so long, cleared, and with it came memories. A hovercraft with medics… and Mage. The mek walking out of the safe room with an unconscious Angelica slung over its shoulder. The keen blade of reality scythed a devastating swath through the blissful numbness that enwrapped him and cleared a path for crippling grief. *Oh, Goddess. Angelica.*

He hadn't protected her. He'd been forced to watch as her enemy strode in and simply took her away. She was certainly dead by now. Why wasn't *he* dead? He was supposed to die. He'd wanted to. It would have been cosmic justice. He'd fulfilled his brother's predictions. He was a supreme disappointment, but this time the cost had been someone of irreplaceable value, both to him and to Verdantia. *Angelica.* She'd never known what she'd meant to him. He'd been too much of a coward to tell her. The emotional pain of her loss clogged his throat and tears threatened behind his eyelids. He took a deep, shuddering breath.

"Tris?" The side of his bed sagged and a large hand enveloped his. He knew the voice—his older brother, Hel. The higher powers truly despised him. "Tris, I know you can hear me. You're in

Nyth Uchel in my bed. Adonia won't move you until you regain consciousness, so I'd appreciate it if you would open your eyes and talk to me. I'd like to have my wife and my bed to myself again."

The dry voice of his brother completed Tristan's rude emergence to reality. He supposed he must open his eyes and face the vilification, the scathing denigration that he richly deserved for failing to protect Angelica. By the Goddess, he'd welcome it. He opened his eyes, blinked to clear the tears from his vision and focused on his brother.

"There. My eyes are open. Happy now?"

"Yes. I'm overjoyed you aren't dead." Hel smiled solemnly. He sat on the side of the bed and studied Tris as if he'd forgotten what his brother looked like and was memorizing his features. He'd yet to release Tristan's hand. "Don't scare me like that again, please. I think I've aged ten years. Adonia spent upwards of three weeks doing nothing but healing you. It was a close thing."

"You? Scared?" *What the fuck?* Hel sounded genuinely moved. Tris grunted. "She should have saved her talents for someone worthy."

"There can be no one more worthy than my much loved brother."

Tris eyed Hel in disbelief. "Right. The sole wart on our illustrious lineage." Hel hung his head. For a moment, he looked… embarrassed? Tris blinked to clear his eyes. He had to have imagined it. His arrogant prick of a brother was never embarrassed. No… the expression remained.

"I have been wrong in my behavior toward you—a fact I have had my nose vigorously rubbed in. A number of people think quite highly of you. It's long overdue, but I'm sorry. I'm sorry for so many things. I intend to do better. I love you, Tris. I'm proud you're my brother. I'm proud of what you have accomplished with your life, and I'm ashamed that you're just now hearing those words from me."

Tris supposed he should feel something; after all, he'd waited over thirty years to hear Hel say them, but nothing could pierce the numbness surrounding his heart. *She's dead.* "I failed to keep her safe," he whispered. "I finally found a woman I loved, a woman I would give my life for, and I failed her."

A corner of Hel's mouth lifted. "I think Dr. Giverny disagrees with you. She told me she felt safer with you and Captain DeLan than at any other time in her life."

"What?"

His brother squeezed his hand and stood. "Why don't I let her tell you?" He stepped back to reveal Mage and Angelica standing in the doorway. They walked toward Tris, smiling, and stood beside his bed. Hel nodded at the pair and slipped out of the room.

Tris attempted to regroup from the staggering shock just dealt him. "Guess I didn't disappoint you after all, princess."

A crooked smile stretched Mage's lips. "No, just scared the shit out of me. You weren't supposed to get all heroic... and don't call me princess."

Tris squinted at Angelica. He forced words through the riot of emotions clogging his throat. "You're not dead. I was certain the meks would kill you."

She sat on his bed and leaned in to kiss his lips. He placed his hands on her waist, her warm *alive* waist, to hold her to him. "No. I'm not dead." Angelica's glorious face clouded. "But you almost died, you know."

"Yeah. Kinda thought I was headed in that direction." He'd been given another chance. He wasn't stupid enough to waste it. "I love you," he whispered.

"I know," she whispered back. "I love you, too."

"Marry me."

She watched her forefinger trace his mouth and then she

replaced her finger with her lips in a kiss. "Yes," she murmured against his mouth. "What about Mage?"

"I'm feeling magnanimous. You can marry him, too, if you want."

Mage smiled at their interchange. Tris caught Mage's eyes and lifted his eyebrows in expectation. Mage rolled his eyes in good humor, straightened and addressed Angelica formally. "Dr. Angelica Giverny, would you do me the honor of becoming my wife? My life would be meaningless without you." His expression softened. "I do mean that."

She chuckled softly. "Yes, Captain DeLan, I would be delighted."

Mage grinned. "Good. That's settled."

Angelica nuzzled Tristan's cheek, placing delicate kisses along his jaw. "You have a kick-ass sister-in-law. She does too have a magick wand—and it is *much* bigger than yours."

Tris drew back and scoffed. "Never."

Mage choked on laughter. "Don't worry. We like yours better."

Tris chuckled, hugged Angelica closer and then reached for Mage's hand and pulled him in. "Give me a day or two and I'll remind you why."

"I think you are being optimistic, Tris," Adonia said as she walked through the door. Hel followed on her heels with several stout men behind him. "Perhaps a week or two… we'll see. But these gentlemen will move you to your own apartments so at least the three of you can share the same bed."

"Thank you, *Carissime Medica*… for everything," Tris said, and grinned when Adonia blushed to the roots of her hair. She paused, linked hands with Hel and then cleared her throat. "Your brother helped me significantly. He refused to leave our chamber until you were out of danger. Just thought you should know."

Tris sobered. "Thank you, big brother."

Hel nodded. A slight smile tugged at his lips. "Anytime." Hel turned to the extra muscle. "Now, will you *please* get him out of here."

The End

EPILOGUE

Anger fuelled his purposeful walk as Ram sought out the gangway to Tok's private vessel. When Primus G'hed had dismembered the meks and Adonia had restored him and his beloved vixen to health, he'd returned to Arkodaenia with one thing burning in his brain. Ensure the Haarb and their vile pets were off the face of his planet. In this one instance, he rejected the thought that the end excused the means. There was never a reason good enough to allow the presence of Haarb to desecrate the surface of his Mother.

There... there Tok was, boarding his vessel. Good. Ram marched to the beginning of the gangway, halted, and stared a hole through the Khlossian.

"Have you come to kill me, Verdantian? You are welcome to try." Devilry gleamed in Tok's eyes. Ram clamped vicious restrain on his desire to pull his sword and answer the behemoth's challenge. "I did serve notice you would not like my methods. I grant you have cause for your anger. I violated your trust. I felt the ultimate goal of saving Dr. Angel's life worth your wrath."

"You are testing my self-control, Khlossian. I'm here to take pleasure in watching you leave." Ramsey crossed his arms over his chest and glared at Tok. "Turn around, get on your ship and go."

"I am leaving Verdantia, but not because I fear your anger." A look of pain crossed the blunt features of the Khlossian, and he suddenly looked immeasurably weary. "The Haarb have struck a crueler blow than one of your daggers. They have stolen Sweet Eva. I am leaving to get her back." Tok turned away and took a few steps toward the open hatch.

To have someone you loved ripped out of your life in an untimely fashion—Ramsey had experienced that agony. The great being in front of Ram had found that person and hauled Ram halfway across the galaxy to be reunited.

"Tok," Ramsey called.

The Khlossian turned back, halfway through the hatch, his expression quizzical. Ram straightened, uncrossed his arms, and held Tok's gaze for a long moment. He released a long sigh and with it most of his rage. He ran a hand through his scalp and shook his head before gazing at Tok once more.

"If I can … ah, help…" Ram gestured awkwardly with one arm.

The corner of Tok's mouth lifted, and he seemed a little less careworn. "Yes, Verdantian. I will call you." With that, Tok entered his ship and the opening in the hull closed and sealed.

Ram stood and watched until the craft lifted from the gantry tower, thundered into the sky and became a mere dot of orange. "*Her* light go with you, Khlossian."

OTHER BOOKS BY PATRICIA:

The Verdantian Series

Hers To Command

Hers To Choose

Hers To Cherish

Hers To Claim

Hers To Captivate

The Heirs & Spares ~ Regency Romance

A Husband For Hire

A Destitute Duke

Lessons For A Lady

The Magic Series

Co-authored with Kris Michaels

An Evidence of Magic

An Incident of Magic

Standalones~Contemporary Romance

Undertow

Adam's Christmas Eve

ABOUT THE AUTHOR

Patricia A. Knight is the pen name for an eternal romantic and dyed-in-the-wool hermit who hides in Dallas, Texas with her horses, dogs and the best man on the face of the earth. With the BMOTFOTE as navigator, Patricia bombs down the highways of the United States in the Taj-ma-haul continuing her life-long search for the best chocolate cake recipe and new pictures of David Gandy. Look for her coming to your state! (Seriously, look for her. Her driving is very suspect.) When forced into it by her PA, Pam, she will actually write.

I love to hear from my readers and can be reached at **www.patriciaaknight.com**.
Or send me an email at **patriciaknight190@gmail.com**.
Join me on my private Facebook group
PAKS PEEPS at https://geni.us/PAKSPeeps, or follow me on:

www.amazon.com/Patricia-A.-Knight/e/B00D7GFZH2
facebook.com/patriciaromancewriter
twitter.com/patriciaaknight
bookbub.com/authors/patricia-a-knight
goodreads.com/author/show/7093656.Patricia_A_Knight
pinterest.com/patriciaknight190

If you would like to receive email notifications on my new *historical* romance releases, free short stories, personal appearances, etc., please subscribe to my ***Regency Readers*'** Group. I send out, perhaps, three emails a year. This is a **separate** listing from those who read my erotic, gay, paranormal, and sci-fi, romance. You will **not** receive any information from me regarding those titles.
If you like your romance hot, sometimes kinky and definitely out of this world, please join the **PAK FANS** group. You may unsubscribe easily and at any time from either group with a simple click.
With many thanks.

Patricia

Join Patricia's *Regency Romance Readers*:
https://eepurl.com/dcJVCn

Join Patricia's **PAK FANS**:
http://eepurl.com/YqckL

And finally, please, leave a review.

Frequently interviewers ask, "What is your favorite part about being an author?" My answer is always the same, "My readers." I adore writing stories that resonate with you so greatly that my characters enter your life. You rejoice with them. You sorrow with them. *This* is why I write.

For readers, the ultimate reward is finding wonderful books—for authors, it is knowing readers love what they have written. Encourage your authors to write. Help your fellow readers find good books. Leave reviews.

Thank you!

GLOSSARY OF TERMS

Adalay—[**a′** da lay]—High mountain range to the east of Sylvan Mintoth and part of the region considered under the governance of House DeHelios.

Aether—[**ee′** thur]—The spiritual realm attained by highborn medical practitioners that allows them to address the seven centers of bodily life and by all other magistrae to communicate with the Great Mother.

Anima—[**ah′** nee mah]—Soul, spirit, internal essence of life.

Arcobaleno—[**ark′** oh bah **lay′** no]—The color that the diamantorre in the sigil towers blaze indicating the highest amount of energy is being transferred, absorbed and transmitted. The color is a pure white at the furthest end of the light spectrum.

Arkodaenia—[Ar ko **day′** nee a]—Verdantia's sole spaceport. Arkodaenia is the only city free from the electromagnetic forces created by the vast deposits of diaman pipes. Because of this, modern technologies are possible in this highly restricted space. It is the one portal for Verdantians into the rest of the settled universes with all the advantages of their technologies.

Ari—[**ah′** ree]—Conte Aristos Camliel DeTano, Primo Signore of the Second Tetriarch, High Lord of Verdantia and the Queen Fleur de Luna Constante's husband and consort.

Bás dtost—[**bas′** toast] – "The Silent Death," Hel's nickname given to him by the Haarb.

Beporza—[**bee** poor za]—A flying beetle type of insect that makes a loud buzzing sound.

Bombom torta—[**bomb** bomb*tor tah]—A decadent tort that consists of layers of heavy, rich, chocolate cake, liquor-flavored butter cream and crushed nuts in a pastry shell.

Bovem—[*bo vem*]—A cow-like creature.

Butyrum—[*butt* **tree** *um*]—A butter-like substance.

Carissime Medica—[*Ca* **riss'** *eh may* * **Med** *i ca*]—"Beloved Healer" After the events in *Hers To Claim*, this was the name given to Adonia by the people of Verdantia.

Chambre Cristalle—[**shaam'** brah***kris'**tall]—the name of the ritual chamber in a sigil tower where the Great Rite is performed. This is the only place the Great Rite is performed. Every sigil tower in Verdantia has a Chambre Cristalle.

Chital—[**she'** tall]—A spotted antelope-like creature with lyre-shaped horns. They travel in herds and occupy the open grasslands.

DeCorvus vs Corvus—In *Hers To Claim*, Adonia is introduced at various times with the last name of "Corvus" and "DeCorvus." In Verdantian society, the "De" prefix indicates the bearer is of one of the thirty-two noble houses originally founded. In the case of Adonia Corvus, her family dropped the "De" prefix when they joined the Mother's Acolytes. Hel introduces Adonia as "Adonia DeCorvus," properly giving her the aristocratic prefix.

Diamantorre [**Dee** ah mahn **tor**]—An immense block of diaman crystal that serves as the central dais in the Chambre Cristalle of each sigil tower. This block of crystal stores the energy of the Great Rite and releases it into the surrounding atmosphere. In an outward display of extravagance, the entire city of Nyth Uchel, its surrounding walls, and the white tower, Torre Bianca, were built entirely of diaman crystal. As such, the overflow of energy from the Great Rite is absorbed by the very building stones to the extent that all of Nyth Uchel is haloed with a soft, luminescent light giving the entire city an appearance of magickal enchantment.

Doral [Doh **rall'**]—Visconte Doral Celestia Agentio DeLorion, Segundo Signore of the Second Tetriarch, lover to Ari and Fleur. While neither Hel nor Doral realizes it, they are distantly related. In fact, the entire Second Tetriarch is distantly related to

Hel as their bloodlines cross repeatedly. This was not by accident. After the schism between Nyth Uchel and Sylvan Mintoth, the High Enclave Elders spent centuries quietly trying to duplicate the genetic makeup of the DeHelios line.

Fell wolf—A genetically engineered hybrid of a large, predatory canine and a giant lizard, similar to Earth's komodo dragon. They are the size of a large pony and have acute senses of smell, hearing and vision. At some point in time, someone added nano-bots to their genetic structure, which makes them heal incredibly fast. It takes beheading or a shot to the brain to put one down. They are highly intelligent and controlled through the use of pulse collars which can be set in varying degrees of severity from mild to stun. They are a favorite of the Haarb.

Fleur—[Fler]—Queen Fleur de Luna Constante, supreme monarch of Verdantia. Her last name does not contain a "De" as she and her father and mother were of questionable nobility. It is the source of one of Hel's reservations about the legitimacy of the Second Tetriarch.

Fricki—[**frick′** ee]—An elusive, elk-like creature living in the mountain regions of Verdantia. They are snow-white in color and very rare. Lore has it that the sight of one of these exotic, shy creatures indicates the active presence of the Great Mother and is very good luck. To kill one is a criminal offense.

Imita mekanikos—[**em′** mi tah*meh **kan′** ni kos]—"Meks" are a highly advanced combination of organic and non-organic cyborg. They are immensely intelligent, can morph into whatever form they wish to mimic, are enormously strong and communicate telepathically. The meks have the capability to absorb power, so they are not vulnerable to conventional weapons that fire blasts of fusion energy or lazer pulses. Firing such weapons at them merely makes them stronger. They were unearthed on Devon III during the cyborg wars on that planet. Their discovery had disastrous consequences for the Devonians. When the planet fell to the cyborgs, the meks were unleashed into the universe.

Magister—[ma **gis′** tur]—A High Enclave-bred and trained nobleman with a specific genetic link to "*Her.*"

Magistra— [ma **gis′** tra]—A High Enclave-bred and trained noblewoman with a specific genetic link to "*Her.*"

Magistrae—[ma **gis′** tray]—Plural form of magistra or magister—gender inclusive. More than one magistra or magister.

Mela—[**may′** la]—A tart, lime green, oval fruit similar to an apple.

Nyth Uchel—[**nith′** oo chel′]—"High Aerie" – The DeHelios family seat – A large palace with a prosperous city below. Nyth Uchel was the original capital of Verdantia.

Nata—[na tah]—A white liquid similar to cream.

Pannis—[**pan** is]—A grain-based type of bread. It can be shaped into multiple forms.

Plains of Vergaza—A vast open grassland west of Sylvan Mintoth and the desert wastelands of the Oshtesh.

Saccharon—[**sack′** ah ron]—The Verdantian equivalent to sugar.

Senzienza—[**sen′** zee **en′** za]—The Planet of Verdantia's sentience. Also referred to as *She* or *Her*

Signore, Primo—[**pree′** mo***sig′** nor eh]—"First gentleman" – the first male in the Tetriarch

Signore, Segundo —[**sah′** gun do***sig′** nor eh]—"Second gentleman" – the second male in the Tetriarch

Tetriarch— [**tet′** tree ark]—A trio of nobles formed by the Senzienza to rule Verdantia. They wield extraordinary mystical power with joined with Mother Verdantia. There have been only two in the five hundred year history of the planet.

Torre Bianca—[**tore bee′** ahn ka]—the "White Tower"—a sigil tower above Nyth Uchel. Torre Bianca is the first, and greatest, of all sigil towers in Verdantia. Her construction, as with all the sigil towers in Verdantia, was accomplished by the First Tetriarch, Tristan's ancestors. Torre Bianca is the only sigil tower constructed entirely of diaman crystal.